THE SEX TRAFFICKERS

NEIL POLLACK

THE SEX TRAFFICKERS

iUniverse books may be ordered through booksellers or by contacting:

iUniverse
1663 Liberty Drive
Bloomington, IN 47403
www.iuniverse.com
844-349-9409

ISBN: 978-1-6632-1413-3 (sc)
ISBN: 978-1-6632-1412-6 (hc)
ISBN: 978-1-6632-1411-9 (e)

Library of Congress Control Number: 2021919137

Print information available on the last page.

iUniverse rev. date: 10/26/2021

To the #MeToo movement

To exact revenge is not only a right; it is an absolute duty.
—Ancient Japanese adage

PROLOGUE

Twenty-Six Years Ago

SHE HAD MADE A PROMISE TO JESUS, WHICH SHE INTENDED to keep, no matter what.

"Morgan, hurry up, or you'll be late for church."

She heard her mother's mild admonition as she powered down her computer, which lay on her old metal desk in the small bedroom she shared with her younger brother. She quickly grabbed her jacket, threw it on, and ambled into the sparsely furnished living room, where her mother stood, car keys in hand.

Morgan Kelly was only eleven years old, but she had suffered through the abandonment by her father, who had left her and her eight-year-old brother three years earlier. Morgan had idolized her handsome father. Being firstborn and a girl, she believed she was his favorite, as he often told the auburn-haired, green-eyed Morgan how pretty she was.

Her father had been coming home late for a few months. Morgan assumed he needed to work late to earn more money. She'd heard her parents arguing at times, but she never really understood what the arguments were about. One day, he simply disappeared. His abrupt departure forced her mother to find waitress jobs to support their meager existence. Morgan overheard hushed conversations her mother had with friends and relatives—he'd moved to Florida and had a new family. For months, Morgan cried herself to sleep under her covers. What had she done to make him want a different family? And if he were to return and spread his arms wide, would she rush into those arms? In her dreams, she envisioned a great cloud being lifted as she fell into his loving embrace. But three years had passed, and she believed those arms would never beckon her again. She'd learned at far too young an age what unrequited love meant. She vowed to one day find and confront him with one question: why?

The void she felt was partially filled by the church, which gave Morgan peace of mind with its rules and routines, and devotion to God. Angels would watch over and protect her. She would never do anything to make the church abandon her.

Morgan followed her mother outside, where their dented old Pontiac was parked in front of their rented two-bedroom Boston row home. Her mother got behind the steering wheel as Morgan climbed onto the passenger seat. Her mother pulled away from the curb and toward the church, where Morgan was a member of the junior choir. The melodious hymns they sang imparted a feeling of warmth and acceptance. It made her feel close to God. She had a decent voice that could hold a tune, and she knew she was one of Father Timothy's favorites.

Morgan's mother turned to her and said, "Something's bothering you lately. Feeling OK?"

Morgan shrugged her skinny shoulders and stared out the window.

Her mother placed a hand on Morgan's shoulder. "Girls your age can become moody, especially around the time of their period. I know you haven't gotten yours yet, but maybe it's coming soon."

Morgan cringed. She hated discussing what her mother had told her was *girl talk*. "Mom, just watch the road, OK?" She shuddered, thinking that that time might soon come. *Disgusting.* She continued to stare out the window.

Her mother nodded as they came within sight of the impressive, solid stone, Gothic-style church located in the heart of Boston. She stopped the car in front of the church. Morgan opened the door, stepped out, and headed for the church doors.

Her mother shouted through an open window, "Pick you up at six."

Morgan waved over her shoulder as she climbed the steps toward the heavy wooden doors. More than just singing in the choir was now required of her. But it was God's will, and she would do whatever he commanded of her. She was guaranteed a place in heaven at the right hand of God. She opened one of the doors and entered the cavernous church, where the sad eyes of Jesus on the cross stared lovingly down at her from above the beautifully appointed altar. Jesus had become her hero and surrogate father, and she would do whatever he wanted in order to please him.

Choir practice often went from 4:30 p.m. to close to 6:00 p.m. On occasion, it would end early, and this was one of those days. As the children were leaving the church to wait outside to be picked up, Father Timothy called Morgan into his office, where he smiled pleasantly and once again asked, "How much do you love Jesus?"

"With all my heart," she answered with sincerity.

The kindly looking, middle-aged father cupped her face with his hands and said, "You are so beautiful. You are God's very special girl. Jesus wants you to do the same thing for me that you did two weeks ago."

She saw him take his thing out of his pants. She knew what he wanted her to do from his instructions the first time. She gingerly began to rub his thing until he made some grunting noises and ejaculated. Her mother had given her a cursory understanding of how babies were made. She was therefore confused by what she had done and witnessed. It felt wrong, but she craved his approval.

He kissed her on her forehead. "Remember, it's our secret. A secret that will guarantee you a place in heaven next to the Lord Jesus."

CHAPTER 1

OFFICER MORGAN KELLY DIDN'T HAVE TO BE A COP TO KNOW that darkness shielded crimes. Having patrolled the streets of Manhattan's Chinatown for the past eleven years, much of it in her 3:00 to 11:00 p.m. shift, she had seen firsthand the increase in criminal activity after sundown. Night magnified everything. Whatever lived in darkness awakened. Most of it didn't scare her anymore.

She was expecting this night to be like other recent summer nights as she cruised the streets in her patrol car with her temporary partner, Officer Mario Fuentes, everything routine. She took pride in providing law-abiding citizens a sense of security, while potentially giving pause to those who might be contemplating crimes such as those she had been involved with—including shoplifting, grand larceny, burglaries, felony assaults, and many domestic disputes.

It was 10:20 p.m., and they were nearing the end of their shift. They passed tenement buildings, some older than one hundred years, whose apartments were cramped, many with bathrooms in hallways, shared among multiple families.

By day, the thirty-seven-year-old Morgan would pass groceries, fishmongers, bakeries, herb stores, bubble tea shops, and crowded streets filled with vendors selling knockoff brands of perfumes, watches, and handbags, attracting many from outside Chinatown, who knew they had arrived by the colorful shop signs with Chinese lettering, the Far Eastern language and music, street signs written in both English and Chinese, and banks and other structures that used Chinese traditional styles for their building facades. With more than three hundred Chinese restaurants, the neighborhood was permeated by a pungent odor—a combination of cooking oils and seasonings.

By night, those same streets were transformed into a kaleidoscope of activity. The buildings became the riverbanks for the never-ending stream of motor vehicles and pedestrians, ebbing and flowing like the tide, with colorful lights emanating from shops and restaurants filled with hungry patrons, perhaps seeking some dim sum or other Chinese delicacies. But those same streets beckoned petty thieves and drug dealers, while prominently displaying clusters of young women who lingered in shadowy areas and smiled at the men leering at them, either from idling cars or having stepped off a bus. Customers paid fifty dollars for oral sex and double for intercourse. Morgan knew that in the five boroughs of New York City, more than a thousand prostitutes were arrested each year on the streets and in subways—as well as in Chinese and Korean massage parlors. Prostitution was a misdemeanor, and most would simply pay a fine and be out on the streets again, participating in the world's oldest enterprise. More disturbing to Morgan was the knowledge that behind many closed doors were trafficked children and young women who were being both used and abused by their traffickers. Seeking out traffickers and freeing their victims was high priority for Morgan and the rest of the NYPD. Although not her usual job, Morgan was always on the lookout for trafficking. She knew firsthand what it meant to be a victim.

Fuentes, in his fourth year with the department—filling in for Morgan's usual partner who was out with the flu—was sitting shotgun as Morgan spotted a couple of scantily and provocatively dressed young hookers standing on a street corner. The hookers smiled and waved at the patrol car, knowing it wasn't against the law to walk the streets; they had to be caught soliciting to be arrested.

Fuentes turned toward Morgan. "My daughter just turned four, but I can't imagine what it would take for her to have to do that." The burly, olive-skinned, twenty-seven-year-old, who Morgan thought smelled of aftershave, slowly shook his head.

Morgan nodded. "Desperation is what it takes." She stopped the car at a red light. "So, you have a daughter."

"And a two-year-old son."

"The million-dollar family."

Fuentes smiled. "And I worry about them a lot, doing this job. How about you? Kids?"

She sighed. "Just a crazy husband who I'm divorcing."

Fuentes turned and stared at her for a moment. "Sorry about the crazy, but *you* won't have any problem finding someone." Many men found her to be disarmingly attractive, with her auburn hair, green eyes, and an Irish face accentuated with freckles. The five-foot-eight Morgan still had a figure most teenagers would be proud of.

She took his borderline sexual harassment compliment in stride. Men had always been attracted to her, even in grade school when her nightmares began. "Not so easy. A lot of garbage out there."

Their placid evening was abruptly interrupted by their patrol car's crackling radio as it announced a ten-thirty—robbery in progress—at a local pharmacy.

Morgan replied that she and Officer Fuentes were responding to the call since they were only a few blocks away. Morgan had worked the streets of Chinatown—a neighborhood that had the highest concentration of Chinese in the Western Hemisphere—as a beat cop walking the streets and for the past five years in a blue and white. She lit up the Crown Victoria and sped toward the reported address, expertly negotiating narrow streets lined with caravans of parked vehicles. Although facing a possibly dangerous situation, she was eager to answer the call.

As Morgan deftly careened around a corner, tires screaming, Fuentes remarked, "Good chance the perps will be gone."

She glanced his way. He seemed understandably nervous, but she hoped he was also feeling what she was—an adrenaline rush. "Just be careful," she cautioned as the car raced through stone and brick canyons of mostly three- and four-story residential buildings that seemed to lean on one another for support. It looked like, if one fell, the rest would topple like dominoes. Their ground floors housed many small businesses.

Like most of the thirty-five thousand members of New York's finest, Morgan had never fired her weapon in the line of duty, and unlike what was seen on TV cop shows, much of her time was spent on more mundane matters like traffic control and issuing citations for motor vehicle infractions.

The cruiser screeched to a halt and double parked in front of the neon-lit pharmacy. Several persons who had been casually walking the sidewalk stopped to observe the scene. The only sign of disturbance was the police car's varicolored lights reflecting off the surrounding vehicles and buildings.

Morgan and Fuentes unclipped their SIG Sauers from their holsters as they exited the vehicle. Everything outside the pharmacy appeared quiet. It was possible that this was another of the many false alarms police officers encountered, or perhaps the robbers had already fled the scene, as Fuentes had speculated, but they knew to be wary. Morgan felt her pulse quickening, her senses on high alert; robbers often wielded guns.

Morgan was able to see into the well-lit pharmacy through the large plate glass windows. She noticed nothing out of the ordinary as she peered down a few of the pharmacy's several aisles. She drew her weapon as she shouldered her way through the door, Fuentes on her six. Some pop song played throughout the store.

Morgan loudly announced, "Police. Someone reported a robbery."

A clerk in her twenties stood stiffly behind a counter. Morgan focused on the clerk, who appeared unnerved and whose eyes directed Morgan's attention toward an aisle just as a man leaped from there and fired several rounds at Morgan and Fuentes. Morgan instinctively crouched and returned fire, hitting the man twice in his upper chest. The man flew backward onto a shelf containing first aid supplies. They littered the floor as Morgan jumped up and kicked the gun away from the thin, scruffy-bearded white male, who appeared to be in his early twenties. His unblinking eyes were wide open. Morgan shouted at the petrified clerk, "Anyone with him?"

"Just him," she barely croaked.

Morgan turned back toward Fuentes, who was flat on his back near the door, staring open-mouthed and not breathing. He had a gaping wound above his left eye. She shouted into her shoulder microphone, "Officer down! Send a bus! Officer down!" She immediately started CPR and shouted to Fuentes, "Stay with me!" even though she believed Fuentes was gone. The department's motto, *Fidelis ad mortem*, Faithful until death, flashed through her mind as she vainly attempted to revive her partner. As tears welled up in her eyes, she envisioned his wife and two young children standing in front of hundreds of men and women in blue, whose white-gloved hands saluted as the hearse rolled slowly by.

Crestfallen, she recalled another partner, a fellow soldier in Iraq who had been killed by her side. She had achieved the rank of corporal in the infantry in 2006. Again, she had survived unscathed—at least physically. For the second time in her life, death had brushed her with its wing. She didn't feel lucky since she knew she was destined to live with still more guilt.

Just as she had to since she was eleven years old.

Three months after the pharmacy shooting, as Morgan stood in the hallway of New York City's Seventh Precinct, whose jurisdiction included much of Chinatown, Detective Ben Chang approached her and said, "Congratulations, *Detective* Kelly." He extended his hand, and Morgan shook it.

Morgan smiled amiably. "Thanks, Ben. I think you and I will make a wonderful couple," she said with a grin.

Ben laughed. "Hey, rookie. It's called partners."

Morgan knew she was teamed with Ben due to department policy, which attempted to partner a highly experienced detective with a newbie. Ben, with more than fifteen years as a homicide detective, fit that bill. She had heard that he'd never been assigned a female partner, and she wondered if the married, forty-nine-year-old Ben, six foot two and a beefy two twenty, would be at ease when bonding with her. She was cognizant that male partners used time-honored techniques of bonding such as talking sports and telling raunchy jokes. She was unsure how comfortable he'd be working many hours every day in close proximity to her. She wondered if he would doubt, like so many men, that she could be as effective in certain situations as a two-hundred-pound male partner. On the plus side, she believed Ben would be appreciative of the fact that if their detective work took them out of town, a female partner meant he wouldn't have to share a room or bathroom.

She had been promoted to detective in large part due to her involvement in the deadly shootout that took the life of her partner. The perpetrator had attempted to storm out of the pharmacy with several opioid pill containers in his pockets. Morgan's killing of the pistol-brandishing robber was a brief media sensation and made Morgan a hero, even though she professed to be only doing her job. She had to "ride the pine"—assigned to desk duty until her shooting was investigated and she underwent a psych evaluation. The department needed assurance that Morgan wouldn't hesitate to fire her piece in a kill-or-be-killed situation.

Her leapfrog to detective irked many men in the department. She heard numerous grumblings by male officers, which made her uncomfortable, sometimes angry. She felt that she shouldn't have to prove herself; she'd been a soldier, after all. You'd think they would respect that.

The commander of the precinct, Captain Martin Graves, middle aged and balding, walked up to the two detectives and said to Ben, "I need you in the interview room." Then, to Morgan, "OK, Detective, you too. Time to start earning your keep."

She respected Graves. She knew him to be a plain talker and straight shooter, with no patience for bullshit.

Morgan wore a stylish dark suit that was in vogue with female detectives. A dress didn't demonstrate as much power and authority, and the suit allowed her to carry her piece on her hip instead of in a purse. She knew female police were better than their male counterparts in many situations. Statistics showed that women cops were less inclined to use unnecessary force, and they deployed their weapons less frequently. They were also better at deescalating domestic violence cases, and many children related to a female officer in the same way they would their mom. Morgan recalled an incident where she was able to break up a fight among young teenagers by initiating a dance-off with them. The bias that still existed against female cops made her determined to change a few attitudes.

Morgan turned to the captain. She was excited to begin her job, hoping to demonstrate an untapped ability as some sort of super sleuth. "What do you need?"

Ben asked, "What are we doing?"

"Ben, I need your expertise with an eleven-year-old girl. A victim of sexual abuse. O'Hara and Jaworski are getting nowhere with her."

"I've interviewed many victims, with some degree of success, but what makes you think I can do any better?"

"The girl is being questioned in regard to accusations by her mother that the mother's ex-boyfriend sexually abused the child on more than one occasion. Maybe Morgan's being there might help."

Morgan stared at Graves. The number eleven leaped out at her, and she felt as though she were being grabbed by the throat, but she managed to keep her composure as the past swept through her. By the time she turned thirteen, she had known for a very long time that what Father Timothy had done was terribly wrong. She finally summoned the courage to make a full confession—not to a priest but to her mother, who was in disbelief until she was provided with the salacious details. To blow the whistle on the priest would lead to embarrassment and shame her mother could not abide for herself and Morgan. She moved the family to New York City.

Jesus was no longer Morgan's hero. She had silently vowed never to feel powerless again.

Morgan took a deep breath and nodded. "Since you're not relying on my vast inexperience, they're *male* detectives, I assume?"

He shrugged. "A female's presence might make a difference. Worth a try."

"Where is she?"

"Interview room two."

Morgan's eyebrows lifted. "Shouldn't we have interviewed her at her home? She's probably scared to death."

"The child opened up a bit to her mother this morning, but she wouldn't give any details. Her mother brought her in about an hour ago and asked us to press the child for specifics."

She slowly shook her head. "I'm no miracle worker." She worried that her first assignment would end in disappointment.

"Don't worry. Ben will handle the interview." He turned toward Ben. "Give it your best shot."

"Her name?"

"Ashleigh."

Graves led Ben and Morgan to the twelve-foot-square interview room. He opened the door and nodded toward the two male detectives who were seated at a metal table opposite a frightened-looking young girl who appeared younger than her eleven years. She had dirty-blond hair tied back in a ponytail that hung halfway down her back. She wore an oversized black T-shirt, faded blue jeans, and time-worn, black high-top Converse sneakers. Morgan envisioned herself in the girl's fearful eyes, and she felt like screaming, but she knew she had to hold it together.

The male detectives took their cue. They stood, and the taller of the two, O'Hara, scowled at Morgan, who was standing in the doorway with Graves. O'Hara said to Graves, "I see you've got Wonder Woman with you."

As they left the room, the other detective, Jaworski, disdainfully said to Morgan as he craned his neck toward the girl, "Good luck with *that* one."

Morgan knew the Wonder Woman moniker wasn't meant as a compliment, but she felt it best to not respond. Without any of the male detectives verbalizing it, she couldn't help feeling that they believed that she, the more experienced of the two, was responsible for Officer Fuentes's death, even though she had been cleared of any procedural wrongdoing. She wondered if they thought that, had she been male, Fuentes would still be alive.

Morgan, Ben, and Graves entered the small, sterile-looking room. Three chairs were grouped around the metal table. The walls were painted what Morgan could only describe as vomit green.

Graves approached the girl and stood over her. As he cast a shadow across the table, he pointed toward the detectives. "Ashleigh, these are Detectives Chang and Kelly, who would like to speak with you."

The girl shifted nervously in her seat and avoided making eye contact.

Morgan and Ben approached and sat in chairs opposite Ashleigh. Morgan smiled warmly. "Call me Morgan, OK?"

Ashleigh shrugged her skinny shoulders and still made no attempt to look at either Morgan or Ben.

Graves left the room and stood outside, observing through the one-way mirror.

The girl was small for her age, and Morgan estimated her weight as not more than seventy-five pounds. She was fair-skinned with a face that Morgan thought might be pretty if the girl weren't so forlorn looking. Ashleigh stared down at hands that were clasped so tightly in her lap that her knuckles were turning white.

Ben gently said, "I know you haven't told the other detectives what happened, but maybe you could change your mind and tell us so that we can punish the person who hurt you."

Ashleigh continued to stare at her clasped hands.

Ben continued, "Would you like something to eat or drink? Anything you want. We can get it for you."

Ben waited, but Ashleigh made no attempt to respond. After a few more futile attempts by Ben to get her to open up, Ben turned toward Morgan. "Any thoughts?"

Morgan had only a cursory idea as to how to handle this, but she knew she had to avoid asking the wrong questions or ones that might make Ashleigh uncomfortable. She allowed her instincts to guide her. Morgan softly said, "Ashleigh, you've already been asked several times about your mother's old boyfriend, and you haven't said what he did to you, so I won't bother to ask you any questions. I am here to tell you this." Morgan inhaled deeply and said with conviction, "It wasn't your fault."

Ashleigh looked up at Morgan but said nothing.

Morgan softly repeated, "It wasn't your fault."

Ashleigh's lower lip quivered slightly, but still she remained silent.

Morgan stretched her hand out over the table.

Ashleigh merely stared at it.

Morgan repeated in an even softer voice, "It wasn't your fault."

Ashleigh's eyes welled up. She slowly lifted an arm and gingerly grasped Morgan's hand.

Ben looked at Ashleigh and then at Morgan. A look of admiration crossed his face.

Almost in a whisper, Morgan said, "It wasn't your fault."

Ashleigh began to sob in a way that broke Morgan's heart. Morgan let go of Ashleigh's hand, stood, walked around the table, bent down, put a mothering arm around Ashleigh, and hugged her. Ashleigh responded by hugging back, more tightly than Morgan expected.

Through her sobs, and as tears spilled out of her eyes, Ashleigh said, "I didn't … want him to." She cried all over Morgan's shirt.

Morgan pulled back from Ashleigh and looked directly into her eyes. "I know. I know. It wasn't your fault, Ashleigh. It was *not* your fault."

With a determined expression, Ashleigh answered with a strong voice, "It wasn't my fault."

"And we don't want him to hurt other girls like you, do we?"

Ashleigh shook her head.

"And in order to stop that, I need you to tell me what he did to you. Do you think you can do that? You don't want him hurting *you* again."

Ashleigh sniffled, and Morgan handed her a tissue from a box on the table. After wiping her eyes and nose, she nodded.

Ben knew to keep silent and let Morgan continue the interview.

Twenty minutes later, Morgan and Ben left the room knowing that the hidden camera had recorded the salacious details, enough to put the pedophile behind bars.

Graves had been watching the interview. He congratulated Morgan and then added, "I think she'll be OK."

Morgan stared at Graves for a moment. "You can fix a broken bone, but a broken spirit might never be repaired." She hoped Graves understood.

Minutes later, after Ashleigh's mother spoke with Graves, the mother found Morgan standing by her desk, speaking with Ben. She approached Morgan, threw her arms around her, and said, "Thank you." Morgan was a bit embarrassed, not expecting such a heartfelt reaction.

The mother let go, and Morgan said, "Just take care of her, and remember, the department has experts who can help her heal."

She thanked Morgan again and left to take Ashleigh home.

Later, when O'Hara and Jaworski asked Morgan what questions she used to get Ashleigh to open up, Morgan replied straight-faced, "I used my Wonder Woman lasso of truth."

A smirking O'Hara said, "OK, funny. What's the real story?"

Morgan, trying not to sound too smug, responded, "I told her it wasn't her fault."

The two male detectives looked at each other. O'Hara said, "Why didn't you think of that?"

Jaworski responded, "Why didn't you?"

Knowing that many men were clueless as to what it meant to be #MeToo, Morgan believed she had found her calling.

The #MeToo movement had awakened something within her that she had relegated to the darkest recesses of her mind, and she now felt as though she had always been #MeToo on steroids, having trusted men from her past, only to be turned into a victim. Dealing with Ashleigh conjured images of her first violation at eleven. She had put her faith and trust in the church, and she was especially thrilled to be chosen by Father Timothy to join the choir. Morgan shook her head, as she had done so many times since, an attempt to erase the memory of her years between eleven and thirteen. Thoughts of revenge sometimes had a paralyzing effect on her emotions, but other times, those thoughts washed over her like a fifteen-foot wave, nearly drowning her in self-pity. Perhaps some form of revenge would be salvation from the shadow of her hidden shame.

As a detective, she was in a position to help the #MeToo movement by finding the most extreme violators and placing them behind bars. She knew that much of the crime in Chinatown—including drugs, gambling, and prostitution—was controlled by two major groups, the Triads, who originated in China, and the Yakuza, who originated in Japan. It was widely reported that the Triads were controlled by a man named Sun Li Fong, and the Yakuza by a man named Satoshi Akita—with Akita's organization known to being the most egregious abuser of girls and young women.

Morgan's past sensitized her to the plight of girls and young women who were being used as prostitutes. Shutting down an illegal brothel or spa here and there seemed to have scant effect on the overall industry. But getting to kingpins like Sun Li Fong and Satoshi Akita might cause a ripple effect that could close numerous establishments. Perhaps it would also serve as a way to assuage violations from her past.

She hoped her nighttime dreams of vigilantism would never materialize, fearing that once the dike was broken, an irresistible sea would roll overwhelmingly in.

CHAPTER

2

MORGAN KNOCKED ON GRAVES'S OPEN DOOR. "CAPTAIN Graves. You wanted to see me?"

He looked up from behind his large metal desk. "Not so formal. Marty will do."

She smiled. "Marty it is."

He motioned at a chair opposite his desk. "Have a seat."

She entered his office, a mostly glass-enclosed space, and seated herself opposite Graves. She wondered why she was there.

Graves immediately came to the point. "I want to more formally congratulate you for a job well done with Ashleigh."

"Thank you, but it was a partnership, with Ben's help."

"I appreciate giving Ben some credit, but I saw how you conducted the interview. I doubt Ben could have accomplished what you did by himself, which leads me to another reason you're here. The Human

Trafficking Unit is working to rid the city of sex trafficking, but they need, in military terms, foot soldiers like you to do the grunt work."

Puzzled, she asked, "You want me to join them?"

"Hell no. You just got here. After what I witnessed with Ashleigh, I don't want to lose you. What I'm getting at is that I coupled you with Ben because he's a top-notch homicide detective. But if and when suspicion of sex trafficking comes our way, I'd like you and Ben to handle some of it. How does that sound?"

She leaned forward. "I'd like nothing better than to put men like Sun Li Fong and Satoshi Akita and the dirtbags who work for them behind bars, and to free their victims. That's exactly what they are, victims." Father Timothy's image appeared before her. Was he still alive? She hoped he died and was burning in hell.

He smiled appreciatively. "Then it's settled, but as you know, detective work can be emotionally taxing. You'll see a lot of garbage out there, sometimes enough to make you want to throw up. Just yesterday, a sicko was arrested for sextortion. He contacted girls between twelve and fifteen using Snapchat. He offered them money in exchange for sexually explicit selfies. Paid them through things like Cash App or in Amazon gift certificates. His intention was to use these girls for sex. If they refused, he planned to spread their photos and videos on the internet. Fortunately, he was caught before any of these girls became trafficked."

She gritted her teeth and shook her head. "Scumbag."

"Therefore, I tell all my newbies to wind down occasionally and try not to take the job home. How do *you* wind down?"

She thought for a moment. "I go to the Neck whenever I get the chance. Lets off some of the steam."

Rodman's Neck in the Bronx was the location of the NYPD shooting range, situated on a fifty-four-acre police training facility.

"Know what you mean." He nodded. "Been there, done that."

She added, "Also, I read a lot. Helps get me to sleep at night."

"The boob tube does that for me. If you don't mind my asking, what kind of stuff do you read?"

"Mostly historical novels and history books."

14

"Reading anything now?"

"Jon Meacham's *The Soul of America*."

"Is that the guy that's on TV a lot?"

"That's the one. He wrote about times where things looked bleak for America, but our better angels always seem to win the day. One particular story stuck with me, which was the fight for women's suffrage."

He cocked his head to the side. "Because you're a woman?"

Annoyed, she retorted, "Because I'm a *human being*." She realized she might have sounded too harsh. She put her hand up apologetically and said, "Sorry."

He seemed lost in thought until he replied, "No, you're right. Equality should be everyone's fight." He stood and extended his hand across his desk. Morgan stood, and they shook hands.

She left the office.

That evening, Morgan made her way to the ladies' department at Macy's. Morgan had feared her out-of-control husband, Paul, might be stalking her; now she was certain of it. She had spotted him watching her, but the moment her brawny, ruddy-complexioned husband knew he had been detected, he vanished like an apparition, perhaps to seek a better stealth position.

Morgan's marriage of two years was about to end in a few weeks. She had initiated it, and he was fighting tooth and nail. She knew Paul suspected she was with another man and was seeking confirmation. She could only guess at his intentions if she was with someone. Knowing he could become violent, she predicted an unpleasant outcome. As a cop for eleven years, she had seen far too many domestic disputes that had turned violent, sometimes leading to a homicide. She wasn't planning on adding to those statistics.

She made her way through the perfumed air to the shoe department while keeping an eye out for her often out-of-work construction worker husband. She approached the salesman, a thin, pasty-looking man in his early thirties, and began to describe the type of shoe she was looking for when Paul rapidly approached.

She turned toward Paul, but before she could get a word out, Paul grabbed the unsuspecting salesman by the shirt collar and shouted, loudly enough for several women shopping nearby to overhear, "Are you screwing my wife?"

The startled salesman yelled, "What the hell?" as he tried to push Paul back, but the much stronger Paul held on tightly.

Morgan grabbed Paul's arm and ordered, "Let him go!"

Paul, over six feet tall and muscular, hung on and, through clenched jaw, demanded, "Are you her boyfriend?"

The struggling and befuddled salesman responded, "I'm the one with a boyfriend."

Paul said, "What?" He realized what the salesman meant and released his grip.

While a growing knot of women gathered around the trio, the salesman shouted, "Will someone please call the police?"

Morgan quickly pulled her badge from her pocket and announced, "I'm a cop, and I'll take care of this. Everyone, please go about your business."

The indignant salesman said, "I hope you arrest this idiot."

Paul looked at the man. "Sorry, buddy. My mistake."

Morgan looked at the salesman. "Do you want to press charges?"

The salesman glanced at Paul and then turned to Morgan. "Just get him the hell out of my face."

Morgan grabbed Paul's arm. "Let's get out of here."

The two turned and rushed outside into the cool mid-September air, where a seething Morgan turned to Paul. "You need to grow up. Our marriage is over."

Paul snarled, "Not yet. And as far as I'm concerned, you're still my wife."

Her eyes flared. "Not for long, and you know it. It's over, and I'm going home now." She turned and strode toward the apartment she had rented after moving out.

She was fuming as she heard Paul shout, "It ain't over till I say so."

Later that evening, she went to the shooting range to relieve her stress, aiming the hard, cold pistol at the target, where she often visualized an imaginary villain or enemy. Although angry with Paul, she didn't envision him. He was his own worst enemy, and if he picked on her, well, she could handle it. The ones she imagined killing were the abusers of girls, such as Sun Li Fong and Satoshi Akita.

Satoshi Akita was sitting at a table in his legal strip club in Chinatown, the Happy Hour, with one of his bodyguards, Yoshi Nomura—forty, small in stature, and highly proficient in martial arts. They were smoking and drinking as they watched two female strippers pole dancing on a small stage, entertaining some customers. Another of his bodyguards, Ichiro Harada, a fierce-looking man of thirty-five, entered the club and approached Akita's table. He bowed to Akita and was instructed to sit next to him.

Satoshi Akita had two families—one he married and one he was born into. He was a family man with a wife and two college-educated adult children, but he was always destined to have a second family in the Yakuza—also referred to as the Japanese Mafia—following in the footsteps of his father. Hardcore Yakuza had their entire bodies tattooed from shoulders to ankles, very often depicting dragons and/or tigers. If a subordinate disobeyed a rule, he was made to cut off the last inch of his pinky finger.

The fifty-year-old—with jet-black hair neatly swept back with gel and black coal for eyes—had managed to survive what was known throughout Japanese society as the circle of death, where every assassination tended to bring another. Funerals mourning the dead often ended up as cues for more bloodshed.

On Akita's mind was a shortage of girls and young women for his brothels. The Yakuza in Japan had an ample source from the nearby Philippines, but the vast distance from there to here required constant replenishment from local talent. He would get his men working on it. But one girl in particular weighed heavily on him. He was deeply disturbed that a nineteen-year-old named Chunhua might jeopardize his relationship with his wife and children.

Akita asked Harada, "What did she tell you?"

"She won't get an abortion."

Akita drew a deep drag from his cigar and blew the smoke toward the ceiling. "You need to convince her."

"I tried. She says it's against her religion."

He took the cigar from his mouth. "What?"

Harada slowly shook his head. "Believe it or not, she says she's a Catholic."

He squinted. "A Chinese Catholic?"

"What do we do about her?"

Akita usually had a quick response, but this case was different. Chunhua had been orphaned in China and placed in a convent, where she was raised by nuns. When she was thirteen, she was kidnapped by Triad traffickers, eventually ending up in Chinatown, where traffickers, in need of money, sold her to the Yakuza. She'd suffered harsh times, but she always believed that Jesus would reward her for keeping the faith. When she was eighteen, she was taught to perform at Akita's club. Her Chinese name meant *spring flowers,* which Akita thought was perfect since she was a breath of fresh air to him. Akita was enamored with her beauty, and it wasn't long before he took her into his back room for sex. That was five months prior. She had hidden her baby bump until it became obvious that she was pregnant.

"Who is she saying is the father?" Akita apprehensively asked.

"She still insists you are the only one she had sex with since she was hired."

"She was supposed to be on the pill."

"She said that was also against her religion and that most men she had sex with, before you, used a condom."

Akita slammed his fist onto the table. "Now she fucking tells us? Where is she?"

"Outside. Nervous as hell."

He wearily rubbed his hand across his face and said, "Bring her in."

Harada left and a minute later appeared with a fearful-looking Chunhua.

Akita stood, smiled at her, and said, "Follow me."

Chunhua followed Akita into the small, empty room that had a bed against the far wall. He closed the door, and they stood facing each other.

Akita placed his hand on her shoulder. "You know you cannot have your baby."

Tears began to flow down her cheeks. "I will end up in hell. And it is *our* baby."

His penetrating eyes glared at her. He removed his hand from her shoulder and pointed at her swollen belly. "How will you support the child? You will be out of work from now until months after you give birth."

She answered meekly, "I was hoping you would help."

Akita nodded slowly. "One last time. Will you have an abortion?"

"I cannot." She began to sob.

He touched her cheek. "All right. I will help."

Chunhua grinned broadly and threw her arms around Akita. She released her grip, and he said, "Come." He led her back to his table, where he spoke with Harada. "Take her home."

Harada knew what Akita meant when he gave the order to take Chunhua home. If she had acquiesced to Akita's demands, she would have been invited to stay. Instead, Nomura was driving, with Chunhua in the front seat and Harada seated behind her.

As they drove through Chinatown, Chunhua excitedly said, "I can't wait to have our baby. I knew Satoshi would help."

Harada liked Chunhua. Not only was he attracted to her, but she had always been polite and respectful. There were times he hated his job. This was one of those times. He threw a garrote around her neck and twisted it. Chunhua frantically kicked at the dashboard and windshield, desperately struggling in a vain attempt to save her and her unborn child's lives, but the garrote quickly cut into her carotid arteries, and she was dead in less than a minute. Harada exhaled and slumped into his seat.

Nomura glanced at the motionless Chunhua, shook his head, and said, "Had to be done."

Their next instructions were to take the body to Akita's thirty-six-foot *Sea Ray*, travel out to sea, and tie a weight around her.

As Akita sat at his table, he imagined Chunhua bringing the child to his office or, far worse, showing up at his home. Money to support the child would be no problem, but he believed his wife and grown children would be appalled. And he would be embarrassed, which was unacceptable. He felt a bit remorseful at having to destroy such a beautiful young woman. But then again, there would be many more beauties who would eventually take her place. More importantly, his problem had been solved. His family was far more important than one Chinese slut.

Satoshi Akita was the gang boss in Chinatown and parts of Lower Manhattan. One of Akita's main sources of income, as was common with Yakuza, was collecting protection fees from establishments doing business in his territory. Akita's group also collected finder's fees from Russian, Irish, and Italian mafiosos and other organizations for guiding Japanese tourists to gambling parlors and brothels, whether legal or illegal. Japanese men on sex tours often desired Western women, particularly blonds. Hence, many in Akita's stable dyed their hair blond.

The Yakuza were relative newcomers to Chinatown. The Triads had their origin in seventeenth-century China and had been operating in America for at least one hundred years. Their name was derived from the Triple Union Society, referring to the union of heaven, earth, and humans. Much of their operation in Chinatown overlapped with his. The Triads were currently engaged in fraud, extortion, money laundering, human trafficking, and prostitution. They also had their fingers in smuggling and counterfeiting goods, such as music, video, software, clothes, watches, and designer handbags.

Akita believed there was enough room for both groups, but there was much evidence that the Triads were attempting to take over some of Yakuza territory.

Bloody turf wars had been waged between rival Chinese gangs in the 1970s and 1980s. There were battles between the Tongs and the Triad group known as the Flying Dragons. Many were killed, some by mere teenagers.

Since the 1980s, crime in Chinatown, as well as in the rest of New York City, had fallen dramatically. Turf wars seemed to be a thing of the past. Akita hoped it would remain so.

He was familiar with the carnage that a war could lead to. He had witnessed wars that lasted for years, with dozens of gang members killed and many more wounded. It always amazed Akita how easy it was to obtain a gun in America. In his former homeland of Japan, strict gun laws resulted in far fewer deaths in a single year than occurred in the United States in a single day.

Akita had risen through the ranks of the Yakuza with cunning and ruthlessness. If he thought someone needed to be killed, it was done. His dark eyes mirrored his dark soul. Anyone who posed a threat to him or his group was fair game. If that meant an eventual war with the Triads, so be it.

CHAPTER 3

THE FOLLOWING MORNING AS MORGAN AND BEN MET IN A hallway at the precinct, Ben asked, "You heading to the briefing room?"

"I heard it's important, and I want to be early," Morgan responded.

"Everyone's talking about how you got the girl to open up about her pedophile. That was great work."

She smiled. "Beginner's luck."

He laughed. "I know better."

Ben Chang had been born and raised in Chinatown and was as familiar as anyone could be with that neighborhood and its surroundings. His family had endured the hard times of New York City in the seventies, and they had lived through the Tong and Triad wars of the eighties. As a teenager, Ben resisted becoming a member of any gang, even though many of his schoolmates had joined. He was well aware of these gangs' reputations, but he also knew the type of young man they attracted. He believed he was not that type.

He had been raised in a loving, stable family that stressed education for Ben and his older brothers and sisters. Ben's grades were above average, which enabled him to attend City College. Crime and murder rates were high in the seventies and early eighties in New York, and Ben had seen the results of much of it, all too often in the media and sometimes personally.

By the time Ben reached twenty-one, two of his former classmates had been killed in a senseless gang war. It was during this time that Ben decided to join the police force. He believed that proper policing could reduce crime and make the city a safer place to live. This goal was met to a great degree; the statistics had borne out that by the time President Obama left office, the city was one of the safest places to live in the United States. Of course, crime still existed there, and Ben felt it his duty to do his utmost to both prevent and solve crimes. As a boy, he had watched numerous police and crime shows. He had envisioned himself driving the streets of Chinatown, seeking out and capturing the bad guys who were responsible for so much death and mayhem. So many young lives destroyed. His parents had hoped he would become a doctor, but he knew they were proud of him in his role of *protecting and serving*.

As a detective, he had seen his share of shootings and stabbings, but the crime that hit him hardest was the exploitation of children. He was the father of a son and a daughter, both college graduates, and the thought of someone victimizing them when they were just kids increased his blood pressure. If someone had done to his kids what he saw had been done to other kids, what would he have done if he found the pervert? *Anything and everything* was as specific as he allowed himself to surmise. He wouldn't permit himself to enter the darkest recesses of his mind.

As soon as Morgan heard she'd be partnered with Ben, she Googled him and asked around about him. Her inquiries led her to believe that Ben was a good guy, a real family man, and one who could be trusted. She desperately wanted to be able to trust someone.

She entered the briefing room and sat on the folding chairs that had been set up for the meeting in which ten detectives were expected. Within five minutes, the room was filled with the chatter of the ten, who settled into their seats as Captain Martin Graves took his place at the lectern in front of the chalkboard. The group took his cue, and the chatter immediately quieted down.

Graves put on his reading glasses, a clear indication that he would be reading from notes. "Good morning, everyone."

The group answered in sporadic fashion, "Good morning."

"First, let me welcome someone a few of you already know, but for the first time as Detective Morgan Kelly."

The group focused on her and applauded as she blushed—a trait she hated but couldn't control since it had been bequeathed by her pale Irish ancestors.

Graves addressed the group. "Every precinct in the city has been asked by the mayor to address the ever-growing problem of human trafficking." He glanced down at the papers on the lectern and began to read aloud. "Although slavery was abolished a hundred and fifty years ago, slavery still exists in this country in the form of sex and labor trafficking. Victims are often emotionally and economically dependent on their abusers, working as domestic servants, restaurant workers, and in the commercial sex industry in massage parlors, strip bars, the porn industry, and in the catch-all phrase of 'escort services.'"

Morgan raised her hand and was recognized by Graves. "Just how bad is the problem in the Big Apple?"

"First, I regret to say that New York *state's* trafficking problem is one of the worst in the nation because of its long international border, major ports of entry, and diverse population." He looked at the audience. "And you better believe that this city, with over eight million ... diverse and densely populated ... is prime for such activity."

Morgan called out, "Where do we go from here?"

Groans could be heard from some of the veteran detectives who wanted nothing more than to have the meeting end as soon as possible. Coffee and cakes were waiting.

Graves answered, "It isn't all bad. In 2007, New York state passed its first law against human trafficking. It's a fairly comprehensive law, a copy of which you can pick up from the table back there at the end of the meeting." He pointed toward a table in the back of the room and read again. "In sum, it changed the way we treat the victims, who were often treated as criminals."

This time, Ben called out, with a touch of sarcasm, "And our great mayor's solution is?" This was met by an acknowledging murmur from the audience.

"I know how you feel. Let him get out in the street and see what we go through every day. But let me say this. Just as with drugs, the best way to stop it is by reducing demand. The same goes for prostitution. But even though laws were passed that increased the penalty for patronizing a prostitute, they're often underused by law enforcement and prosecutors who arrest and prosecute those patronized far more than their patrons."

Once again, Ben called out, "So the reason for this meeting is?"

Graves paused for a moment. "The way to go is to find and prosecute the perpetrators of the trafficking. Which means finding our victims and getting them to give us information on their traffickers. It would be great if we could get to the major players, such as Satoshi Akita."

Ben said, "We've tried to get him several times over the years. We haven't been able to penetrate his organization."

Morgan angrily said, "We've known all this time that the SOB is behind so much crime, even murder, and yet he's never been arrested?"

Graves responded, "Not as simple as you might think. Guys like him insulate themselves from the bottom rungs, similar to what many of the mafia chieftains did, where we always had trouble linking them directly to a crime. Look what it took to get Al Capone, with all the crap he did. They got him on tax evasion."

"OK, so how about something like that?" Morgan asked.

"He operates several legitimate businesses, like bars, restaurants, motels. Akita uses legitimate lawyers and accountants to ensure he doesn't get caught like Capone. He hangs out at one of his strip clubs, the Happy Hour, acting like some king."

"So, he'll continue his dirty deeds?"

"To get a high-echelon member to inform on the group—as Joseph Valachi did years ago to the Mafia, when we first learned about the Cosa Nostra—is rare. They placed a bounty on his head of a hundred thousand dollars. That's over a million in today's dollars. That's how badly they wanted him dead. He died of a heart attack in federal prison, with the bounty still on his head. Let's try and get these guys."

Morgan asked, "Aren't we trying every single day?"

"Look, I know the mayor makes it sound like we aren't doing our jobs. But to appease him, let's redouble our efforts and do whatever we can to try and get the scumbags who profit from this trafficking. That's all I can ask of you. I've done what the mayor has asked of me. If there are no more questions, go get 'em."

The group eased out of their chairs and left the room for the corridor. As Morgan and Ben walked toward the detective's squad room, Ben said, "A bunch of bullshit, as usual."

Morgan looked at him. "But he has a point. We need to get to the kingpins. Maybe we save one, maybe we save hundreds of victims."

"It's what we do every day. The mayor is just trying to cover his own ass."

Morgan merely nodded. Politics was never her thing. She envisioned taking Akita out, using her marksmanship at long range and placing a bullet between his eyes.

They walked into the squad room—a thirty-by-forty-foot space lit with flickering overhead fluorescent lights—and sat at their desks, waiting for the morning's itinerary to arrive while partaking in the morning's refreshments.

With a cup of coffee in hand, she once again fought against spiraling into the darkest recesses of her mind. The reminder of her unfulfilled retribution against violators from her past conjured fantasies that ran counter to her oath to uphold the law. She took that oath seriously, but her urge for revenge was powerful and persistent. She had been violently attacked by a fellow soldier prior to serving in a combat zone in Iraq. She thought back to when she was stationed at Fort Hood, Texas. Her ambition to join a police force had been kick-started by that fellow soldier. She needed a ride somewhere, and she asked a group of soldiers sitting at a picnic table if one of them would drive her. She would give gas money. A wiry, pockmarked soldier, sporting a blond crew cut, said to follow him to his barracks to talk about the details. There, he tried to kiss her, but she pulled away. He told her she was beautiful, choked her, and threw her onto the ground on her stomach. As he was trying to tear her pants off from behind, she yelled for help and yelled for him to stop. Fortunately, she had excelled in hand-to-hand combat in basic training. She threw her elbow back, striking him squarely on his nose. As he grabbed his nose, she was able to kick her leg over, which flipped him onto his back. She rolled away from him, stood, and threw a violent kick at his midsection. He grunted, and as he grabbed his side, she was able to run out of the barracks.

She immediately went to the office of her first lieutenant, Marie Caldwell, where, out of breath and clearly distressed, she stated, "Some guy just tried to rape me!"

Caldwell, in her late thirties, short and stocky, rose from behind her desk. "Who was it?"

"A soldier named Chuck something. I never got his last name, but I know what he looks like."

"Where did this happen?"

"I needed a ride and said I would pay gas money. He told me to follow him to his barracks. It happened there."

"Any witnesses?"

Taken aback, she countered, "Do I need any? Look at me. My shirt is ripped, and I've got a scratch on my neck."

Caldwell shrugged. "So, no witness, and you were in the men's barracks. You probably shouldn't have gone there, and it'll be your word against his."

Morgan's face turned red as her body quaked with rage. "You going to do something or not!"

"I'm sorry, but maybe you should see the base commander."

Morgan told the base commander, who said he would look into it, but nothing was ever done. Morgan learned the hard way that sexual attacks in the army were almost always swept under the rug. Bad publicity wasn't good for recruitment in a volunteer army.

Objectively, she knew that nothing those bastards did to her was her fault, yet she couldn't shake the guilt and searing shame she'd carried with her since grade school. She often wondered, if she could find and kill her violators and not get caught, would she carry out the deed?

She didn't know for sure. She wouldn't pursue them, but if it was in her power, and the circumstances were just right … who could say? On the other hand, she had trust in the law. She had worn a uniform to help her country kill people. After the attempted rape, she decided to wear another uniform to help *save* people. Upon completing her three-year stint in the army, she attended City College and majored in criminal justice, graduating with honors. She applied to the Police Academy and became a police officer. She believed that even tempting circumstances would not turn her into a vigilante. She would follow the law and arrest the bastards who violated her. She would not only let the system do its job; she would make sure it did.

Later that night, while watching nothing of interest on TV, images of being on her knees in front of Father Timothy suddenly appeared, something she hadn't conjured in a long time. She wondered if it was due to dealing with Ashleigh and being assigned to sex trafficking.

She thought about Satoshi Akita. What kind of man treated girls as items to be discarded like trash when they were no longer useful?

Feeling restless, and for reasons she couldn't define for herself, she decided to scout out the Happy Hour. She drove there and walked into the dimly lit strip club, where she immediately detected a conglomeration of odors that included alcohol, marijuana, and perfume. On a small spotlight-lit stage was an Asian woman performing acrobatic moves on a metal pole. There were people at the bar, most of whom seemed to be paying little attention to the stripper, while some patrons were seated at tables in front of the stage, shouting encouragement and throwing money onto the stage.

Morgan walked to the bar and asked a bartender if Satoshi Akita was there.

The bartender pointed to a table in a rear corner of the room. She thought, *What am I doing here?* But curiosity got the better of her. *What does the animal look like?*

She approached the table where Akita sat with Nomura and Harada, all three dressed nattily in suits and ties.

"Which one of you is Satoshi Akita?"

Akita rolled an unlit cigar from one side of his mouth to the other and smiled a handsome, toothy grin. "I'm Akita. Who wants to know?"

Morgan had expected a thug rather than someone who appeared as though he was attending an affair with sophisticated people. She flashed her badge and said, "I'm Detective Morgan Kelly, from the Seventh Precinct."

Akita's eyes opened wide. "Detective? You're much too pretty to be a cop." With a smirk, he said, "Are you applying for a job?"

Nomura and Harada laughed.

She leaned toward him. "I wanted to see what a monster who kills girls and young women looks like."

Akita's grin faded. He leaned back in his chair. "I believe you've overstayed your welcome here."

"I just wanted to let you know I'm watching you."

Akita pointed a finger at her and said, "And I'm watching *you*."

She turned and walked out of the club. She now knew who she was up against.

Akita said to Nomura and Harada, "If the bitch comes alone again, we'll have a surprise for her."

Masahiro Araki was told it was the world's oldest profession. He was pleased to play a part in it, but he saw nothing of promise as he surveyed the area in front of an aging Chinatown high school. He tried to appear nonchalant as he sniffed the fragrant September air, replete with the scent of delphinium and hydrangea lining the flowerboxes in front of the school, but he was becoming increasingly impatient since he knew that Ogura would shortly be picking him up.

He'd scouted the area for several days to no avail. Unless he was lucky enough to find one in the next few minutes, it promised to be a poor week's pay. Nineteen, Masahiro Araki could pass for much younger, a trait that had served him well. The nice-looking Japanese American, who had the gift of gab, eyed the group of teenaged girls who were ending their conversation and heading in separate directions, except for the one he'd never seen before. She stood by the curb.

These past few days, the high school dropout had spotted many teenaged girls, but none fit the strict criteria he was looking for. He fancied himself a talent scout, something he was proud of since he never failed to fail at almost everything else—school, sports, and as a son to his single-parent mother. He had always seemed to disappoint her, but the disappointment was mutual. He was making enough money to support his drug habit and afford the rent on a tiny studio apartment in a run-down building, but nobody gave it to him; he had earned it. His mother had predicted he would end up as a dishwasher or work in a car wash.

It was Saturday, and many school kids congregated around the school, some playing ball on the field in back, some flirting, and some just messing around—kid stuff. He had seen most of this group this past week as they had exited the school, but this new one had said goodbye to the group, which left her alone by the curb, possibly waiting for a car or bus ride. He was certain he had never seen her before. She was much better looking than most; he would have remembered her. She had shiny, straight black hair that hung down past her shoulders, a slim figure, and perfect Asian facial features. He approached her, smiled pleasantly, and said, "Hi. I don't remember you. Are you new to the school?"

She turned to face him. "I used to go here but still have friends here. Do you go to this school?"

"Yeah. Just moved here a few months ago. What's your name?"

"Wendy. And you?"

"Masahiro, but my friends call me Hiro."

31

She smiled. "You're Japanese. Me too."

"And you're one of the prettiest girls I've ever seen." Now that he was seeing her up close, she was beautiful. He would love to get his hands on her. The coincidence of her being Japanese was a bonus. He hoped his instincts were right about her.

Her smile quickly faded as she stared at the ground.

"Hey, I didn't mean to embarrass you. Just speaking the truth."

She looked up at him. "How old are you?"

"Sixteen," he lied. "And you?"

"Fourteen … but almost fifteen," she quickly added.

Hiro glanced left and right. "Why are you standing here?"

"Waiting for the bus to take me to the Long Island Railroad and then to Great Neck."

"Hey, you know what? My father will be picking me up in a couple of minutes, taking me to soccer practice. I'm on a traveling team. We go right past Great Neck. We could give you a ride."

She hesitated. "I don't think so."

"Why not? You'd save time and money. And we could get to know each other better." His handsome face brightened.

A shiny, late-model Lexus pulled up to the curb across the street, with an adult male at the wheel. He opened his window and waved at Hiro.

Hiro waved back and said, "Hi, Dad. Can we give my new friend a lift to Great Neck?"

"Of course. Jump in," the man pleasantly replied.

Wendy peered across the street at the man who appeared to be Japanese, about forty or so.

Hiro pointed at the sky. "I hear thunder, and it's gonna pour any second. Come on. I don't bite." He smiled broadly and extended his hand toward Wendy. "It's starting to rain. You'll be home really fast. And my dad's a very safe driver."

Large raindrops began to fall. She took his hand and crossed the street.

She liked Hiro, and she would much rather be in a car than take the subway and train. If she decided to go with him, she would have to text her father to tell him he didn't have to pick her up at the train station, but she still wasn't convinced that it was the right thing to do.

Wendy stood at the curb as Hiro stepped into the street to speak with his father through the open, driver's side window. Wendy discreetly snapped a photo of Hiro with her phone and quickly typed something she would send to her father if she decided to go with him.

Hiro walked back to Wendy and again extended his hand. "Come on. It's beginning to pour."

Wendy's parents had ingrained in her never to take a ride with a stranger. But heavy rain had begun to fall, it was daylight in midafternoon, and Hiro, a fellow Japanese American, seemed nice— and was very good-looking. Besides, it was his father who'd be driving her home. She glanced at her phone and sent the photo and text to her father. She stepped into the back seat, next to Hiro, and the car pulled away from the curb.

After two minutes of small talk, the car turned away from the bridge that would take them to Great Neck.

Wendy noticed. "Why aren't we going over the bridge?"

Hiro answered flatly, "Just have to make a slight detour."

Something felt terribly wrong. Wendy could feel her stomach churning. As calmly as she could, she said, "Let me out here. I'll take the subway."

The car picked up speed as the driver said, "We'll let you out soon enough."

Wendy pulled her phone from her pocket. Hiro snatched it out of her hand. She fought to grab it as she shouted, "Give it back!"

Hiro opened the window and tossed the phone onto the street, where it was immediately crushed by the traffic.

A terrified Wendy began to scream at the top of her lungs.

The driver, Tadashi Ogura, a huge, bald-headed man, pulled the car over and double-parked. He quickly turned toward Wendy, who was anxiously pushing on the handle of the locked door, and punched her in her jaw, knocking her almost unconscious. He reached into his pocket,

33

pulled out a syringe, and injected a small quantity of heroin into her arm. "That will shut her up for a while." He drove off.

Minutes later, they parked in front of a Chinese restaurant. Ogura exited the vehicle and opened a rear door. With Hiro's help, he placed Wendy into a duffel bag, zipped it, and carried Wendy, who weighed less than one hundred pounds, up two flights of stairs and into an apartment above the restaurant.

The door opened into the dilapidated living room where two topless teenaged girls sat on a threadbare couch. Hiro and the big man, Tadashi Ogura, opened the duffel bag and pulled the groggy Wendy from the bag, laying her on her back on the hardwood floor. Still feeling the effects of the heroin, all she could do was look up and stammer, "Where … am I? W … what's happening?"

Hideki Fujita, a small, wiry, middle-aged man with a full head of graying hair, walked into the room from the only bedroom in the two-room apartment. He passed a window that overlooked Mott Street, located in the heart of Chinatown. The apartment was in a pre–First World War building, indifferently maintained. The pungent odors of Chinese takeout consistently wafted up to their apartment, whose yellowed walls were sloughing leaded paint like a molting reptile. Although they were not in love with the area, Chinatown had been chosen as a place where two Japanese could blend in, inconspicuously able to come and go as they checked on their girls in this and other run-down apartments.

The two teenagers, a Chinese American named Alice and a Guatemalan named Maria, sat expressionless on the couch. Maria—who referred to herself as Mariposa to her customers, due to the large butterfly tattooed on her lower back—was drifting in and out of a self-inflicted drug stupor. She leaned over and rested her head on Alice's shoulder. Alice pushed her aside, and Maria keeled over sideways onto the couch.

Fujita and Ogura proceeded to remove Wendy's shoes and then her pants. Wendy made a vain effort to hold onto her pants while pleading through tears, "Stop! Please don't! Stop!" They pulled her arms over her head as she struggled, then pulled her shirt off over her head. Ogura rolled her onto her side, unclipped her bra, and yanked it off, revealing two well-developed breasts. Fujita then pulled her panties down and over her ankles, rendering a crying Wendy totally naked. The last male to have seen her naked body was her father when she was three years old, yet she lay there more fearful than embarrassed.

Hiro pointed at the dark triangle between her legs. "She'll soon have to be shaved. Let me pop her cherry."

Ogura firmly said, "I'm first."

The powerful Ogura picked up the sobbing Wendy, carried her into the bedroom, and tossed her onto the bed, whose sheets were gray with filth. Ogura pulled down his pants, climbed on top of Wendy, and forcefully penetrated her. A wretched and weeping Wendy gagged at his fetid breath and body odor as Ogura pulled out. He sat on his knees next to Wendy's head, and proceeded to masturbate. He laughed at the sight and stood up.

Wendy was awake enough to know what was happening, but the heroin made her muscles feel like lead weights. The thought that she was no longer a virgin thudded through her. She had all she could do to keep from vomiting as her hand made a fruitless effort to wipe her face. Thoughts of contracting a venereal disease or even AIDS from unprotected sex careened through her mind. This had to be a nightmare. Less than half an hour ago, she was talking with her friends! She envisioned her father coming to rescue her and cutting off their heads with a samurai sword. As she lay there sobbing, she prayed that her ancestral spirits would come to her aid.

Ogura pulled up his pants and walked back to the living room. "Our customers are going to like her. Who is next?"

Hiro stepped into the bedroom where the nubile beauty lay spread-eagle on her back.

Wendy saw him approach, and she braced herself, knowing what was coming next. She wished she could castrate the smirking Hiro. He stepped next to the bed and saw what Ogura had done on her face. He walked back into the living room. "Jesus, Ogura, you could at least have cleaned her up."

Ogura laughed. "You don't fuck the face, but maybe I'll teach her how to give a great blowjob." He turned toward the two girls on the couch. "Right, girls?"

Alice merely smiled and nodded in his direction, while Maria drifted to unconsciousness.

Fujita said, "Enough shit," and then turned toward Hiro. "I assume she met our standards."

Hiro swallowed hard. He knew what standards Fujita meant. The girls he procured were supposed to be runaways, homeless, or immigrant girls who needed a place to stay, to be fed and protected. Some of them needed to earn money to pay off illegal traffickers who threatened to harm their families back home if the debt wasn't paid off. Some needed to earn money to feed their drug habits. Hiro wasn't certain that Wendy fit any of these criteria, but she had been standing in front of a school in a run-down part of Chinatown, alone. It was possible she was homeless or a runaway, although the shiny hair and clean clothes suggested otherwise. He had been enamored of her looks, and he needed the money he would now earn. Therefore, he took a chance he should not have taken. But it was too late now. "Sure. She'll be great."

"She better be. Our tribute to Satoshi Akita is due."

CHAPTER

4

MORGAN WAS AT HER DESK, FINISHING HER CUP OF COFFEE, when Ben approached her. She looked up and said, "What's up?"

"Got a dead female, found in a garbage dumpster. I'll fill you in on the way."

They hurried out of the precinct.

Morgan felt a rush of excitement. This was her first murder investigation as a detective.

Upon entering the Ford Taurus, Ben stated, "Female corpse was found in a garbage dumpster behind Tasty Dumpling, across from Columbus Park. Forensic guys are already there."

"Who found her?"

"Around eight this morning, a worker was throwing out some trash when he noticed what he thought was a finger sticking out of the garbage. He pushed some of it aside and realized it was a whole person. The owner called it in, and a couple of officers initially responded."

Ben lit up a cigarette with his Zippo lighter. He cracked open a window, which sucked out most of the smoke.

Morgan said, "That's a nasty habit."

"My wife, Doreen, tells me that every day. You ever smoked?"

"Here and there in high school, to look cool. Gave it up when I enlisted. You should give it up." She hoped she didn't sound like a nagging wife.

"Tried, several times." He took a drag. "Frankly, it makes police work seem easy."

Morgan could relate to that. She knew what to do on the job. Personal demons were quite another story.

Within minutes, they arrived at the scene, which was a blur of activity. They parked in the street and walked behind the restaurant where the dumpster stood. Yellow crime scene tape looped an area around the dumpster. Ben and Morgan approached the CSI unit as the body was being loaded onto a gurney, ready for transport to the morgue in the coroner's van. Ben asked, "What do we have here, Frank?"

Frank DeMarco was the chief forensics expert in the CSI unit, and he had dealt with Ben on homicides on numerous occasions. He had also met Morgan once before, having been on duty for her shooting incident. "Young female, possibly Hispanic, maybe seventeen, eighteen. Preliminary shows evidence of an overdose. Track marks on her arms. Lab guys will tell us more."

Morgan asked, "Time of death?"

"We put it between eight and ten hours ago, so probably expired and dumped here sometime after midnight. The way she was covered up meant that whoever buried her figured she'd be picked up and buried forever in a landfill. Didn't manage to cover her entirely. Probably too dark to see. We're dusting the dumpster for prints."

"Any ID on her?" Ben asked.

"Nothing. She was wearing panties. That's it. Good chance she was a hooker of some kind. No jewelry, though she does have pierced ears and greenish-colored nail polish on her fingers and toes. Oh, and a large tat of a butterfly on her lower back."

"Any cameras in the area?" Morgan asked.

"We're surveying the area now. I didn't see any in this alleyway, but maybe we'll get lucky from the street."

Morgan and Ben snapped on a pair of latex gloves and walked around the area, searching for anything that might catch their attention. After examining the area, they questioned the worker who found the body and the owners and workers of that establishment and those adjacent to it. Finding nothing of value, they returned to the precinct to file their report. Without mentioning it, if she was a prostitute, they knew this would probably be another case that wouldn't get solved. That's how it went with prostitute homicides. If she was a runaway, they would periodically check to see if anyone filed a missing person's report describing a young female with that butterfly tattoo.

After discussing the event and filing their report, Morgan and Ben talked about lunch.

"I know a great place on Moyers Street," Morgan offered.

"Which place?"

"Gam Wah Tea Parlor."

"Yeah, I know it but never ate there. I'll take your word for it, and I could go for some tea."

A short while later, as they approached the entrance to the restaurant, they detected the sweet and pungent aromas, an invisible lure reeling in patrons. They entered the restaurant, a small storefront establishment with only seven tables, of which three were occupied. Many framed photographs of China papered the walls. They were seated and handed menus.

"What's good here?" Ben asked.

"The stuffed eggplant is good, but I usually get one or two of the hargaw, minced shrimp in a handmade wheat wrapper, and one or two of the house-special pan-fried dumplings, which are pork and shrimp."

"Sounds good. I'll let you order for both of us. But I gotta let you in on a little secret. I don't love Chinese food." He saw her surprised look. "I know, you noticed I'm Chinese."

"Chinese? I thought you were Swedish." She smiled like the Cheshire Cat, and he laughed.

"I ate Chinese my whole life. Still surrounded by it. I'd take a burger and fries anytime." Ben then asked, "How's it feel not to have to wear a uniform?"

"Feels great. No matter where I went, I couldn't help seeing the stares of people. Some good stares, some not so good, but I always stuck out like a sore thumb. Took a while to get used to."

"Know what you mean."

The waiter poured hot tea into their ceramic cups and shuffled off. Morgan tore open a packet of Sweet'N Low and stirred it in. Ben preferred his tea as is. They each blew on the steaming cups of tea and then took a sip. Ben made an *ah* sound.

"Not bad tea," Ben said. "You know, so long as we're going to be partners, I think we should get to know one another better."

Morgan's eyes tracked up from her teacup. She was always reluctant to discuss her past, but this low-key fellow detective, whom she believed she could trust to some degree, based on her prior inquiries, put her at ease, although she knew to remain guarded in her disclosures. "What would you like to know?"

"I heard you were in the service, served in Iraq, and have a reputation of someone not to be messed with. How was it over there?"

She looked off into the distance and said, "The only quote I ever fully memorized was by the French philosopher Voltaire. He stated, 'It is forbidden to kill; therefore, all murderers are punished, unless they kill in large numbers and to the sound of trumpets.'"

"Profound. When did he write that?"

"The early seventeen hundreds."

"Geez, way before the World Wars, Vietnam …"

"And Iraq."

He nodded and then glanced at her hands. No rings. "I believe you're single."

She smiled coyly. "Are you hitting on me?" She knew he wasn't.

"If I were single, that might not be out of the question."

She sighed jokingly. "Married. Thought so. All the good ones are."

"Wife and two kids. Son and a daughter. Both grown. College graduates," he said with obvious pride. "Parents are both gone. I was the youngest with two older brothers and sisters. Always got hand-me-downs until I became bigger than my brothers at sixteen." He paused. "Jesus, I'm running off at the mouth. First time I ever discussed so much personal stuff at any one time with a partner."

She smiled. "Maybe I'm exposing your feminine side."

He laughed.

"I understand you speak Chinese."

"Cantonese, actually. My parents emigrated from southern China, and Cantonese was spoken at home. China's national language is Mandarin. China's influence is so great that even Cantonese-speaking families want their kids to learn Mandarin. What about you?"

She was always apprehensive about discussing her personal life with someone she'd only known a short while, even if she believed he was one of the good guys. But the death of her partner had changed something. She wanted to let this new partner into her life. Not too far, of course; she would never fully reveal the events that had shaped her relationships with men.

"Unlike your family, mine's nothing to brag about." She inhaled deeply. "When I was eight, my father ran off with a younger woman. He moved somewhere around Tampa and raised a new family. It hit us pretty hard. My mother never remarried but had some shitty boyfriends. I joined the army and found my direction in life."

She withheld that, for a very long time, she still hoped that Daddy would return, mainly because she believed he still loved her. After not seeing her father for over a week, the eight-year-old Morgan asked her mother where Daddy was. Her mother told her that Daddy had a new family he loved more than them and that they might never see him again. Her father, who had called her sweetheart and told her how pretty she was, was never going to come home? Morgan blamed herself. She wasn't a good enough daughter. She cried for days and was inconsolable. Her mother then turned to the church for support.

Three years ago, she was able to track down her father in a suburb of Tampa. She had a deep-seated need to see him, perhaps to confront him and let him see the woman she turned out to be in spite of his absence. She flew to Tampa and knocked on his door. A young man in his early twenties answered. She was taken aback since the resemblance to her father was unmistakable. She quickly caught her composure and asked if Chris Kelly was home. Seconds later, her father appeared in the doorway. He was older with graying hair but still handsome. A whirlwind of emotions coursed through her. She hadn't known what to expect. She held her breath.

"Yes?" he asked.

She thought he'd immediately recognize her, but it was almost thirty years since he'd seen her—and she was only eight at the time.

"Do my hair and eyes mean anything to you?" She took a step toward him.

He stared intently at her. His eyes told her that he absolutely recognized her, yet he answered coldly, "I don't know you."

She answered firmly, "Yes, you do. I served in Iraq and am a New York City police officer. Mom and Bobby are doing just fine, in spite of you. Just thought you'd like to know."

"Listen, sweetheart. I have a family inside. I don't know you and don't want to know you. Is that clear?"

She stared at the father she once loved. "Crystal." She smiled wryly and turned toward her rental car. He'd called her sweetheart all those years ago. Her mother had been right all along. He was an asshole. She never again felt the urge to see him.

The waiter came over and asked, "Ready to order?"

Morgan nodded and ordered for both of them. The waiter left for the kitchen.

"Ever been married?" Ben asked.

"I'm actually married now. Getting an annulment. Didn't work out. We were married only eighteen months when I accidentally opened a letter addressed to him. Not only did he not tell me he was married before, but he was only legally separated. Therefore, still married when he married me, and grounds for an annulment."

"Kids?"

"No, thank God. Married Paul on the rebound after being dumped by someone I thought loved me. My future ex turned out to be a real creep too. Very happy not to have to share a kid with him." She smiled wryly to herself. Two more men whom she had managed, in spite of herself, to place some trust in, only to be disappointed again and again.

"How long to make it final?"

"Signing final papers in a few weeks, but it's taken almost half a year and a lot of my paycheck. He's fighting the annulment all the way."

"You think he still loves you?"

Appearing melancholy, she said, "I know he still thinks he does. It's taking a lot for me to try to convince him it's over. I know he's not accepting it."

"If it's not too personal, what was the attraction?"

For some strange reason, discussing some of her personal life, which she hadn't discussed with anyone, seemed to be having a positive effect on her. She hesitated and then said, "I thought I was marrying a man's man, you know? He worked construction, was a big, strong, tough guy, and I was attracted to him. Good-looking too. But it took me a while to realize what a man's man should be like."

The waiter served Morgan and Ben their lunch.

Ben took a bite. "Pretty good."

"I knew you'd like it."

Ben continued, "And what's your interpretation now of a man's man?"

"Paul liked to drink. Way too much. He also liked his freedom. He was thirty-eight when we married. Wasn't used to being with only one woman, if you get my drift. His drinking got him laid off jobs, and I was often the sole breadwinner. My interpretation now of a man's man is one who cares deeply for his wife, through thick and thin. Like what our marriage vows stated. Anyway, it all came to a head when he became violent ... even tried to force himself on me one time. This was right after he was served the annulment papers. He was drunk. Made it easy for me to flip him on his back and pull my piece on him."

Ben's eyes opened wide. "Jesus! You're a cop. What did you do?"

"Do? You mean report it? Yeah, I could just see me going into my precinct and saying my own husband tried to rape me. Can you picture that?"

He rubbed his chin. "Yeah, gotcha."

She started to say something, paused, and then said with a sullen tone, "I still have a problem with him."

"What do you mean?"

"I know he's stalking me."

Ben cocked his head.

She explained what happened at Macy's.

"Do you think he means you any harm?"

"I know he wants to see if I'm with another man."

"OK. Keep an eye out. If it keeps happening, you might want to get a restraining order."

"I'll think about it. And here I sit, a future divorcee at thirty-seven." She smiled sadly.

"Seeing anyone special now?"

"Not really." She took a sip of her tea.

Ben finished his cup of tea.

Morgan quickly changed the subject. "What did you think about yesterday's briefing? Is he often so long-winded?"

"Almost never, only when the higher-ups ask him to give some speech about this or that."

"But I do think the subject is an important one. I skimmed some of the info we picked up. Do you know that the average age of initial victimization is only thirteen years old?"

"Average is thirteen? Man!"

"Think about it. Average. That means for every kid who's fifteen, there's probably one who's only eleven. Makes my blood boil."

"Yeah, me too. But we're doing our best."

"It also said there are anywhere from as little as a hundred thousand to as many as three hundred thousand US citizen children currently involved in sex trafficking."

He made a whistling sound. "I knew it was a lot but didn't know it was that much."

"And at least eighty percent of them are female."

"*That* number I thought would have been higher." He took a bite out of his meal.

She shook her head slowly. "A lot of perverts out there, victimizing young girls *and* boys."

"I wonder what percentage of those boys are victims of the Catholic Church," he casually pondered.

"And girls," she assertively said.

"What?"

"Many *girls* were victims of the Catholic Church too," she said harshly.

"Of course, girls too."

A couple walked in and was seated at a nearby table.

"Maybe the mayor is right. Maybe we *can* do more to alleviate the problem." She struck her knuckles on the table several times, making the teacups jump.

"I'm certain we can."

"What do you think about today's case? Good chance she was trafficked."

"The stats you mentioned make me think she probably was. Young girls like that are traffickers' meal tickets."

"I hope we get the bastards."

Ben nodded.

The waiter came by and asked if they would like anything else. Morgan responded, "Just the check, thank you."

"By the way, I have my psych meeting tomorrow at two."

"How's it going?"

"Piece of cake. Only nine more months to go."

She was required to have PTS therapy for one year after the shooting incident. She had already seen the psychologist—Dr. Kathryn Lambert, a thin, middle-aged woman with stringy silver hair—on three occasions. Officers involved in shootings reacted in unpredictable ways. Some showed signs of PTSD, but not Morgan. Morgan had opened up a bit to Dr. Lambert, stating that she'd seen death in Iraq—bodies lying on the side of the road, sometimes of children. But that was as far as Morgan was willing to go regarding her service. She liked Lambert, but she wasn't going to fully open up to a cop department psychologist.

She never mentioned her prior violations.

Lambert's report stated that Morgan had already been through unsettling situations before and seemed relatively unscathed. Her life experiences had apparently prepared Morgan for further stressful events. Her report concluded that Morgan was doing remarkably well. She would probably schedule Morgan for only a few more appointments.

After paying for the meal, they left for the precinct.

CHAPTER 5

AT THE PRECINCT THE NEXT MORNING, A REPORT OF A MISSING
person crossed Morgan's desk regarding a fourteen-year-old named
Wendy Kagawa, who was last seen outside a high school in Chinatown.
Until more information ensued, the report was temporarily added to the
backlog of potential runaways since so many teenagers were eventually
found or simply made their way back home. The case would initially be
handled by precincts in Nassau County, where the girl resided.

Morgan, with Ben at her side, was sitting and watching a computer
monitor, examining the one video gathered from the street that showed
the entrance to the alleyway where the girl was found in the dumpster.
Since the ME's office determined the time of death as sometime around
midnight, she chose to view the video from 11:00 p.m. onward, using
fast-forward to cut down on the viewing time.

What she saw was the darkened street, sporadically lit by a few streetlights. An occasional car passed by. Then, around one in the morning, a car turned the corner and turned off its headlights.

"Maybe we got something," Morgan said. She slowed the video to normal speed.

The dark-colored vehicle slowed down, passed the alleyway, and then backed in, out of sight of the camera.

Morgan posited, "If this car dumped her body there, it might take only a few minutes to back the car to the dumpster, open the trunk and lid to the dumpster, pull her body from the trunk, drop it in, attempt to cover the body, close the lid, and then leave."

"Let's see if and when this car leaves."

They sat watching the screen. About four minutes later, the vehicle was seen exiting the alley and turning back toward the direction it came from. The car's lights were not turned on until the car was swallowed by darkness.

"Apparently, this guy was fearful of cameras catching a view of the license plate," Ben said.

Morgan looked at him. "Or this gal. Let's not be sexist," she gently admonished.

Ben smiled. "OK. Or gal."

A female perpetrator was possible, but they both knew that crimes such as this were almost always committed by men.

"What do you make of the vehicle?" Ben asked.

They replayed the video in slow motion.

"Looks black, maybe dark blue or dark green," Morgan guessed. "Hard to tell in such bad lighting. Could be a Ford … maybe a Chevy or Toyota. They all look so much alike."

"We'll have to survey the area. Maybe some camera got a view of the license after the car's lights were turned back on."

She nodded agreement.

The two detectives knew that local newspapers and television had given short shrift to the death of an unidentified female found in a dumpster behind Tasty Dumpling on Mulberry Street. Even so, they gave a number to call if anyone had any information regarding the case. Perhaps someone would come forward with something useful.

Fujita and Ogura had seen the report about the Guatemalan girl on the five o'clock news as they sat in the apartment they shared in the Tribeca section of Manhattan. The apartment was on the tenth floor of a twenty-story building that boasted a doorman. The rent wasn't cheap. It was a two-bedroom apartment with two full bathrooms and a fair-sized living room, along with a view of Thomas Paine Park.

They had done well since arriving in New York from Kyoto, Japan, twenty years prior. Neither man had ever married. Their life of petty crimes, prostitution, and dealing drugs didn't mesh with the idea of matrimony. Besides, they both enjoyed the freedom to come and go as they pleased, and they especially loved the women who were a never-ending river of pleasure. But the two men were small-time. The only way to make it big-time was to become a member of the Yakuza, also known as the Japanese mafia.

Although only affiliated with the Yakuza, the two men benefitted from the deception that they *were* Yakuza. They knew that fear was power, and they used that power freely. Being Japanese, they were allowed to do business, so long as they paid a handsome tribute each week to the Yakuza.

The Yakuza was a transnational organized crime syndicate with membership topping one hundred thousand. Fujita and Ogura knew from frequent mentions in the Japanese media as well as talk on the street that the Yakuza were notorious for their strict codes of conduct and organized fiefdom nature. With no connections, Fujita and Ogura were never accepted as Yakuza in Japan.

They had met in a bar in Kyoto twenty years earlier. Fujita was a petty thief with no gang affiliation. He struck up a conversation with Ogura and learned that the hotheaded Ogura had been fired from his job in a Mitsubishi factory for fighting with fellow workers. Ogura's size was impressive, and Fujita thought he might be able to use it to his advantage. They teamed up, and Fujita used Ogura to intimidate small businesses into paying protection money. The scheme worked until a local gang threatened them with torture and death if they continued.

Fujita heard that the Yakuza had a large presence in the United States. The Yakuza owned half of the skyscrapers built in the 1980s in downtown Chicago, were major owners of several American banks, and were the unpublicized kingpins in dope and human trafficking in America. The two men had thought that perhaps the grass was greener across the great pond. Maybe they could hook up with American Yakuza. They arrived in Los Angeles but believed that prospects would be better for them in the great city of New York.

Fujita had hoped the death of the Guatemalan girl would never see the light of day—a person who never existed. The authorities were looking for the killer or killers of a person who indeed did exist, though from the news report, little was known about her, not even her name, and nothing about her killer. The reports had said that she appeared to be in her late teens, about five three, possibly Latina.

Fujita wasn't happy. "I thought you said you buried her under the trash."

Ogura answered meekly, "I did. Maybe somebody moved the trash aside and saw her."

Fujita waved a hand. "Ah, it probably won't matter. No one will claim her. Maybe they'll slice her up in some medical school."

Morgan was at her desk when a call came in from a Mr. Kagawa, who said he had reported his daughter missing two days ago.

Morgan shuffled some papers around until she found the report of a fourteen-year-old named Wendy Kagawa who had been last seen outside her former high school in Chinatown.

"Mr. Kagawa. Since the missing girl resides in Nassau County, the case is being handled by a precinct there."

"I realize that, but I have information that might be of interest to persons in your precinct."

"And why is that?"

"At exactly two forty-seven, around the time she was to take the subway to Penn Station, I received a text message and photo that stated she was being driven home by a friend's father."

"Did she give you any names?"

"No. But she snapped a photo of the young man whose father was to drive her home. Obviously, she never made it home."

"Sir, I still don't know why it would involve my precinct."

"Because several hours ago, I realized that the photo was taken in front of her former high school in Chinatown."

"Didn't you tell the Nassau police?"

"Immediately. They said they would also contact your precinct, but I got the impression they're still treating this as a runaway. My wife and I know this is impossible, so I thought I would contact your precinct myself, and they put me through to you. If you knew my daughter, you would agree. I believe she was kidnapped, probably in front of the school."

Morgan tapped her finger on her desk, deep in thought. "Let me understand you clearly. You received a message that instead of taking the train home, she was being driven home by a friend's father, and you never heard from her again?"

"Exactly. If she had changed her mind and done something else, she would have texted or called me so that I would know to pick her up at the train station, which was our original and usual plan."

"Can you send me the text and photo now?"

"Certainly. What's the number?"

She gave him the number and received the text in less than a minute. She placed Kagawa on hold so that she could examine its contents. The photo was a clear headshot of a young man who appeared Asian. In the background was a school that Morgan knew was in Chinatown. The text read, "Cute & 16. His dad driving me home. W."

Morgan picked up the phone. "Mr. Kagawa. Do you recognize the young man?"

"No, but she had many friends and acquaintances there. Could have been anyone."

"Would she normally take a ride with someone you didn't know?"

"No, but it started to rain heavily that afternoon, and the subway was several blocks away from her school. I guess that sealed the deal. But understand, if there was another change of plans, she would have immediately contacted me. My daughter is an honor student and always reliable."

"I'm sure the detectives there attempted to trace her whereabouts through her phone."

"They did. Her cell's last location was in Chinatown. After that, nothing. She would never turn her phone off. I believe something more sinister must have happened."

"Let me make a couple of calls." She intended to check out his story with Nassau. "Perhaps we can take over some of the investigation."

"That would be wonderful. Any help would be greatly appreciated."

The call ended. Morgan discussed the call with Captain Graves, who contacted the Nassau precinct. Detectives there confirmed Kagawa's story and were more than happy to turn over part of the investigation to a local Chinatown precinct.

Morgan brought Ben up to date on the missing Wendy Kagawa. Their first step was to take the photo of the young man to the high school, hoping to identify him. They drove there and met with the principal and two vice principals. None of them were able to identify the young man, but they admitted that with some two thousand pupils, that didn't mean he wasn't a student.

Morgan and Ben were given permission to circulate throughout the school, showing the photo to dozens of students, some of whom had attended the school for three years. No one was able to confirm that the boy in the photo ever went there. The one real break came when a girl stated that she was certain she had seen him hanging around the outside of the school on more than one occasion as school was being dismissed.

Morgan asked, "How certain are you that this is the same person?"

The girl shyly answered, "Very. Because he's so nice-looking."

Morgan and Ben decided to stake out the school, arriving prior to it letting out. If he had hung out at the school before, perhaps he would do it again.

They intended to stake out the school for the next few days, at around two twenty, before the end of the school day. They would wait until the majority of the students left. If they saw nothing, they would return to the precinct.

They sat in their unmarked car, looking up and down the block. Ben turned on the radio to a classical music station.

Morgan asked, "You like this stuff?"

"Sometimes. I grew up with it. My parents tried to get me to play the cello. I got turned on by The Grateful Dead."

"*You* were a Deadhead?"

"I didn't follow them around the country, but Jerry Garcia inspired me to play the guitar. So I also like pop music."

"How well do you play?"

"I'm no professional, but I can play. What music do you like?"

"Both rock and rap."

He smiled sardonically. "Rap crap? I can never understand the words."

"Maybe you're not listening close enough. Some powerful stuff there."

He nodded. "Maybe so."

Day one offered no results, but on day two, with the two of them compromising and listening to a rock station, they believed they hit pay dirt. Standing on the street, across from the school, was a young man who resembled the person in the photo. As school was letting out, the short, slightly built young man seemed to be watching the students leaving, as though studying them.

Morgan felt her pulse quickening. If that little twerp had something to do with Wendy's disappearance, she would make certain he spent many years behind bars. And if he worked for others, perhaps she might nab them as well.

Morgan and Ben made their move. They exited their vehicle and quickly strode up to the young man. Morgan stopped on one side of him, while Ben stopped on the other side. It was apparent that this was indeed the person in the photo. The young man was stone-faced as Morgan introduced themselves as detectives, flashing their IDs.

Not appearing at all nervous, he shrugged. "What do you want with me? I ain't done nothin'."

Ben immediately showed the young man the photo. "This is you."

The young man flinched ever so slightly. "How did you get that?"

Morgan asked, "You have ID on you?"

"Sure." He reached into his back pocket and extracted his wallet. Taking out his driver's license, he handed it to Morgan.

"Masahiro Araki. Is that your real name?"

"No. It's really Bruce Lee."

"You can cut the sarcasm. You live at this address?"

"Yeah."

"And according to this license, you're nineteen?"

"If that's what it says," he testily replied. "Listen, I got stuff to do. I gotta go."

Ben said, "We would like you to voluntarily come with us to the precinct to answer some questions. Otherwise, we can read you your rights and handcuff you right here and still take you to our precinct."

"About what? What did I do?"

Morgan stated, "Nothing that we know of. We just need some things cleared up. Again, your choice. The easy way or the hard way."

"Then I'm not under arrest?"

"Not if you cooperate," Ben answered.

"OK, but then I got stuff to do."

Morgan asked, "Do you need to call your parents?"

"I live alone. No parents."

They drove Hiro to the station house and began their inquiry in the interview room, with both detectives sitting across from Hiro at the metal table.

Ben began. "This photo was taken by a girl named Wendy Kagawa. It shows you in front of her former high school. Look at the caption. It reads, 'Cute & 16. His dad driving me home. W.'"

"She thought I'm cute. So what?"

"You said you had no parents," Morgan stated. "Why would your father be driving her home?"

"How should I know? She must be a mixed-up kid. First, she gets my age wrong. Then she says my father is driving her home? I don't have a father. Never did."

"How long did you know her?" Ben asked.

"I just met her."

"Why would she snap your photo?"

"I told you, I didn't even know she took it."

Morgan asked, "Why did you talk to her?"

"I like good-looking girls. Is that a crime? We spoke for a couple of minutes, and then I left for home because it started to rain."

Morgan stared at the seemingly self-assured young man. She was fairly certain he was lying.

"Do you own a car?" Ben asked.

"A real piece of crap."

"Where do you keep it? We would like to examine it," Morgan said.

"Examine it? For what?"

Ben said, "You might have been the last person to see her before she disappeared. If you gave her a ride in your car, we would like to search it."

Hiro looked at Ben and then at Morgan. "What's going on? You think something happened to this girl, and I got something to do with it?"

Morgan asked, "Again, why would she state your father was going to drive her home, and why did you tell her you were sixteen? You do look young for nineteen."

"Like I said, she must be a mixed-up kid. You can search my car all you want." He smirked and added, "Gee, but don't look in the trunk."

"And how about your apartment?" Ben asked.

"I watch a lot of cop shows on TV. Don't you guys need a search warrant?"

Morgan rapped her knuckles on the metal table. "I assure you, we can get one."

"OK, I'll show you where my car is parked. And you can look in my apartment, but bring a knife so you can cut this girl loose. But then you gotta let me go. Deal?"

Morgan knew he seemed too confident about the searches, but maybe he was good at bluffing, and maybe there were clues he didn't know he'd left. She would still check out the car and apartment.

Morgan said, "Let's assume that she didn't get into your car and she's not in your apartment. Then whose car did she get into?"

"How should I know?"

"What happened after she took the photo?" Ben asked.

"Again, I didn't even know she took it."

"OK. What did you see her do?" Morgan asked.

"It started to rain, so I said, 'See ya,' and ran home. Left her there and never saw her again."

"What do you do for a living?" Ben asked.

"Odd jobs."

"Who for?" Morgan asked.

"Different people."

Morgan continued. "What are their names?"

"I never ask. They ask me to deliver something, so I do it, and they pay cash."

"How do they find you?" Ben asked.

"I hang out at different bars. I got a reputation. They seem to find me."

"What's your relationship with the Yakuza?" Morgan asked.

"Never heard of 'em."

Morgan leaned forward in her chair. "How about Satoshi Akita? Ever do any work for him?"

He shrugged his shoulders. "Never heard of him either."

"Why do you hang out at the school?" Ben asked.

"I like to meet foxes. If I see one, I go talk to her."

"Like Wendy?" Morgan asked.

"Sure. She's real pretty. But like I keep telling you, it started to rain real bad, so I got out of there."

Morgan asked, "Did you know she's only fourteen? That's jailbait."

"Fourteen? She told me she was eighteen."

The questioning went on for two more hours, with Araki never wavering in his story.

They ushered Araki downstairs to their Ford. They seated him in the rear seat and closed the door. Before getting into the car, Morgan turned to Ben and said, "It doesn't smell right. He stands outside a high school just to meet girls? And I believe the text. He probably told her he was sixteen."

"Unfortunately," Ben answered, "there's no law against lying to pick up a girl."

"Yeah, but for what purpose?"

"That's what we hope to find out."

They asked forensics to meet at the location of his car. They thoroughly examined the beat-up, white 2002 Chevy, finding nothing of value.

Hiro then let them into his apartment in a run-down building in Chinatown. It was a tiny studio, about five hundred square feet, with a bed at the end near a window and a kitchenette and bathroom at the other end. At first glance, the place appeared to be typical of many a young bachelors' pads, with empty beer bottles here and there, clothing strewn about helter-skelter, dishes piled high in the sink, cigarette butts floating in a coffee mug, and a fork congealed in the remains of whatever he'd eaten in the past few days. Since they had no search warrant, they had to be careful not to go too far. They had no compelling reason to believe Wendy Kagawa was or had been there, and courts routinely threw out evidence obtained without a lawful warrant. Their main interest was satisfied; Wendy Kagawa wasn't being held captive in the apartment.

Morgan and Ben had to release the smirking Araki, but he remained high on their list of suspects. They left the apartment for their car.

Back at the precinct, a seated Morgan pounded her desk with her fist and said to Ben, who was standing, "Something smells fishy with that kid. I know it's a crappy apartment, but even that one would carry a rent that would be out of reach for a guy that *does errands* for people whose names and addresses he doesn't know."

"Agreed. But let's fill out the report and ask around about him."

Morgan and Ben included in their report that it was still possible that Wendy Kagawa was merely a runaway and would soon be found or return home on her own. It often ended that way. But the photo and text had them suspecting otherwise.

Morgan and Ben then canvassed various bars in Chinatown, attempting to find any friends and associates and what jobs Araki may have held. They discovered he was well known in the area as a small-time hustler who called himself Hiro. He hung around local bars and strip clubs, very often with some young girl at his side. Some of the locals leaned toward him being a pimp, lining up customers that he'd met at the bars and strip clubs, prime territory for introducing men to prostitutes. The detectives made a note to bring Araki back for questioning regarding his possible involvement in prostitution.

That evening, Morgan's phone indicated Paul was calling. She let it ring several times and took a deep breath before deciding to answer. "Yes, Paul."

"Listen, I was wondering if you would meet me for a drink. For old time's sake."

She felt a quiver of anger. She didn't want Paul anymore, but it wasn't easy to give up on a marriage. She didn't want to think about the good times. *I loved you once, you fool.* "I'm dead tired. Been a long day. I work, remember?" She didn't mean for it to sound like a dig; she just wanted to get off the phone.

He took it as such. "I'm lining up a job with a local construction company."

That wheedling tone in his voice. She hated it six different ways. "That's great, but I really need my rest. Thanks anyway. Good night, Paul." She hung up.

An irritated Morgan hoped that once the divorce was final, he would get the picture. Maybe someday she could look back on her marriage with clear eyes. Not yet. She opened Jon Meacham's book and had faith that enough reading would make her forget about Paul and put her to sleep.

But her mind kept drifting from the book to that smirking Akita. Somehow, she would wipe that smile off his face. A bullet in each eye would probably do it.

CHAPTER 6

BARRY SLOAN DIDN'T JOG TO STAY IN SHAPE, ALTHOUGH IT
was a welcome by-product. Running relieved the tension of his job as a
stockbroker, where the highs never seemed to counterbalance the lows.

His usual routine was navigating the well-lit streets of Long Island's
south shore after work, often post sundown. But by every full moon's
light, he and his dog, Merrill, would run along the shore of the local
beach between the shoreline's iridescent white foam and the beachgrass-
covered sand dunes. Merrill enjoyed running unleashed alongside her
master.

Normally, he would run to the last house situated above the dunes—
whose backyard lemon lights drew scores of fluttering moths—and then
turn and head for home, but the cool late-September air and gentle
breeze made him feel especially strong, and he was determined to run
another mile toward the marshland. He heard the thunderous crashing
of waves tirelessly attacking the slowly eroding shore, the nocturnal

chirping of crickets, and the sound of his shoes slapping against the wet sand. His pace was set by a rhythmic metronome of breathing and panting. He could taste the salty ocean air.

Barry reached the marshland and turned to go back, expecting Merrill to do likewise, but she uncharacteristically began to bark. He turned to see her run into the thicket of tall marsh grass.

"Hey, girl. Get out of there!" he shouted.

Merrill stopped fifty feet into the grass and continued to bark at something.

As though she could understand English, he yelled, "There could be snakes and ticks in there. Come here!" he commanded. "We're going home." He turned and began a slow, mock jog toward home, peering over his shoulder to make sure she followed, but she stood still, barking repeatedly.

He stopped and turned toward Merrill. "Merrill, let's go!" He briefly thought of going in and retrieving her, but his admonition about ticks and snakes resonated with himself, especially as he was dressed only in jogging shorts.

The wind shifted for a moment, and he detected the stench of a decaying animal. He thought that might be what was attracting Merrill's attention.

He hated to trick her, but he whistled the brief tune telling her that food was in her bowl, and Merrill dutifully bounded out of the grass, catching up to him with something in her jaw.

"What do you have there, girl?" He bent down, squinting in the moon's dim light, and exclaimed, "Shit!" He wasn't certain, but it appeared to be a human thigh bone.

"Drop it," he commanded, and she set the bone at his feet. He extracted his cell from his pocket and dialed 911, telling the operator what he'd found. She replied that she would take his name and phone number and have the proper authorities contact him.

Later that night, two Nassau County detectives arrived and, guided by Barry, Merrill, and flashlights, strode into the area where Merrill had picked up the bone. The detectives covered their noses as they detected the stench of rotting flesh. To their horror, they discovered what appeared to be at least three different bodies in various stages of decomposition. Apparently, they had been haphazardly buried but were exposed by the action of severe high tides during storms. A CSI unit examined the area, and the remains were carted off by the coroner to the morgue.

The autopsies determined that one of the victims was a female, possibly Asian, in her early teens. The ME stated that the victim had been dead for about a week when discovered, enough time for decay and various animals and insects to chew on the body, making visual identification difficult. Her tissues told the tale of death due to a massive overdose of heroin.

Two other bodies had been there at least several months to perhaps a year, making it difficult to pin down exact cause of death. They would attempt to match the descriptions, dental records, tattoos, scars, and DNA profiles to the list of missing persons to hopefully identify the remains. From the skeletal remains, the medical examiner was able to quickly determine that both of these victims were female, with one estimated as twelve or thirteen and the other as sixteen or seventeen.

The description of the female with Asian features matched that of a Nassau County girl named Wendy Kagawa, recently listed as missing. Nassau County detectives intended to contact the Kagawas and ask them to meet at the morgue in Nassau.

Mike and Amy Kagawa had been waiting and worrying for almost two weeks when word regarding their daughter, Wendy, had mercifully arrived. She was originally supposed to have been at the Great Neck train station after visiting friends from her former high school, something she had done regularly since the family moved to a single-family home in Great Neck one year earlier.

Wendy was their only child, the bright light of their lives. They were told that her body had been found in a marshland on the south shore of Long Island. DNA proved positive that it was her, information the

Kagawas needed to believe that the horribly decayed and partially eaten thing they had viewed in the morgue was indeed their beautiful child. She had been blossoming into a wonderful young lady who played a lustrous violin and was on her school volleyball team.

It had been one excruciating day after another, three hundred and fifty-three hours by Mike Kagawa's count, played out one unbearable minute at a time. Amy was now more despondent than he could ever have imagined. The light of their lives had been extinguished—their legacy gone forever.

He had met Amy Tanaka through a mutual friend. She had just finished college, having majored in finance, and was newly hired by a department store as their bookkeeper. It was the type of job that suited her well since she was good with mathematics but extremely shy. Numbers she could deal with; people were another story. Yet it was her shyness that attracted him to her. There was something innocent about her, and he loved her for it. She became his rock, his best friend, and the loving mother to his daughter, their only child. They had thought about having another child, but Amy had developed endometriosis and needed to have a hysterectomy.

Mike Kagawa had taken a leave of absence from his teaching job, but now that Wendy had been found and the arrangements for cremation had been made, he intended to return to his classroom with the hope of alleviating some of the pain. His wife, Amy, could not yet bring herself to return to her bookkeeping job. Kagawa often saw Amy staring at a photo of Wendy, sometimes for hours without speaking. He tried to make her talk about her grief and suggested counseling for the two of them, to no avail. He hoped that with his help and perhaps counseling, they could put some of the pieces of their shattered lives back together.

When he returned home that late afternoon, he used his remote to open the garage door, expecting to pull his car in beside his wife's car, except that she had parked her car in the middle of the garage. He got out of his car and strode into the garage, where he detected the odor of exhaust fumes. He quickly looked inside the car and saw Amy slumped over toward the passenger side. Kagawa screamed, "No, no, no!" as he opened the door, dragged the limp body out of the car, and frantically attempted to perform CPR. He used his cell phone to dial 911, but her body felt cold as ice. He knew she was gone. Wracked with pain, all Kagawa could think of was that he would now have to make arrangements for *two* cremations. Losing Wendy, the love of his life, had been a stab through his heart. But at least he had Amy, the first love of his life, to grieve with. Who else could possibly understand? They'd had visions of attending a wedding one day and doting on grandchildren. Now there was nothing but darkness.

Other than the cremations and funerals, he could think of no reason to continue to go on living. He believed he would meet his beloved Wendy and Amy in the afterlife, and he would soon decide how to take his own life.

The Nassau detectives painstakingly searched their databases of missing persons, which was narrowed down when it was determined that the other two were also Asian. Dental records and DNA helped determine that one girl of thirteen was named Patty Chen, while the sixteen-year-old was named Li Huang, with both girls' last known residences in Chinatown. In both cases, a parent had listed them as missing, and they had been treated by the authorities as potential runaways. The investigations of these two were now handed over to Morgan and Ben, since they appeared related to Wendy Kagawa's case.

Patty Chen had two parents, an eighteen-year-old sister, and two older brothers in their early twenties. Morgan and Ben met with them in their small apartment. The five Chens sat on two couches while Morgan and Ben stood.

The father, Yong Chen, stated, "We knew our daughter was troubled, but she was a free spirit. Always a mind of her own. But no matter what she did, she did not deserve to be dumped in a swamp like a piece of garbage." He held back a sob, while Mrs. Chen dabbed her eyes with a tissue.

Ben asked, "How long had she been missing?"

Mr. Chen answered, "Over seven months. Nothing left but bones." He shook his head sadly.

Morgan asked, "Do you know anything at all about what she did during that time, or who might have killed her?"

They all shook their heads.

Both brothers vowed to, in some way, help with the investigation.

One of the brothers, a twenty-one-year-old named Lyle, was incensed as he stated, "If I could find the person or persons who did this, I would kill them." Lyle, well built with short-cropped black hair, continued, "I've had some training in mixed martial arts and wouldn't hesitate to strangle the sons of bitches."

Morgan responded, "I know this is difficult to handle, but don't even think of doing something that would place you in prison for the rest of your life. Your parents have suffered enough losing one child. Let us do our jobs. We'll do everything in our power to bring the guilty party to justice."

A choked-up Lyle said, "She was only thirteen. I loved my kid sister."

Morgan and Ben left. In their car, Ben driving, Morgan said, "I hope Lyle cools down. He needs to go through the agony of mourning his sister and then go on with his life."

Ben stopped at a light and turned to Morgan. "The impulse to become a vigilante is understandable. Fortunately, few ever act on those thoughts."

Morgan knew that, although it was rare, families in need sold their children into slavery, but she could find no indication that this was the case with the Chen family. It was also possible that any or all of the Chen, Huang, or Kagawa girls were abused by a father or other family member, causing them to end up a victim of trafficking. That possibility would have to be checked out.

Li Huang's unwed teenaged mother had immediately given Li up for adoption. Li was then adopted at the age of two by the Huangs after doctors determined that Mrs. Huang would never be able to conceive another child. The Huangs had one natural-born child, a boy of five at that time, now nineteen. Again, Morgan, whose job it was to suspect everyone, considered the possibility of the Huangs selling their adopted child into slavery or abusing her, but she had no evidence of it having occurred. Li Huang had been reported missing for almost nine months, and like Patty Chen, all that was left were mostly skeletal remains.

As they interviewed the Huang family in their apartment, the Huangs' guilt was palpable to Morgan, especially that of the father, Jimmy Huang. "We had chosen Li for adoption and had pledged to nurture her in every way possible. But Li was always affected by not knowing who her birth parents were. She would often ask why she was given up for adoption. Does she look like them? Does she have any brothers or sisters? Who were her grandparents? Questions like these seemed to haunt her. One day, Li just disappeared."

Jimmy Huang felt responsible, perhaps unduly, for her demise. "I had promised to raise Li as though of my own flesh and blood." He looked down at his clasped hands. "I must have failed her." He looked up at Morgan and Ben. "Without saying it, I feel that friends and relatives believe that we treated Li differently from our other child, and perhaps this led to her running away. But this was never the case." It left him inconsolable.

Like the Chen family, the Huang family could offer no aid in finding the perpetrators.

At the precinct, Morgan and Ben searched their databases and contacted Child Protective Services. There were no records of abuse for any of the Chen, Huang, or Kagawa females.

Now that Wendy Kagawa and two others were declared homicide victims, it was time to bring Masahiro Araki back in for further questioning.

Morgan and Ben sat at a table in the interview room, opposite Araki.

Ben began, "The reason for this second interview is that the girl who took your photo is now lying in the morgue, along with two other young women who were discovered at the same location. It follows that whoever killed Wendy is probably also responsible for the deaths of the other two. Since you were the last person known to have seen her alive, we believe you might have had something to do with her death."

Morgan observed him for a reaction, but he was expressionless.

"Like I told you before, it rained. I left. Someone else obviously killed her."

Morgan said, "We did some research on you. It appears you like to call yourself Hiro, and some of your so-called odd jobs may have included pimping for some person or group." She watched for any change in his expression but saw none. He was either telling the truth or was a very good liar.

"That's bull. I don't do that stuff. Like I said, I hang out at different bars. A guy says, 'Deliver this to a certain address,' and I do it. He pays cash in advance."

"What are some of these addresses?" Ben asked.

"Once the job is done, I forget them."

"Do you know a girl named Patty Chen?" Morgan asked.

"Who?"

"Patty Chen."

"Never heard of her."

"What about Li Huang?" Ben asked.

"What about her?"

Ben, who was almost twice Hiro's size, attempted to intimidate Hiro by getting in his face. With a raised voice, Ben said, "Patty Chen and Li Huang are the two girls found with Wendy. We know you killed them. Did you do it alone, or did you have help?"

Hiro leaned back in his chair. "This is all bullshit. I never heard of those two. Yeah, I met Wendy, but who those other two are, I have no idea."

Morgan felt like punching the little shit in his face. Maybe that would get him to confess.

Morgan's gut told her he knew more than he was admitting. Was the name Masahiro Araki going to be added to the list of sexual offenders who got away with their filthy deeds?

The questioning went on for another hour, with no crack in Araki's story. During that hour, Morgan felt like her stomach was full of stones grinding against one another.

Morgan was almost certain he was lying, at least where Wendy was concerned, but the possibility still existed that he was telling the truth. Perhaps once it rained, he left, and someone else picked her up. They continued to try to poke holes in his story, but Araki never wavered. They eventually had to let him go. Maybe forensics would come up with some evidence from the three bodies, but unless that occurred, they were momentarily at a dead end.

Morgan ended with an admonition. "I suggest you don't return to that school. Find yourself another place to hang out."

"You got it. I don't need you guys harassing me."

There was something about Araki that bothered Morgan. He was too cocky, too confident. At some point in the interview, an innocent nineteen-year-old would have appeared nervous, even scared. After all, they weren't discussing some petty theft. This was murder. But not Araki. It was as though he'd practiced for an interview such as this his whole life. She looked forward to finding any shred of evidence that might bring Araki back.

CHAPTER

THEY RECEIVED THE MEDICAL EXAMINER'S FOLLOW-UP REPORT
on Wendy, Patty, and Li. The ME determined that Wendy had been
killed by a massive drug overdose only days after she was reported
missing. She had been sexually and physically abused. The other two
young women were so badly decomposed it was impossible to rule on
the cause of death. The ME found no further evidence that might lead
to the perpetrators.

Morgan hoped this was only a temporary dead end in the
investigation of the three young women's deaths. The one case that
occupied much of her and Ben's time over the following two days
involved the young Jane Doe they now referred to as Butterfly, although
the other three girls were never far from their minds. Also, they had
received several calls from the Chen, Huang, and Kagawa families
asking about the progress of the investigation. The families were told
that even if they had a person of interest, they wouldn't be able to

divulge the name to the public unless an arrest was made. Morgan and Ben promised to keep them informed if and when progress was made. Mr. Kagawa had asked Morgan if they had identified the young man in the photo. Protocol required police not to divulge such information to the public in an ongoing investigation. She answered no.

Regarding Butterfly, they had obtained a postmortem photo of the girl's face and of the butterfly tattoo and had frequented many food and shopping establishments with the hope that someone would recognize her, unfortunately with no luck.

They worked the many tattoo parlors in the area, searching for the one that might have painted her. Perhaps they would have a record of Butterfly's name and/or address. After time-consuming visits to every parlor in the area—some in which Ben's Cantonese came in handy—they again had no luck.

"It's possible," Morgan said as they stood on the sidewalk on the corner of Delancey Street and the Bowery, "that if Butterfly was here illegally, she may have been tattooed in her native country."

Ben nodded. "And, of course, there would be no record anywhere of her entering the country. No name, nothing."

"Lending credence to that thought is the fact that no one has reported anyone missing who matches the description of Butterfly. Pretty easy to do with that tat."

"So, what we might have here is a girl from some Latin-American country, here illegally, who forensics found had semen on her skin, and who died of a drug overdose. Maybe DNA analysis can come up with something. Sounds like a typical case of sex trafficking."

"That would be my guess too, but if it is, as Graves said, it would be just one of many thousands of kids forced into trafficking." Morgan shook her head slowly.

"You OK?"

Morgan turned and pointed down the block. "I thought I saw Paul for a split second. But maybe I'm becoming paranoid where he's concerned."

Ben turned and peered down the block. Many people were strolling this way and that. "But maybe it *was* him. Like you said, he's stalking you. Maybe you should confront him."

"I have, but what I'm hoping is that he'll get tired of this crap. Maybe he'll get a job and won't have time for this. Or maybe he'll find some woman and forget about me."

"OK. Maybe. But be careful. You know that stalkers can become dangerous."

"I know, I know. But I don't think he would hurt me."

"You and I both know we've heard that song before … until."

She nodded. "I'll be careful."

In a serious tone, Ben said, "And you'll contact me if anything funny happens. Got it?"

She smiled appreciatively. "Got it."

She hadn't had a real father since she was eight. Although Ben was only about a dozen years older, she was beginning to view him almost as a father figure.

That evening, after polishing off two glasses of merlot, visions of her abuse by Father Timothy flashed through her mind. She felt immense anger building inside her, which made her restless. She began to pace back and forth in her apartment. She stopped pacing and decided to pay another visit to Akita's club. She left her apartment, got into her Ford, and arrived at the Happy Hour. She strode to Akita's table, where he was sitting with Nomura and Harada.

Akita looked up at her. "Back so soon, Detective?"

She wasted no time. "Does the name Wendy Kagawa mean anything?"

He put an unlit cigar in his mouth. "Should it?"

Nomura got up and disappeared as she asked, "What about Patty Chen or Li Huang?"

"Never heard of them."

"How about a Hispanic girl with a large butterfly tat on her lower back?"

"Why would I know any of them?"

"Because you deal in sex trafficking."

He took the cigar out of his mouth and pointed it at her. "That's a horrible accusation."

"Not as horrible as it would be if I arrest you," she forcefully said.

"You're so pretty when you're angry. I could use a good-looking woman like you on my stage."

"And our prisons need dirtbags like you."

Harada suddenly stood menacingly, chest out.

Akita grabbed his arm and calmly said, "It's OK."

Harada sat down, glaring at her.

"Detective. I don't know why you have a bug up your ass about me, but you either arrest me or get the hell out of my establishment. I run a legitimate business here."

"We'll be seeing each other again. Guaranteed."

She strode out of the club with a satisfied smile.

Harada asked Akita, "Chunhua?"

He shook his head. "Let's see how she handles tonight."

Morgan was pleased with herself as she entered her Ford. She gasped as she looked at the windshield. Splattered across the windshield was a bloody tampon. Disgusted, she turned on her windshield wipers, but they merely streaked blood farther across the windshield. She pressed the button for the washer fluid, which cleared away most of the blood, but the tampon itself had become stuck under the wiper blade. She stepped out of the car, gingerly grasped the tampon's string, freed it from the blade, and threw it to the ground.

"Cocksuckers," she said, bristling with anger.

She rushed back into the club, where she confronted the three seated men, angrily shouting, "I guess you think this is a game we're playing. It's not. Sooner or later, I'll see you behind bars." She stormed out of the club without waiting for a response.

Akita said to the two men, "She really is quite pretty when she's angry."

The men all laughed.

Tadashi Ogura was sitting on the old threadbare couch in the Mott Street apartment with Alice and a new teenaged girl, May Ling, sitting topless on either side of him, when Hideki Fujita asked, "Where is Hiro? He should have called by now."

Ogura bristled. "I told you we cannot trust that kid. Makes too many mistakes." Ogura stood and strode next to Fujita, towering over him. Ogura was the opposite of Fujita in many ways, being over six feet tall, weighing almost three hundred pounds, and with a shaved head, but he differed especially in temperament. Ogura was swift to mete out justice with violence.

They walked into the bedroom, out of earshot of the two girls.

"Right now, he's the best we have. Good with young girls," Fujita said.

Ogura looked down at Fujita. "Except for the Japanese girl."

"Everyone makes mistakes. We wait a bit longer, then check on the other places."

"We're running short." Ogura snorted. "That stupid Guatemalan slut had to go and OD."

"You're certain there will be no connection to us?" Fujita asked dubiously.

He shrugged noncommittally "The dumb shit arrived from Central America through Mexico. No form of ID when she got here. I'm not even sure her real name was Maria. No family, no friends, just us and the johns who would never admit to knowing her."

"And the Japanese girl?"

"I didn't think using a dumpster so soon after Maria was smart, so I went to our old burial spot."

Fujita nodded approval. "That *was* smart."

Ogura smiled.

They walked back to the living room, where they waited impatiently for Hiro's call for ten more minutes. Fujita told the girls they would be back later that night to collect the day's earnings. They left the two girls alone to wait for the day's lineup of customers.

May Ling had just that day been transferred to that apartment, taking the place of the dead Guatemalan girl, Maria, so this was the first time they had a chance to get to know each other.

Alice had been working and living at that apartment for just under one year.

With the two of them still sitting on the couch, Alice turned to May Ling. "What's your story, and how old are you? You look older than some of us." The two of them could have passed for sisters, each with long, straight jet-black hair, both about five foot two with ample breasts and slim figures.

May Ling answered haltingly, "I seventeen. I from small town China. Smugglers promise bring me New York. Find me good job in nail salon for fifty thousand dollar American. They say I pay back from wages. They take all ID. Say I must sell body to pay debt. They say, I do not, they tell immigration, and smugglers will hurt family in China. I no choice. They give apartment to share, and food."

Alice acknowledged with a nod. "I'm only fifteen. My grandparents came from China a long time ago, ya know, so I don't speak Chinese. I was born and raised in the Bronx. My mother's piece-of-shit boyfriend forced me to have sex with him when I was just thirteen. I go and tell my mother, and guess what? She throws *me* out. I had no idea where to go, ya know, so I wound up at a bus terminal, where Hiro sees me and tells me how beautiful I am and that he would take care of me as my boyfriend. I lived with him for a month. He turned me on to coke, then tells me we need money and that turning tricks was the only way to earn it. Hiro supplied me with coke to take the edge off. I figure, what the hell, if that piece-of-shit boyfriend could take it for free, why not give it for cash? I don't really see any of it, ya know, but like you said, we eat and have a roof over our head. The drugs are pretty good too. The worst part of this is some of the johns are disgusting. I once tried to refuse this one guy, so big, ugly Ogura beat me and threatened to tell my mother that I was a prostitute. So here I am."

May Ling said, "Many men, how you say, dis … gus … ding."

Alice wistfully said, "One day I'm getting out of here."

"Where you go?"

"That's the thing. I don't know. I dream some rich family, like on TV, will take care of me. Ya know, buy me nice clothes, take me to movies, restaurants." She bit a fingernail and said, "I had friends in school. Now, anyone I get close to ends up being transferred, kicked onto the street, or dead."

May Ling was taken aback. "Dead?"

Alice hesitated. "Listen. Be careful. Two girls OD'd and died right here, only a few days ago. I can't get it out of my mind. Try to stay off too much H. Understand?"

There was a knock at the door. A man's voice called through the door, "I love Peking Duck."

The girls both knew what that meant. May Ling's first customer of the day had arrived.

That evening, Morgan was in her apartment, getting ready to meet someone she knew only as Tyler at the Smith, a trendy American restaurant on Second Avenue in midtown. She had moved out of her apartment that she had shared with her husband, Paul Sperling, and was glad she had chosen to keep her last name of Kelly. It had made it easier with her job, and now it would make it easier after her annulment.

They had lived in a one-bedroom apartment in Tribeca, where he was still living, and she had moved to a studio apartment in Soho. Manhattan was a big town, and she knew the crossings of their paths were more than coincidence.

Her new apartment contained a twin bed, a small couch, a kitchenette table that could seat two, and bare walls. She had left Paul with the few posters and cheap paintings that adorned her old apartment.

She had met Tyler at the Broome Street Bar in Soho one week earlier when she was feeling down on herself and didn't want to sit home alone. Going out by herself wasn't something she normally did since the bar scene for her had ended years earlier, before she met Paul. She had been sitting at the bar, enjoying a lite beer, when Tyler took the stool next to hers. He ordered a Southern Comfort, which he downed in one big gulp. She noticed this and said, "Slow down. That drink was meant to be savored."

He turned to look at her and smiled. "Yeah, it *usually* is."

She took a guess. "Female problems?"

He laughed. "You a mind reader?"

"Hey, bud. I know where you're coming from."

"I hope you're not having female problems also," he said half-jokingly.

She swiveled in her stool and looked squarely at his face for the first time. It was a handsome face, she thought. Blond hair, cut short, aquiline nose, and square chin. She was expecting to see someone in his twenties or early thirties, but this man seemed closer to forty. "No, my problems stem from the male being-an-asshole syndrome."

He laughed again, a full hearty laugh this time. "Then we're kind of in the same boat."

"If it's the *Titanic* you're talking about, yeah," she remarked in a droll way.

He smiled and extended his hand. "I'm Tyler."

She glanced at the hand, shook it briefly, and said, "Morgan."

"Pleased to make your acquaintance, Morgan."

"Is that a southern accent I'm detecting?"

"Why yes, ma'am. It most certainly is," he said with a purposely exaggerated twang.

She smiled. "Where from?"

"Born and raised in Asheville, North Carolina. But, you know, I detect a slight accent of yours, and it's not Brooklyn."

"You have a good ear. I was raised in Boston. Lived there until thirteen. Never totally lost that accent."

He seemed to be admiring her face when he asked, "Hey, Miss Morgan. How would you like to have dinner with me sometime? My treat."

She was both flattered and flustered. It had been a long time since she had been asked out on a date. "How do I know you're not some serial killer?" She instantly regretted her lame attempt at humor.

He didn't laugh. "Tell you what. You tell me when you're free, and we can meet at a favorite restaurant of mine, the Smith on Second Avenue. We can get to know each other better, and you can decide if my real name is Jeffrey Dahmer."

She wanted to laugh but didn't. She thought the worst that could happen was that she would get a free meal. "OK, but it would have to be in about a week. Say, next Thursday?"

"Thursday would be great."

"Let's meet there. Eight sound good?"

"Sure. Shouldn't we exchange cell numbers?"

She pondered the question. "Not at this point. I know if one of us can't make it for any reason, we'll never see each other again. And that would be fine. If it's not that important to either one of us, then it was never meant to be." She was accustomed to being disappointed by men, forever on guard where relationships were concerned.

He grinned. "Then if it's karma for us to have met, it will be karma for us to be there."

"I couldn't have said it better." She smiled.

They parted ways, not knowing if there would be a first date.

Thursday had arrived, and she was applying a small amount of makeup, the finishing touches to what she hoped might be a fun evening—providing he showed up. Even if he did, it could still be a total disaster. She looked in the mirror and was happy with what she saw. She wore an off-white silk blouse and black pants. She left, hailed a taxi, and arrived at the restaurant at 7:55. Five minutes early. The busy restaurant had a wood-lined ceiling that seemed to warm the entire restaurant, whose booths and tables were filled with a noisy crowd. Upon entering, she apprehensively asked the maître d' if a Tyler had made a reservation for two at eight. To Morgan's relief, the young man said that Tyler was already there. A waitress showed her to his booth.

Tyler slid out of the booth to greet her with a firm handshake. He eyeballed her from head to toe and exclaimed, "Wow!"

She blushed. "You look OK yourself." He wore a navy V-neck sweater and dark slacks. They slid into opposite sides of the booth.

He said, "I'm glad you didn't stand me up."

"Likewise."

"You know, before we order drinks, maybe we should at least know each other's full names."

"OK. You first."

"Tyler Anderson. And you?"

"Morgan Kelly."

The waitress handed them menus and asked if they would like a drink. Morgan ordered a lite beer, and he ordered the same. The waitress shuffled off.

"No Southern Comfort tonight?"

"Only when I'm down. I drink beer when someone makes me happy."

She looked him straight in the eye. Was he merely a smooth-talking con artist? Or was he speaking truth? "And why are you happy tonight?" She anticipated his answer.

"Because I'm here in this fine establishment with a beautiful woman."

This time, she did not blush. Maybe he thought a couple of compliments would woo her into his bed tonight. "Is that your normal pickup line?"

He seemed genuinely hurt. "I've always believed that telling the truth can't get you into too much trouble. But I can see, in your case, I'm wrong,"

She stared at him for a moment. She believed that by the end of the dinner, she would know if he wasn't just any old con artist but a master.

The waitress brought their beers and asked if they were ready to order, which they were not.

In an apologetic manner, he said, "Look. Maybe I've come on too strong, but once you get to know me, you'll see that I'm a nice guy who likes to speak truth."

She sighed. "Okay, Mister Truth. Tell me about yourself. What do you do for a living?"

"I'm an accountant—CPA actually. Just made partner at Eisner-Amper, a midtown accounting firm with over twelve hundred employees."

She showed no sign of being impressed. "Where did you go to school?"

"Did my undergrad at Duke and then got my MBA here at NYU. I loved being in the city and sought a job here, and here I am."

"I have to confess. The first thing I looked at last week was your finger."

"I can make the same confession. No ring there either." He pointed at her hand. "Were you ever married?"

"Once. Divorced now." She felt it better to lie, knowing it was soon to be true. "No kids. And you?"

"Came close recently. Was dating a woman for four years. We broke up about a month ago."

"What got in the way?"

"We sort of drifted apart. Hard to explain."

"Sorry."

"Don't be. I wouldn't have met you." He grinned.

There he goes again, she thought. He was beginning to annoy her.

"What about you?" he asked.

She braced herself for his expected reaction. "I'm a cop. Detective actually."

His eyebrows raised. "No kidding? Are all the cops as pretty as you?"

Jesus, he doesn't stop, she thought. "No. They're all better looking. Maybe you should go out with one of *them*." Her voice was biting.

He seemed put off. "Why is it so hard for you to accept a compliment?"

It was an interesting question. Why *was* it so hard? "Let's say under certain circumstances, I'm not averse to someone paying me compliments for my looks. I'd much rather get a compliment for what I do."

He nodded as though he understood. "Fair enough. Maybe if I get to know you, I might be able to do just that." He picked up his menu. "Maybe we should order."

The waitress arrived. Morgan ordered the little gem Caesar salad and the brick-pressed chicken. He ordered the jumbo shrimp cocktail and the seared tuna.

The rest of the evening consisted of small talk, from politics to favorite movies to hobbies. He said, "I like to jog or go to the gym. Helps clear my head."

She said, "I go to the shooting range whenever I get the chance. Helps to relieve some of the tension of the job."

He asked her to describe her duties as a detective, which she did in general terms.

After paying the bill, Tyler noticed an old-fashioned photo machine at the rear of the restaurant that took six photos for five dollars. He enthusiastically led her toward the machine.

"Are you kidding?" she asked.

"I used to take photos like this when I was a kid. Come on. We'll keep three each."

She acquiesced. They entered the tight booth, pulled the curtain closed, and sat on the small bench, which was hardly built for two. He paid the five dollars, and the machine lit up six times. In less than a minute, six photos of the two of them, smiling and mugging for the camera, emerged from a slot. They examined them and laughed. He handed her three, and he kept three.

They left the restaurant, but as soon as they stepped onto the sidewalk, Morgan abruptly turned away from him.

"Are you OK?" he asked, concerned.

She caught her composure. "I'm fine."

"You sure?"

She forced a smile. "Really. I'm fine. I had a good time tonight."

"Can I see you again?" For the first time, he seemed a bit nervous.

She looked at him. Maybe she was being too critical of him. "OK, but I can't say when right now."

"Let's exchange cell numbers, and I'll call you."

She took out her cell, and he did likewise. They added the numbers to their cells.

He hailed a taxi for her, and she left with only a limp handshake.

In the taxi, she was bristling with anger. She had seen Paul across the street, staring at them.

She immediately called Paul's cell, but all she got was his voice mail. There was no holding back as she angrily said, "Listen, asshole. If you don't stop stalking me, I'll put the cuffs on you myself. I mean it!" She ended the call as her body quaked with rage.

Fujita and Ogura opened the door to the apartment on Mott Street and entered the room while arguing over some bridge hands, having played bridge at the club that evening. The two naked girls, Alice and May Ling, were sitting on the couch watching television. Ogura requested they be butt naked each night when they came to collect the day's profits since he loved viewing the girls that way. Their bodies were totally shaved except for the hair on their heads. Ogura had an insatiable sexual appetite, and the girls knew that if he wanted it, it had to be given with as much fake enjoyment as they could muster.

While standing in the center of the room, Fujita pointed at Ogura. "We would have come in third if you had gone to slam. You had an eighteen count. How could you not go?"

Ogura answered sharply, "How about you leaving me in no trump when you had no stopper in their suit?"

Fujita waved his hand in disgust. He turned to the girls, who were staring at the two of them as though they were speaking Greek, and asked, "How did we do today?"

Alice replied with trepidation, knowing that a bad day did not bode well for them, especially knowing Ogura's temper. "Not so good."

"What does that mean?" Fujita asked, eyebrows raised.

Both girls defensively drew their knees to their chests.

Having worked in this apartment for almost a year, Alice had seen far more than most people saw in a lifetime. Not only was she the victim of beatings—and not always by Fujita and Ogura but also a couple of times by some asshole johns who couldn't get it up and blamed her for it—she was also a witness to the deaths of two other girls. First, it was Maria, who didn't know how to control her own drug habit, and then it was the stupid Japanese girl, Wendy, who just wouldn't cooperate. She knew Ogura had thrown Maria into a garbage dumpster, and she fervently hoped that wouldn't be her fate. She had never envisioned herself ending up in a place like this. But she couldn't go home and had nowhere else to go. If she were older, she could get a regular job—maybe—but nothing she could do, other than sex work, paid enough to live in the city; she knew that much. Thinking about it made her feel like the whole world was falling on her head. So she didn't think too often. She survived by living from moment to moment.

Alice nervously reached under the couch cushion, extracted a wad of bills, and handed it to Fujita. She braced herself for a beating.

Fujita counted the money and then looked sternly at both girls. "Where's the rest of it?" he demanded.

Ogura stepped menacingly closer to the couch. "If you hold out on us …" He balled his thick hand into a fist.

May Ling had been with them at another apartment for the past two years, and she had never been caught stiffing them before. Cowering, she said, "Many regular come. But no new."

"Didn't Hiro send some new blood?" Fujita asked.

"We wait for knock at door. New men say, 'Peking Duck' for me, 'Wonderland' for Alice, but no one say the words."

Ogura had been especially proud of the code word *Wonderland* he had picked for Alice. *Peking Duck* was Fujita's idea.

"That little shit," Ogura said. "I'll break him in two when I see him."

Fujita had already begun dialing Hiro's cell. It immediately went to voice mail. "Hiro, you better call. Where the fuck *are* you?" He ended the call. Addressing the girls, he said, "OK, I believe you."

Both girls slumped with relief.

Ogura stepped up to the couch. "But since you can't be very tired, you'll do me now." He unbuckled his belt and let his pants and shorts drop to his massive ankles. The girls didn't need to be prompted as to what to do next. Getting on their knees, they each took turns at him until he achieved release onto the girls' faces, which took less than two minutes. He picked up his pants, patted each one on the head, and said, "That's my good girls."

Fujita handed a roll of paper towels to them and then tossed a small plastic bag containing a white powder onto the couch. Fujita and Ogura left the apartment as the girls wiped their faces.

The girls were happy to see the two men leave without either of them being punched or kicked. But they wondered, where was Hiro? It was very unlike him to miss work.

Alice picked up the plastic bag. They turned to each other and giggled. They looked forward to powdering their noses.

After snorting the coke, a feeling of melancholy washed over Alice. She recalled a time in seventh grade when an eighth-grade boy kissed her on her lips. It was her first real kiss, and a warm glow coursed through her. Little did she know that it would also be her last kiss before her mother's boyfriend violated her. She longed for the feeling of that first kiss, and she was afraid she might never have a real romance. Who would want a dirty slut?

CHAPTER 8

TO EXACT REVENGE IS NOT ONLY A RIGHT; IT IS AN ABSOLUTE *duty*. Mike Kagawa was aware of this in spoken and unspoken ways, but he'd never imagined it would apply to him. His father had repeatedly stated that human beings were natural-born killers—that given the right circumstances, anyone might kill another person. His deceased father had said you needed only to follow history to see that even the most sophisticated societies were capable of mass destruction.

His father had witnessed the heinous acts of both Germany and his family's former homeland of Japan. The elder Kagawa had been only eight years old when the United States government chose to place his family in an internment camp at Manzanar in the Sierra Nevada of California, even though he and two-thirds of all Japanese Americans interned there were American citizens by birth, while Caucasian German Americans were never interned. It left an indelible mark on his family. But his son, Michael, hadn't been convinced of this natural predisposition for killing until recently. His life had been shattered, and all Mike Kagawa's thoughts had been focused on how to avenge his losses. This had been a reason to live, at least temporarily.

Standing in his living room, now devoid of most furniture, he glanced at the wall over the fireplace where the portrait of him with his wife and child still hung. In the corner of the room had stood an antique mahogany breakfront in which his wife had proudly displayed fine crystal and glass figurines, including vintage Japanese hand-painted porcelains with high-gloss finishes, finely detailed and accentuated in gold. Photos of his wife and daughter had been prominently displayed in the breakfront. His wife, Amy, had been his best friend these past twenty-five years. His fourteen-year-old daughter, Wendy, had been the joy of his life.

He glanced through the window at his favorite maple tree, standing regally in his side yard, just as it must have stood since the construction of the house some sixty years earlier. It was early October, and the leaves had begun turning color as though painted by an artist's brush, a harbinger of the winter that was to come.

But his winter had already arrived. Wendy had disappeared in September when the earth was still blossoming with life. Late summer would never have that same effect upon him again.

Kagawa knew that loss could come in many ways. Above all else was the loss of his daughter to murder and his dear wife to suicide. Whether warranted or not, he and his wife had felt guilty about not being able to protect their only child. But the search for their daughter had cost them their meager life savings and their home, the sum of which led them to feel a severe loss of respect. The Japanese called it loss of face. His wife had chosen to take her own life, as so many of her heritage had done before.

Kagawa ran his hand over his thinning gray hair as he approached the one television that remained. He turned the volume up high to whatever afternoon talk show happened to be playing. He would decide how soon to confront Masahiro Araki, held captive in his basement. But first, he would go to the mantel above the fireplace and speak to the two multicolored cremation urns that sat on it.

After he finished speaking to the ashes of his wife and child, Kagawa opened the door to the basement and closed it behind him. He stepped into the finished part of the basement and opened another door, which led to the unfinished section with its concrete walls and floor that housed the boiler and oil tank. Thick wooden beams supporting the first floor ran across the ceiling.

Sitting on a heavy wooden chair in the center of that room was a young man of Japanese descent whose name Kagawa knew from his driver's license. Normally, his most prominent feature wouldn't be his squinting eyes that spewed hatred at Kagawa as he entered the room. Hiro's perfectly shaped mouth was the first thing one would notice if it wasn't for the silver duct tape that totally obscured it, having been wrapped from his mouth to the back of his long dark hair and back again. His arms were likewise taped to the arms of the chair from hand to elbow. His legs were taped to the chair's legs from ankle to knee. Hiro tried speaking, but he was only able to make muffled sounds.

Kagawa bent down in front of the young man and stared into his eyes. He detected no fear in them, and he wondered how long that might last.

"I'm going to remove the tape from your mouth." He pointed toward the ceiling. "As you can hear, the TV upstairs is very loud, and in this basement, no one will hear you even if you scream at the top of your lungs, so don't bother."

Kagawa reached for the end of the tape and removed it from Hiro's mouth. The tape made scratching noises as it unraveled.

Hiro took a deep breath and shouted, "Who the fuck're you? What the fuck am I doing here? Are you some kind of pervert? If you are, I'm gonna fuck you up real good!"

"Hold on a second," Kagawa calmly answered. "All I want is some information, that's all. Then you go free."

"Information about what?" he said with a sneer. "And why am I in this chair? And how did I get here? And did you steal my wallet and phone? I had a couple hundred dollars."

"All very fair questions." Kagawa stood and began to slowly pace back and forth in front of the chair. "First, I grabbed you last night when you were either drunk or high on something as you staggered out of that bar. As you got to your car door and opened it—and by the way, you shouldn't drink and drive—I placed a rag saturated with ether over your mouth. You collapsed onto the front seat of your car, which I backed up to my car. I taped you up, threw you into the back seat of my car, and, around three last night, dragged you down here. I waited until I was certain you were awake. So here we are. By the way, I tossed your phone down a sewer so it couldn't be tracked."

Hiro shouted, "You fucking bastard! I need that phone. And why me? What do you want? Are you fucking nuts?"

Kagawa stopped pacing and shook his head slowly. "No, not nuts. Just angry most of the time, and sad all of the time," he wistfully said.

"OK, why me? And what do you want?" His eyes flared.

"Like I said, information."

"I don't know nothin'," he answered defiantly.

"How do you know? I haven't asked a single question."

"OK. Untie me, and I'll tell you anything you want."

He nodded at Hiro. "First, my answers. Then I let you loose." He looked down at Hiro and folded his arms across his chest. "Do you know a young woman, just a girl really, named Wendy Kagawa?"

Kagawa thought Hiro's eyes betrayed him for a split second as Hiro answered with assurance, "Don't know no Wendys or Kagawas. And the cops already asked me a lot of questions about her, but they let me go 'cause I didn't do nothing."

Kagawa studied him, and then he said, as though a bone were caught in his throat, "But I know you did. She was fourteen and very pretty. I would say beautiful, in fact." Kagawa inhaled deeply at the thought of his daughter. He felt the muscles in his stomach tighten.

"Never heard of her and never saw her," he retorted sharply. "OK, I answered you. Now cut me the fuck loose." He struggled against the tape.

Calmly, Kagawa continued. "My only child disappeared a few weeks ago. A blessing to us, as we never thought we could have children, but then one day, a miracle, my Wendy was born. I quit my job to search for her. The police surmised that she was a runaway, but we knew that was impossible. I hired a private investigator at considerable cost, to no avail. We spent three hundred and fifty-three hours of pure agony with sweaty, sleepless nights, and when sleep mercifully came, it came with nightmares and endless days of not knowing if Wendy was alive or not. Where was she? Who took her? What was happening to her? Would we ever get her back, the only child we would ever have? But we never gave up hope in finding our little girl. Can you understand that?" His voice had reached a crescendo.

Hiro didn't answer.

Kagawa drew a calming breath before continuing. "Then, last week, her remains were found in a marshland on the south shore of Long Island along with the remains of other poor young girls. We had to view her decomposed body. My wife was so distraught she committed suicide. I had cremations for the two of them on the same day. They are both sitting on my mantelpiece upstairs. Nothing but ashes." His face became distorted as a tear rolled down his cheek.

"Hey, sorry, man. But what's that got to do with me?"

"I was the one who gave the police the text with your photo, which is why they questioned you."

"Wow, what a great story." The sarcasm was thick as tar. "I need to use the bathroom. Gotta piss bad."

"You'll have to piss in your pants until I get what I want," he answered testily.

Hiro shouted, "Well what the fuck do you want?"

"I thought, *Why didn't this person's father drive her home? How could she be abducted in front of a school in broad daylight? Maybe this person took her with the help of his so-called father.*"

"Again, nice story. Got nothin' to do with me."

"I staked out the school at the end of each day for the past several days, just like the police did. I parked by the school and saw the police take you away. I called the police and was told that no one had been arrested. I returned to the school for the next few days, hoping you would be there again. I spotted you acting like a high school student and followed you to your car. By the way, you could pass for sixteen … lie number one. Your driver's license says nineteen. I then followed you to your apartment. I left quickly, drove to my high school, got some ether from the science storeroom, went back to your apartment, waited until you left, and followed you last night to the bar. Now you are here, Masahiro Araki. A very Japanese name for someone so American."

"My family came from Japan when I was an infant. My friends call me Hiro. I like the nickname. Sounds like—"

"Got it. You're a real hero. You probably struck up a conversation. She thought you were sixteen, didn't she? You're probably a smooth talker and offered her a lift home. She would never accept a ride home with a stranger, but I guess when someone pulled up in a car, an adult Japanese male, I assume, she believed it was your father and thought it would be OK. Besides, it rained heavily that afternoon, and that may have sealed the deal."

Hiro struggled against the tape. "Bullshit! All bullshit!" Spittle flew out of his mouth. "It wasn't me. And I didn't kill her."

Kagawa pointed a crooked finger at him. "Then you must know who did."

He shrugged. "How should I know?"

"I think the man in the car might know something. Who is he?"

"Listen, I gotta piss. Unless you want it all over your floor, let me get to a bathroom."

"This house is up for sale. I can't bear all the memories. Piss on the floor all you want. I don't give a shit." It was the first time he let his anger take hold.

"What are you gonna do, shoot me? I doubt you're a killer."

With serene calmness, Kagawa answered, "I don't even own a gun, although now I have yours." He pulled a pistol from his pants pocket and showed it to Hiro. "It was tucked neatly away in the small of your back. I guess every person your age carries a concealed weapon, don't they, you big *hero*."

Hiro shrugged. "I need it for protection."

Ignoring Hiro, Kagawa said, "My father always told me that under certain conditions, we're all natural-born killers. If I don't get my answers, you become useless to me. I kill you, I get at least a bit of revenge, and then I go upstairs and talk to the ashes of my wife and daughter."

"Look, you know you're not a killer. Do you want blood all over the floor for the next owner to see?"

"You're right. I'm not a killer. And I don't relish trying to clean blood off my floor. But you will, in effect, be killing yourself."

The blood drained from Hiro's face. "What? I'm not killing myself. You want me dead, you'll have to fucking do it! But I don't think you can. And I have powerful friends who will find you and pour sulfuric acid all over you. Your skin will melt off of you as you scream in agonizing pain. They say it can take a full day for a person to die like that. Is that what you want?"

Kagawa reached into his pocket, extracted a plastic bag, and said flatly, "I simply place the bag over your head. You will live as long as you hold your breath. If not, you will, like I said, be killing yourself."

Perspiration was now beading up on Hiro's forehead. "You're bluffing. You'd be wanted for murder. You're Wendy's father. They'll suspect you."

"I thought of that. I plan to call them right after they find your body in the trunk of your car, asking them if they found the boy in the photo. Do I look like a killer to you?"

Kagawa took a photo from his pocket. It showed him with his wife and daughter at the Bronx Zoo, smiling broadly for the camera. He stared at the photo and then at Hiro and said with resigned sadness, "I have nothing to live for." Kagawa approached Hiro's head with the plastic bag.

Hiro leaned back in the chair and shouted, "What the fuck!"

Kagawa slipped the bag over Hiro's wildly gyrating head.

Hiro was still able to breathe through the opening at the bottom of the bag, and he cried out, "Don't do this! I beg you."

Kagawa picked up the roll of duct tape that was lying on the floor behind the chair and began to peel off a piece large enough to encircle Hiro's neck.

The plastic bag began to expand and contract more rapidly and fogged up with each and every breath inhaled and exhaled. As the tape wrapped around his neck, he shouted, "Wait! I know stuff. I can tell you. Take the bag off!"

Kagawa continued to wrap the tape around Hiro's neck as Hiro's head twisted violently from side to side in a vain attempt to stop Kagawa.

Kagawa suddenly pulled back. "Tell me what you know and speak quickly. If you hesitate, I'll know you're trying to think up some phony story, and that will be the end of your life. I will take maybe eighty years from you, about the same my daughter lost. You'll be nothing but food for worms. My legacy was to continue with her children. Now …" He choked up. "OK, *Hiro* … what do you know?"

Hiro's clothing was saturated with sweat. Through the plastic bag, he pleaded, "Then you let me go?"

"I let you go." Kagawa yanked the bag off his head. "Now start talking."

The words came pouring out. "There are these two guys, came from Japan about twenty years ago. Said they're Yakuza but maybe not. You know what that is?"

Kagawa nodded. "Japanese mafia."

"Right. You don't mess with these guys. I got a job working for them. They pay me to find young girls and bring them to them."

"For what purpose?"

He hesitated. "You know what they do."

"I want to hear it from you."

"You know, prostitution, porn, that kind of stuff. They have ways of getting girls to do whatever they want, like by getting them hooked on drugs or promising to take care of them while turning them into prostitutes. They're into other shit also. Drugs, gambling."

Kagawa took a shuddering breath as he asked, almost regretting the question, "What happened to Wendy?" He braced himself for the answer.

"She was a mistake. I try to find girls who are runaways, girls on drugs, abandoned, like that. Mostly in poor neighborhoods. Seeing her in that area, I thought she might be the type."

"Because she's Japanese?"

He squirmed a bit before answering. "I don't know. Maybe I was attracted to her. So pretty and in a shitty neighborhood. Maybe I was hoping she was the type, but she wasn't. She was trouble from the start."

"Trouble?"

"Wouldn't cooperate. They told me she fought like a demon. No matter what these guys did, she always kept trying to escape. No matter how much they drugged her ... and did other stuff ... she wouldn't do what they wanted. They told me that, finally, they pumped so much shit into her she OD'd and died."

Kagawa's lower lip quivered, and his misty eyes blinked in rapid succession as though trying to erase the horrible visions from his mind. He took a deep breath and audibly exhaled. "Thank you for not telling me what other things they did to her."

"No problem."

"What are their names?"

"If I tell you, they'll kill me," he pleaded.

"How would that matter if I kill you first?"

Hiro answered sheepishly, "Good point."

Kagawa waved the plastic bag in Hiro's direction. He'd had enough. "Their names, goddamn it!"

"OK, OK. Hideki Fujita and Tadashi Ogura." He cocked his head. "What are you thinking? Taking these guys out? No way. You probably don't know how to use a gun. And they have protection."

"Don't worry about that. But I do have your gun, don't I? Where do they live?"

He shook his head. "I really don't know. I swear it. We meet at different bars, restaurants, sometimes in a parking lot. I deliver a girl. They pay me. I also line up johns for them."

He was puzzled. "Why would these girls go with you?"

"I promise to do stuff for them."

"Like what?"

"I promise to give them money, food, and a place to stay. Sometimes it's drugs."

"Wendy would never fall for any of that," he said with conviction.

"When Ogura pulled up, I said it was my father. It was starting to rain. She got in. When she realized we were going in the opposite direction, she freaked out. Started screaming. Ogura gave her a shot of heroin to knock her out. The rest you know."

Kagawa's shoulders slumped at the thought of what the rest must have been for her. "What do they do when not working?"

"The only thing I ever heard them talking about besides money was bridge."

Kagawa's forehead creased. "Bridge?"

"The card game. These guys seem addicted to it."

"Do you know where?"

"Some bridge club. I don't know where. I swear it."

"What do these two animals look like?"

"Fujita is small but wiry. Clean-shaven. About fifty-five or sixty. Full head of gray hair. Ogura is a bull. Maybe forty. Big, tough as they come. Shaves his head. Makes him look even scarier, like some kind of sumo wrestler."

"What else can you tell me? Are those their real names?"

"I think so. They take in a ton of money. More coming in all the time. Run a big outfit but are small potatoes compared to the real Yakuza here in New York. I think they make cash payments to the guys higher up the ladder. That's all I know. I didn't kill your daughter. She was a mistake. I'm sorry about her. I really am."

Kagawa stared at Hiro, digesting all he'd heard. "And all those other girls?" It was a rhetorical question.

Hiro didn't answer.

Kagawa rubbed his unshaven chin for a moment. "I need to go upstairs. Check something out." He turned toward the stairs.

"Wait. I gotta piss."

Kagawa ignored his plea and went upstairs. He lowered the volume on the TV and called Jerry Silverstein, who he knew played at bridge clubs, and asked if it was possible to find where Hideki Fujita and Tadashi Ogura played bridge. Jerry said, "If they play a lot, they probably belong to the American Contract Bridge League that lists names and scores on the internet." Twenty minutes later, Jerry was able to tell Kagawa where Fujita and Ogura played bridge.

Hiro had told the truth. Had he met him under different circumstances, Kagawa believed he would have liked him. A nice-looking boy with a certain amount of charm. Possibly some intelligence there too. And his Wendy had liked him.

He walked into a bedroom that had served as an office. Fastened to one wall, five feet from the floor, was a Shinto shrine consisting of a pale yellow, wood kamidana household altar, about one foot wide and two feet high, with two small doors depicting hand carvings of tigers. It had been handed down for generations of Kagawas and was considered a God shelf containing memorial tablets of deceased relatives. Like most Japanese, Kagawa was not a religious man but was spiritual. He walked up to the shrine, bowed his head, and attempted to evoke some divine inspiration as to how to proceed.

When he believed he had his answer, Kagawa left the room and walked back down into the basement, where he saw a relieved Hiro smiling slightly at him. Kagawa quickly strode to Hiro and, in a flash, slipped the bag over his head. Before Hiro had time to react, the tape was wrapped around Hiro's neck, completing the seal. The shocked expression on Hiro's face didn't last very long as he struggled to grab the last ounce of air in the bag. Soon, nothing but plastic was being sucked into his gaping mouth. His face turned blue as his eyes bulged out of their sockets. His body shook violently as in a last-ditch effort to free itself. Losing all control of himself, Hiro was finally able to have his piss, urinating over himself and onto the concrete floor. His head slumped forward. Dead in less than two minutes.

Kagawa stood frozen in place as a flood of emotions buzzed through his body like an electric current. He stared at the motionless body and, for a fleeting moment, felt pity for the young man. But he immediately rebuked himself. That young man had kidnapped his innocent daughter, and he was therefore responsible for her torture and death. No. He would reserve his pity for those who deserved it.

As dispassionately as was possible, Kagawa turned and walked upstairs. Justice was partially done, and he had further plans to make.

Kagawa sat dejectedly on a folding chair in his living room. Earlier that day, he had killed a man—no, murdered him. But he had done his duty. He had taken revenge on the young man he knew was at least in part responsible for Wendy's death—and probably other girls' deaths too—but he'd received no relief from the anguish he felt. Just a few days ago, an act like this was unthinkable—the act of a madman. Perhaps his father was correct all along; everyone is a natural-born killer and, given the right circumstance, would be able to kill anyone. His circumstance, in the worst way possible, had arrived like an unforecasted tsunami.

In planning his next moves, he knew that Hiro was correct. He was no killer, and certainly not with a pistol—he'd never even used one. To carry out his plan, he would have to purchase bullets for the gun and then travel upstate to some deserted forest where he could practice using it. He needed to determine whether he could walk into a gun shop and purchase bullets, no questions asked. He Googled his question and found the answer. New York state law stated that a firearms dealer may not sell any ammunition designed exclusively for use in a handgun to any person who is not authorized to possess a pistol or revolver. But Google also informed him that you could purchase ammunition for a handgun online, so long as you are at least twenty-one.

He took the pistol from his pocket and examined it. It was a Glock G19. When he Googled it, he learned that it was one of the most well-known handguns in the world—reliable, lightweight, powerful, and small. He decided to order ammunition online, a box of fifty 9mm bullets from American Eagle. It would be shipped UPS overnight.

Kagawa had seen the movie *The Godfather* numerous times. He recalled the scene where Michael Corleone got explicit instructions on how to kill two people in the middle of a restaurant and get away with it. Michael was to fire bullets into both men's heads and then calmly turn and walk out, dropping the untraceable gun on the way out.

Kagawa knew that it might not be as simple as the movie made it seem. He would have to scout out the bridge club to determine entrances and exits. He would also need to be able to positively identify Fujita and Ogura. Using Hiro's descriptions of them, he believed he would be able to spot the two Japanese without too much trouble. He would find out the club's schedule and visit each time the games were to be played. If he spotted two men who looked like Fujita and Ogura, he could check for their names on the sheet that everyone signed in on. He would wear a disguise. Once the shots were fired, he believed pandemonium would break out, with people screaming, ducking for cover, and running for exits, with chairs and tables knocked out of the way and turned over. It sounded good on paper.

Kagawa dragged Hiro's limp body up the stairs from the basement. The stench of body odor, sweat, and urine made Kagawa gag, but he knew what had to be done. He dragged the body into the closed two-car garage where his late-model Toyota sat next to his wife's Volvo. It was said that a Volvo was an especially safe vehicle, which was why he had bought it for Amy. She was not a great driver. Living in Queens meant they needed only one car, since public transportation was readily available. But when they moved to the island in Great Neck, they needed a second car. Little did Kagawa know that the Volvo would become the vector for Amy's suicide. It had almost been too much to bear. He had considered shutting the garage door, climbing onto the front passenger seat, and sitting next to his beloved wife, who was no longer in torment. His torment had been doubled by her suicide. All he needed to do was close the door and keep the engine running, and he would join Amy and Wendy in the afterlife.

Now he hated to look at the Volvo. He opened the trunk to his Toyota, lifted the reeking body, and tossed it into the trunk.

At 4:00 a.m., after dumping Hiro into the trunk of Hiro's car, Kagawa paced the floor of his living room, wearing only a T-shirt and shorts. The killing of Hiro, though warranted, weighed heavily on him. He had never thought of himself as a murderer and didn't even now. Were soldiers who killed in war murderers? Or were they heroes? Was the killing of a murderer murder? When the government executes someone, is that murder? No, he told himself. The killing of Hiro was justice. Justice for the other girls whose lives were ruined, justice for his Wendy, and justice for Amy.

He intended to travel upstate to a deserted forest where he could practice shooting Hiro's Glock. He recalled reading that the most dangerous person on earth was the one who not only had no fear of death but also welcomed it. Perhaps he'd read it in relation to Muslims who believed they became martyrs by killing themselves in suicide bombings in the name of Allah. Martyred men were guaranteed seventy-two virgins in heaven. Kagawa thought, *What if one billion Muslim men became martyrs? Where would they find seventy-two billion virgins?* It didn't make sense to him, but then, nothing these days made much sense.

CHAPTER 9

THAT EVENING, AFTER BEN HAD GONE HOME TO HIS FAMILY, Morgan, who had no one to go home to, decided to park her unmarked Ford down the block from the Happy Hour. She planned to drink coffee from her thermos, eat a sandwich, listen to her favorite music, and watch who went in and out. She had no idea what she was actually looking for.

At 11:00 p.m., she saw Harada exit the club, walk up the block, and enter a car. The car pulled out. Morgan decided to follow him. She knew this might lead to nothing. He could be going home, and it would be a wasted evening.

Minutes later, Harada parked on Ludlow Street, in a tow-away zone, which made Morgan believe he wouldn't be parked there for long. He left the vehicle. Morgan parked in front of a fire hydrant. She got out of her car and saw him enter an ancient, five-story, walk-up apartment building. She followed him in to the foul-smelling, tiny atrium that housed a bank of mailboxes.

She heard his footsteps stopping at the fourth floor. She silently climbed halfway up between the third and fourth-floor staircase. She heard him knocking on a door. Someone inside answered, "Who's there?"

"Harada."

Morgan peeked around the banister and saw Harada enter 4D. The door closed, and Morgan climbed the stairs past the fourth floor and halfway up to the fifth floor, out of sight, where she heard Harada shout, "Where's the rest of it?"

The man inside answered, "You'll get it by tomorrow, I swear."

The door opened, and Harada rushed down the stairs as the door slammed shut.

Morgan was about to follow Harada when the door suddenly opened again, and a man stormed out and ran down the stairs. Morgan followed.

She carefully exited the building and saw Harada head toward his car, while the other man ran up the street to the corner where a woman stood, alone. Morgan decided to see what the man was up to. She stood back in a darkened doorway, about fifty feet away, and saw the man shake the woman's shoulders. She couldn't hear the conversation, but she could tell they knew each other. The woman nodded several times as the man pointed a finger in her face. He left her there, passed the hidden Morgan, and entered his building.

Morgan knew what was transpiring. From the way the woman was dressed, it was evident the man was her pimp. The man needed money to pay Harada, and she would have to work harder. Morgan went back into the building and looked for the name on mailbox 4D. Jiro Kimura.

She left for home.

The next day, after obtaining the rap sheet on Jiro Kimura, Morgan described the prior night's events to Ben. Kimura had been arrested for petty larceny and robbery, spending eighteen months in prison, and was known to have had a drug habit. Morgan knew that, sooner or later, this kind of robber got caught, since they usually got away with enough cash to temporarily supply their drug habit, and they soon needed to rob again. Somewhere along the line, they'd be collared—hopefully before they killed someone.

Ben asked, "How were you able to ID Harada as one of Akita's men?"

Morgan inhaled deeply and said, "I have a confession to make."

"Confession?"

"I spoke with Akita twice before at the Happy Hour."

"When? And why?"

"I wanted to see what the animal looked like. Maybe get under his skin. I told him I'd be watching him."

Ben rubbed his cheek. "You know how dangerous this guy can be."

"It was just something I needed to do."

He nodded and said, "OK, but be careful around this guy."

Morgan said, "We need to pay a visit to this Kimura. Since he's involved with Harada, he's probably involved with Akita. Is six tonight good with you?"

"No problem."

Morgan and Ben then received word that a body had been found in the trunk of a car in a bar's parking lot in Chinatown. The owner of the bar had noticed that someone had left a car in his tiny lot two nights ago. The next day, he noticed that the car was still there, and by the morning, when the car still hadn't moved, he investigated. He went to the car and saw that it was unlocked. He figured if he could find the registration, he might be able to contact the person and make him move his car. But just as he opened the car's door, he detected a terrible stench. He reached down beside the driver's seat and lifted the handle that unlocked the trunk. He walked to the rear of the car, opened the trunk, and, to his horror, found a body. It made him retch. He slammed the trunk door shut and called 911.

Morgan and Ben arrived at the scene minutes after the CSI crew with Frank DeMarco began their investigation. Upon arrival, the detectives were surprised to see Masahiro Araki's car.

"I have a bad feeling about this. Are we going to find another young victim in that trunk?" Morgan slowly shook her head.

Frank said, "We haven't opened the trunk yet, but even out here, you can smell something decaying in there. But we examined the glove compartment and saw that the vehicle is registered to a Masahiro Araki."

Morgan said, "We searched that vehicle a few days ago. The owner is a person of interest in a missing person's case, which now is listed as a homicide."

Ben said to Frank, "Pop the trunk, and let's see what we got."

Frank opened the trunk. A horrible stench emanated from it.

Frank, wearing gloves and a mask, examined the body that lay in the trunk. "Got a young Asian male … late teens possibly … maybe five six … hundred thirty, thirty-five pounds."

Morgan and Ben exchanged glances. "Sounds like it might be our person of interest. Let me have a look," Ben said.

Both Ben and Morgan held their noses as they stepped forward and looked into the trunk.

"That's him," Morgan stated. "Masahiro Araki." In spite of herself, she felt sorry for him.

Ben asked, "Can you determine the cause and time of death?"

Frank took a few minutes to further examine the body. "As far as cause goes, from the pallor of the skin, appears to be asphyxiation, yet"—he examined the neck—"there are no ligature marks around the neck. Possibly suffocated, like from a bag over his head. There's evidence of some type of sticky substance, possibly from some kind of tape, around the base of his neck. Uncertain as to time of death right now, but I think it might be at least twenty-four hours ago."

"Sounds like this was more a rubout than robbery," Ben offered.

"Seems that way. We'll know more later. But the suffocation theory is bolstered by the fact that this guy pissed all over himself. Stinks to high hell."

"Someone wanted him dead real bad," Ben said. "The unfortunate jerk must have gotten in over his head. Seems he was lying to us all along. Probably had something to do with one or more murders. Just too coincidental that after we accuse him of being involved with the Kagawa murder, he gets rubbed out."

Morgan remarked, "If he was associated in any way with some mob, we might have contributed to his death by bringing him in for questioning on two occasions. It might have given the impression that he was ratting on them. Doesn't take much for mafioso types to suspect and then kill someone, especially a nobody like Araki."

Ben said to Frank, "He said he had no parents and no real job. We need to find out who he's associated with and what kind of job he held, which might be related to sex trafficking, and locate any next of kin, if possible. I would also like to know if he was a druggie."

"We'll get you the results as soon as we can," Frank said.

"Thanks, Frank."

They intended to obtain a search warrant ASAP for Araki's apartment and again canvass the area with a photo of Araki. They reviewed the murder book for people they'd already interviewed in Chinatown regarding Araki's friends and associates. They revisited those people to press them for information they might not have divulged in their first interview. They gleaned no further helpful information.

Araki's murder had all the markings of a gangland hit. They knew there was much work to be done on this case and the one involving Butterfly, although the investigation on her death was growing cold.

Araki's body would be taken to the medical examiner's office, and his car flat-bedded to the police impound lot for further examination.

Back at the precinct, Morgan fielded another phone call from Michael Kagawa, who asked, "Were you able to make any progress?"

Protocol had dictated that they not reveal the name of a person of interest to anyone outside the investigation, but now it was different since it would be all over the news by that afternoon. She took a deep breath before answering, "We recently did. Does the name Masahiro Araki mean anything to you?"

"Other than sounding Japanese, no."

"That's the name of the young man in the photo. Unfortunately, his body was carted off to the morgue about an hour ago."

"What?"

"His body was found earlier today. Probably killed two days ago."

"The boy in the photo? Are you certain?"

"Yes."

There was silence for several seconds. "My daughter talks to this boy, she disappears and is killed, and then he's murdered? How was he killed?"

"He was suffocated."

"What do you make of this?"

"We twice brought him in for questioning, but his story never wavered. He said it started to rain, and he ran home."

"But what about the text? His father driving her home?"

"We knew his story sounded fishy. For one thing, she said he was sixteen. He was actually nineteen, but he said she was mistaken. We still believed he was somehow involved. Now, it seems far more certain."

Silence at the end of the phone again. Somberly, Kagawa said, "If he was involved, now that he's dead, we will never know what he knew."

She understood what he was feeling. "His death was unfortunate, but it doesn't mean our investigation ends. His death seems more than coincidence. He was probably involved with traffickers, and I believe we'll get to the bottom of this. We might know more after we search his apartment."

He sighed audibly. "I hope so. Thank you for your time."

"Wait. Before you hang up, please avail yourself of counseling. It has helped many who have tragically lost loved ones."

He paused. "I'll think about it."

The call ended. Dealing with people's greatest loss was never easy for her.

Later that day, this time with a search warrant, Morgan, Ben, and Frank DeMarco's crew entered Araki's apartment. The apartment was no cleaner than it had been the first time Ben and Morgan were there. Again, there was no sign of any foul play, but while tearing the apartment apart, Morgan pulled the drawers out of the one dresser and found, behind one of those drawers, photos of dozens of naked girls and young women, some perhaps as young as ten. The girls were in various sexual poses, sometimes with other young girls, and sometimes with men whose faces were never revealed. Examining the photos further, she concluded that they were not taken in this apartment. She was reminded of herself at their age: innocent and vulnerable. Horrible memories flashed through her as she slammed the drawer shut.

Ben turned to her and said, "Everything OK?"

"Look at these photos. Enough to make you sick."

She handed him the photos. He viewed them while shaking his head. "Incredible." He gave them back to Morgan.

Also found were several ounces of what appeared to be cocaine. The lab would have to determine the exact drug and quantity. Perhaps he had been involved in drug deals.

Morgan viewed the photos again, with gritted teeth. "Scumbags like this deserve what they get." She no longer felt sorry for Hiro. She silently vowed to get the perpetrators of such filth—especially kingpins like Satoshi Akita.

"Drugs, child porn, human trafficking. Exactly what the captain wants us to solve. But looking at this place." Ben swept an arm across the room. "Araki was small-time."

"Yeah, but where are these kids now? We know they're being used … no … *abused,* but by whom?" She was disgusted.

"Maybe there's a diary of some kind or phone book. There was no cell phone on him when he was found. Probably taken by the killer, but maybe there's one here."

They searched the place for anything that might lead to associates of the deceased or to the whereabouts of any of the girls in the photos. They found nothing of value.

"I didn't think we'd find anything written," Ben said. "Today, everything is kept in their iPhones. Be great if we had it."

Morgan nodded agreement.

The CSI unit would continue to examine the apartment, dust for prints, and search every nook and cranny with a fine-tooth comb.

Morgan and Ben spent most of the day asking the locals if they had seen anyone coming and going or anything unusual. They came up empty-handed.

At four that afternoon, they entered the morgue, waiting to attend Masahiro Araki's autopsy. In his fifteen years as a detective, Ben had viewed numerous autopsies, but this was Morgan's first.

As they waited to be summoned by the ME, Morgan asked, "What should I expect?"

Ben answered, "Besides the smell and gore, don't expect a whole lot of emotion from the ME. To these guys, it's a job to be done, day in, day out. I've seen some strange shit at times. Probably breaks up the monotony."

"Like what?"

"I heard one ME say while removing a scalp, 'That's a hair-raising experience.' Some MEs practically roll on the floor over jokes like these, especially ones with sexual overtones. I saw fingers probing orifices from the outside in and sometimes freakishly from the inside out." He shook his head. "I guess respecting the dead isn't easy when the dead are cut up like meat."

Morgan had seen horrible things happen to live people in Iraq, so this didn't shock her.

They entered the examining room.

The ME, Raj Chawla, nodded in recognition toward Ben. His plastic face shield and gloves were covered in blood and brain matter, which was also splattered across his white Tyvek jumpsuit.

As they entered the room, the thick, pungent odor of formalin—used in preserving tissue for study—immediately hit Morgan's nostrils, even though she and Ben wore masks. Morgan was uncertain what to expect but certainly not a song with a Caribbean beat, playing the lyrics, "In every life we have some trouble, but when you worry you make it double. Don't worry, be happy." It seemed incongruous to her in that setting, but on second thought, the dead weren't listening.

The lifeless, naked body lay on a stainless steel autopsy table. An identification tag hung by a wire from the body's big toe. Araki's chest cavity was already opened up, with some of Araki's internal organs lying grotesquely next to the body on the examining table, allowing the ME to take samples of his organs in order to test for drugs. Some of his organs had already been examined and deposited into a one-pound silver gut bucket, which held a gruesome stew of some already examined internal organs. It would eventually contain all of his internal organs. Morgan was surprised to learn that everyone's internal organs fit into that bucket, no matter what size or shape person.

Morgan had feared she would faint or vomit and thoroughly embarrass herself, but to her surprise, she was able to keep her composure. Perhaps, she thought, it was her experience in Iraq that had inoculated her.

The ME's examination showed evidence of cocaine and marijuana in Araki's system but not enough to have killed him. It was determined that he was asphyxiated, probably with a plastic bag, as traces of plastic were found around his mouth and neck, along with traces of duct tape around his mouth, arms, and legs.

Later, after reading through the entire report, Ben and Morgan concluded that nothing in it offered immediate clues.

"Obviously," Morgan stated, "he was involved in some form with trafficking, child porn, and possibly drug deals."

"And our questioning him probably did get him killed. The list of potential assassins just grew," Ben said.

"You said it. It would include anyone from any crime syndicate to any of the relatives of the females he was involved with, to anyone he 'delivered stuff to,' possibly drugs. But the way he was killed, it was probably a gangland hit."

"I thought about the families, especially that Lyle kid. But there was no way for him to know about Araki."

"If it was some group, such as the Tongs, the Triads, or the Yakuza, we might never know who offed this kid."

News of police finding a body in the trunk of a car hit the media that afternoon. The person had been identified as Masahiro Araki, nineteen years old, whose last address was in Chinatown. Newscasters announced that anyone having information regarding this crime should call the police hotline.

Fujita and Ogura were getting ready to leave their building and make their rounds to their girls in the various apartments when they heard the news. Hiro had been found dead in his car's trunk.

"Shit," Ogura exclaimed, wide-eyed, as he put on a light fall jacket.

Fujita sat heavily on a chair at the kitchen table. "This is bad. I hope it's not the work of one of our competitors."

"Maybe just a robbery."

"They would have killed him and run off. Why take the time to put him in his trunk?"

Ogura asked, "You think we might be next?"

Fujita was deep in thought for almost a full minute. Then he looked up at Ogura. "It's a possibility. But by who?"

Ogura contemplated the question. "We make all our payments, and always on time. The Yakuza likes us. Everyone knows not to mess with us."

They knew the power of the Yakuza in New York. They had heard numerous stories in which dealing with them led to trouble. One such story involved O. J. Simpson. Several months before the double murder for which he was accused, five Yakuza strong-arms operating five cars tried to murder Simpson by running him off the road because a business deal he had with them went sour. They later attempted to muscle in on O. J.'s chain of restaurants.

It was also reported that the popular restaurant Benihana was founded and owned by a member of the Yakuza. Apparently, some American judges believed they could push around some of the Japanese firms, as if the companies and their officials were not entitled to due process and fair proceedings in American courts. But judges were human, and many heeded the caution that a foolhardy court officer might end up someday as a judge-burger, carved up and cooked right in front of unsuspecting patrons at Benihana. It seemed that no person, no matter how well known, was beyond their ability to influence.

"First," Fujita offered, "we watch our backs. We need to reassure the girls that everything is OK. We don't want them scared once they find out about Hiro. I will try to see Akita and ask if he knows anything."

"Good. If anyone knows, Akita will."

They knew that Satoshi Akita was one of the leaders of the Yakuza in New York, whose territory included all of Chinatown, and that their weekly tributes eventually wound up in his hands. He ruled his flock with an iron hand, and he seemed to have powers beyond that of the average man. It would be to Fujita and Ogura's benefit to get to the bottom of Hiro's death—unless, of course, the hit was ordered by Akita himself.

CHAPTER

10

MORGAN AND BEN HAD NO SOLID LEADS REGARDING THE deaths of the Jane Doe, Butterfly, who was found in the dumpster, or on Masahiro Araki, who was found in the trunk of his car. As per protocol, they attempted to determine if there was a connection between the two deaths, especially since they were of approximately the same age and had a connection to Chinatown. But almost nothing was known of Butterfly. They would again circulate the photo taken by the ME's office, hoping it would lead to her identification. That would be the first step. They knew it would be a long shot since no one had notified the police of a missing person fitting the general description of their Jane Doe. They were resigned to the fact that the circumstances surrounding her death might never be known.

Was Araki's death related to his so-called work? Morgan knew that the nefarious activities of pimps very often led to murder, sometimes of prostitutes and sometimes of the men who dealt with them. Although she couldn't be certain, the possibility of Araki being involved with the Kagawa murder seemed likely. Perhaps he was also involved with the Chen and Huang girls' murders.

At 6:00 p.m., Ben, with Morgan sitting shotgun, drove their unmarked black Ford Taurus—bumping down some ancient cobblestone streets—to Ludlow Street and parked.

Her shooting event at the pharmacy was very much on her mind, although she was feeling an adrenaline rush from the prospect of catching a dirtbag who might lead them to Akita. Morgan apprehensively wondered, if Jiro Kimura resisted arrest, would she hesitate to use her weapon? Dr. Lambert didn't think so.

They exited the Ford, found the five-story, one-hundred-year-old building, and walked up the five concrete steps to the front door. As before, there was no lock on the door leading to the five floors of apartments. Morgan knew there was no elevator in the walk-up, and they would have to walk the three flights to apartment 4D.

Upon entering the building, they were immediately hit with a conglomeration of pungent odors.

Morgan placed a hand over her nose and whispered, "Jesus, same stench as last time. Is that food we're smelling or human waste?"

"Probably both."

They began the climb to the fourth floor. Once there, Ben stopped a moment to catch his breath.

Morgan looked sternly at him as she put two fingers to her mouth as though smoking.

Apologetically, he mouthed, *I know, I know.*

After giving the thumbs-up that he was OK, they turned the corner and approached 4D. The corridor was eerily lit by the naked lemon light bulb overhead. Morgan stood to the side of the metal door while Ben rapped his knuckles on it. He then stood off to the other side of the door, out of sight of the peephole. Reaching around, he knocked again.

Morgan's pulse was increasing with anticipation.

A voice was heard through the door. "Who's there?"

Ben called out, "Jiro Kimura. Police. We want to ask you some questions."

No answer for thirty seconds, but they could hear rustling inside and what sounded like the opening of a window.

"He's going for the fire escape!" Morgan shouted.

The detectives turned and bolted down the three flights, drawing their pistols on the way. They threw open the front door and bounded down the five steps to the sidewalk just as the man leaped from the bottom rungs of the fire escape, practically into the arms of Morgan, whose gun was inadvertently knocked out of her hand. Morgan grabbed the man around his waist and, in a flash, tripped the man with her leg. The man fell onto his back, with Morgan landing on top of him with all her weight. The man made an *oomph* sound as the air was knocked out of him.

Ben bent down and grabbed the man's arms while Morgan sat on his stomach. She climbed off him and helped Ben turn the cursing and shouting man onto his stomach. Morgan grabbed the man's arms, pinning them behind him as Ben immediately cuffed the man. The two detectives stood the man up. Morgan reached down, picked up her weapon, and holstered it.

An out-of-breath and pissed-off Morgan shouted, "Are you Jiro Kimura?"

"Fuck you," he said. He glanced from one face to the other and snorted. "Great. A chink and white bitch." He then turned toward the small but growing crowd that was gathering around to watch the spectacle and shouted, "Police brutality! Police brutality!"

Ben reached into the man's back pocket and extracted his wallet. He found his driver's license with the name of Jiro Kimura.

"Why'd you run?" Ben asked, peeved.

"Who said I was running? Needed some fresh air."

Morgan said, "OK, you're a comedian. But as soon as you heard the word *police*, you fled the scene. We're taking you to the precinct for questioning."

"For what, asshole?"

"Suspicion of solicitation," she firmly responded.

Kimura emphatically answered, "No way."

Ben read a smirking Kimura his Miranda Rights. They then pushed Kimura through the crowd of curious sidewalk gawkers and deposited him into the back of their Ford.

Ben and Morgan climbed in, with Ben driving. He turned toward Morgan. "Nice work. Learn that move in the service?"

"That and a lot more," she said, looking straight ahead. This was nothing compared to Iraq. But she was thrilled to have aided in collaring a possibly dangerous suspect.

Minutes later, they arrived at the precinct, where they intended to interrogate Kimura. Of course, pimping wasn't the worst crime imaginable, but he might have run due to some crime totally unrelated to being a pimp.

After obtaining a search warrant, CSI was sent to Kimura's apartment while Ben and Morgan sat in the interview room, filming the interrogation.

Morgan and Ben sat on one side of the metal table, while Kimura sat opposite them. Morgan began, "Mr. Kimura. We know you have dealings with a man named Ichiro Harada and that you pimp for at least one prostitute."

"First of all, I don't know anyone by that name, and I don't pimp. And you can call me Joey."

Morgan continued. "OK, Joey. Here's the deal. I witnessed Harada entering your apartment. I heard him demand more money from you. I also saw you telling your woman at the corner that she needed to earn more money."

Joey leaned way back in his chair. "Who are you? Houdini?"

"Just doing my job. Look, I'm not here to send you away for a few years. What I want is information on Harada. Also, I want to know what you know about the Yakuza, and especially someone named Satoshi Akita."

He sat silent for a few seconds. "Listen, Harada expects a tribute from me. I know he's a member of the Yakuza. I also know the Yakuza here is run by Akita. But I would never testify to any of this. I'm not stupid. Besides, that's really all I know. Harada comes weekly, and I pay."

The interrogation went on until, about two hours later, CSI returned with an unlicensed gun, an ounce of marijuana, and two ounces of cocaine.

Morgan believed she would get nothing more out of this two-bit pimp. If the gun was unlicensed, they might charge him. They intended to keep him overnight and decide what to do with him the next day. Morgan thought at least word would get back to Harada and Akita that she was on their tail. She hoped it pissed him off.

While Ben was working through Kimura's paperwork, Morgan was sitting at her desk, sifting through the photos confiscated from Masahiro Araki's apartment. She was mortified and disgusted by the photos that depicted girls as young as possibly ten in sexual situations she hoped no mother would ever want to see her daughter in.

She viewed the photos one at a time, hoping to see something that might lead to the arrest of others involved. She also wanted, although she knew it was a long shot, to be able to locate and free these girls from their enslavement and addiction.

Photos of one particular girl caught her eye. She opened her desk drawer, pulled out a magnifying glass, and examined the photos more closely. There it was. She was certain of it. Most of the girls were photographed more than once. This particular girl had photos taken front and back. Tattooed on the lower back of this girl was a butterfly. Morgan quickly opened another drawer and whipped out Butterfly's file. She pulled the photo given by the ME's office, and voila! A perfect match.

"Ben, look at this."

Ben went to Morgan's desk. "What do you have?"

She handed him the two photos and the magnifying glass.

"Look at the butterfly tat on each of these photos."

He did so and remarked, "Holy shit. It's our Butterfly."

"Whomever Araki worked with or for was probably responsible for this and perhaps other murders. I'm pretty certain that kid didn't work alone."

"Agreed."

Morgan felt energized by the possibilities. Time to put the scumbags away.

Harada rushed into the Happy Hour and over to Akita's table.

Akita looked up and said, "Something wrong?"

"I went to collect the rest of the money from a guy named Kimura, but he wasn't there. Instead, his worker saw me and told me he'd been arrested last night."

"Not unusual. He won't talk."

"Yeah, but she described the detectives who arrested him."

Akita stood. "And?"

"It was a big Chinese guy and a tall, white, redheaded woman."

Akita slammed his fist on the table. "She's targeting me. Trying to piss me off. She needs to be taught a lesson."

Fujita and Ogura had made an appointment to meet with Satoshi Akita at the Happy Hour. They had never met Akita, but they knew of his reputation: no nonsense, very powerful, but fair. Normally, he would never agree to see the two non-Yakuza unless it was of some importance. Fujita and Ogura, along with other non-Yakuza, paid weekly protection fees for their activities.

Fujita and Ogura apprehensively entered the darkened club. Two bored-looking female strippers, one blond, one Asian, were pole-dancing on a small stage, entertaining customers. Fujita and Ogura paid no attention to them, focusing only on following a man who ushered them to a table where Akita sat with three hard-looking men, two of whom were Yoshi Nomura and Ichiro Harada. As usual, they all wore dark suits and ties.

Fujita and Ogura were dressed casually in shirts and jeans. Ogura nervously whispered, "Should we have worn suits?"

Fujita, equally nervous, ignored him as he approached the table and bowed. Ogura did likewise.

Akita was rolling an unlit cigar in his mouth. He snapped his fingers and pointed at two chairs. Fujita and Ogura immediately bowed respectfully and sat. They said nothing, knowing not to speak until spoken to.

Akita took the cigar from his mouth and pointed it at them. "Which one is Fujita?"

"I am, sir," Fujita answered with due respect.

"I understand we may have a problem. A subordinate of yours was found dead in his trunk. We know that he was questioned by police at least twice. What is the probability that this young man's activities will lead the authorities back to you?"

The question caught the two of them off guard. Fujita and Ogura glanced at each other, since they had no idea that Hiro had been questioned by police. They were expecting the conversation to center around who might have had Hiro killed. Instead, Fujita and Ogura were being put on the spot because the higher-ups were concerned about being insulated from the bottom rung of the hierarchy. The two men knew that they were the bottom rung and, as such, expendable.

Fujita began to perspire. "There is no trail from Hiro to us. We paid Hiro in cash for any services he provided. Besides, we owe our loyalty to you. We would never discuss our relationship with the authorities, even under torture."

Akita struck a long wooden match against the table. The match burst into flame, sending the harsh odor of phosphorous drifting to their nostrils. He put the flame to the tip of the cigar. The tip glowed brightly, and he drew a deep drag, exhaling the gray smoke toward the two men. They ignored the smoke, as did everyone else in the club, even though New York City law prohibited smoking in all restaurants and bars. The smoke was far better for their health and well-being than was protesting to Akita.

"You are not Yakuza. How can we be assured of your loyalty?"

Ogura twitched nervously.

Fujita didn't hesitate. "We have been operating in this area for twenty years. We have never been arrested for any crime. We know the power of the Yakuza. And we know that we would rather feel the wrath of the local police than that of the Yakuza. At worst, we would serve time in prison and be out in a few years. This would be a far better fate than the one we would face if we were ever disloyal to you."

Fujita's leg bounced nervously. He envisioned being dipped in a large vat of acid and having his burning flesh melt away as he writhed in agony.

After what seemed to Fujita to be an interminable pause, Akita spoke. "You have always made your payments and on time. I respect that. As such, you may continue your work, and we will work to try to get to the bottom of this Hiro thing. But I expect a twenty percent increase in your weekly tribute. That is all."

The two men needed no prompting to get up and leave. They bowed toward Akita, exhaled silently, and quickly left the club. The air-conditioning had been working full blast in the club, but the two of them were perspiring as though exiting a sauna.

Once outside, they looked at each other with relief.

Fujita asked, "Do you think Akita killed Hiro? He knew that Hiro had talked to the cops."

"How does he know that?"

"He has eyes everywhere. But if he did kill Hiro, we might be next."

Ogura spat. "That fucking kid. I should have killed him for bringing us that Wendy girl."

But for now, they could continue their operation, although an additional 20 percent meant the girls would have to produce even more than before. A replacement for Hiro had to be found, and soon.

Akita turned his chair toward the three other men in suits. In a low voice, he said, "We might have to deal with those two before long. But right now, I'm concerned about the Triads moving in on some of our territory. Maybe the Triads killed that kid to send a message. If things escalate for any reason, it could lead to a war no one wants. Do everything you can to find out if the Triads are using muscle against us."

The three men stood, bowed to Akita, and strode out of the club.

Akita knew Fujita and Ogura played bridge several nights each week. It would be easy to kill them at their bridge club. His main concern was if Fujita and Ogura were arrested, to save their own skins, they might rat on the Yakuza. They didn't know a lot, but they knew enough to be trouble. As of now, he was leaning toward eliminating them. He would make inquiries into the two men. If he had to order the killing of minor players like Fujita and Ogura, so be it.

CHAPTER

11

HIRO WAS VERY GOOD AT WHAT HE DID. NOT ONLY DID HE
procure clients for their girls, something that Fujita and Ogura also did,
Hiro was one of the best at finding new girls for their stable. His youth,
good looks, and charm meant Hiro could warm up and be trusted by
young girls in a way both Fujita and Ogura never could.

They had to scour the bars and strip clubs in search of another
unemployed young man who wouldn't mind making a decent living
working for them. It was simply a matter of time before they would find
the right person. They hoped it would be soon. The 20 percent increase
loomed like a shroud.

The one thing they couldn't afford was to have one or more of their
girls not producing. When they visited one of their other four locations,
the twelve-year-old complained that she needed a rest because, as she
said it, her pussy was sore. This was bad timing for her. With an open

hand, Fujita smacked the girl's face, leaving a welt. The stunned girl, who was wearing only panties, was picked up by Ogura and thrown onto an old two-seater couch as though she were a sack of potatoes. The girl, whose breasts had barely begun to develop, whimpered as she covered her chest and face with her arms. Ogura's powerful hand reached under the girl's arms, grabbed one of her nipples, and began to squeeze and twist it. The girl screamed and promised to continue to work. The two other girls in the room were made to promise to inform them if the twelve-year-old refused to work again. The 20 percent had to be met.

Morgan and Ben decided to get out in the street again. Although they had interviewed several people twice regarding Araki, they did so a third time with photos of their Jane Doe, Butterfly. No one admitted to knowing her. They decided to expand their area of search. After three hours of shoving the photos in the face of everyone they saw, both on the street and in the many storefront businesses, a woman clerk at a Starbucks recognized the photo of Masahiro Araki.

The woman, in her thirties, plump with a pleasant face, was taken aback as she was told the reason for the headshot, which showed Araki with his eyes closed, was that the photo was taken by police postmortem. She said, "I know him ... or at least knew him. Came in here a few times a week. Ordered the same latte every time. Liked to talk, mostly small talk. Called himself Hero. Never could understand a person calling themselves a hero."

Morgan said, "Actually, his name was Masahiro. Used the last four letters of h-i-r-o as his nickname."

"Oh," she responded.

"Did you see him talk or meet with anyone?" Ben asked.

"Not really. Sometimes he would order out for himself and two others."

"Any idea who the two others were?" Morgan asked.

She shook her head. "Can't help you there."

Ben and Morgan left. They spent the rest of the afternoon showing the photos to the locals. No one else recognized Jane Doe or Masahiro, or if they did, they weren't saying, probably not wanting to get involved, as had happened far too often in police investigations. As of now, they were no closer to solving either crime than they were days prior.

That evening at six o'clock, Morgan received a call from Tyler. She smiled as she recognized the number from the caller ID. "Hi."

"It's Tyler. Did I catch you at a bad time?"

"Not at all."

"I was a little concerned about you, you know, the way you left."

"I have to apologize. It had nothing to do with you. I remembered something that happened on the job and got a little upset, that's all," she white-lied.

"OK. Listen, are you free this Sunday?"

She paused, trying to remember. "Yes, why?"

"Have you ever been to Governors Island?"

"No, why?" Living in New York, she had heard of the island, but she knew very little about it.

"I thought we could spend the afternoon there."

"What's there to do?"

"A friend of mine has been there a couple of times and said there are lots of things. There are buildings full of history, parks, great walkways, pedal bikes for two, great views of Lower Manhattan. We could have lunch there."

An afternoon away from work, spending it with someone she was beginning to like. Why not? "Sounds like it might be fun."

"Great. How about we meet at the Governors Island Ferry at eleven. It's only about a ten-minute ride to the island. It's at the corner of Whitehall and South Streets. Look for the Battery Maritime Building, just to the left of the Staten Island Ferry. I'll meet you in the line inside."

"The ferry at eleven. See you there." *And hopefully without my stupid, soon-to-be-ex-husband following me.*

"By the way," he added. "No weapons are allowed on the island. I know cops might be an exception, but …"

She laughed. "Don't worry. I can live without my piece for one afternoon."

The next morning brought rain slanting down from a charcoal sky. Ben and Morgan splashed through puddles as they went barhopping, badging scores of people, believing that someone had to know something more about the young man who called himself Hiro.

They got their first break at a bar on Pike Street. A bartender, standing behind the bar in the empty pub, recalled Hiro meeting two other men there on several occasions. His memory needed jogging, and Ben said he had twenty reasons in his pocket to help him remember. The bartender said that fifty reasons would really help his recollection. Ben reached into his wallet and waved the fifty-dollar bill. "It's yours if your info is good enough."

"What do you want to know?"

"Can we sit at a table?" Ben asked.

It was ten in the morning, and the place was deserted but still smelled of beer and wood polish since the bartender had just finished polishing the bar. He pointed to a table, led them over to it, and they pulled chairs around it and sat. The stocky, Caucasian, mustachioed man appeared to be older than fifty, and he seemed nervous as his eyes darted around the room, making certain no one else was around.

"What can you tell us about these two men?" Morgan inquired.

Speaking softly, he said, "If we weren't alone, we wouldn't be having this conversation, fifty bucks or no fifty bucks."

"We understand," Ben answered as he opened a small pad to a blank page and extracted a pen from his pocket. "What's your name?"

The bartender was taken aback by the question. "I ain't giving you my name."

"We can easily find it out from the owner," Morgan said.

"Then do it that way. You want information, you play by my rules."

The two detectives glanced at each other. Good information was worth far more than the bartender's name. And if need be, they knew where to find him. They looked back at the man, and Ben agreed, "OK, no names. What can you tell us?"

He continued. "This kid liked to talk. Called himself a hero or something. The two men he met with didn't seem to be the kind of guys who would be friends of his."

"What do you mean?" Morgan asked.

"This one guy could have been around sixty. The other guy maybe forty or so. They never entered the bar together. Usually, this hero kid would find a table, order a beer, and then a while later, these two other guys would show up and sit at his table. I never heard much of their conversations, but I did manage to see them handing him some cash, and more than once, like he was working for them. Don't know their names."

Morgan asked, "What did the other men look like?"

He thought for a moment. "They both looked Chinese. Could have been Korean or something. The older guy had a lot of gray hair, regular build, average height. The younger one was a big son-of-a-gun, tall, maybe weighed three hundred. Completely bald."

Ben was writing on the pad as Morgan asked, "How were they dressed?"

"Nothing special. Regular clothes. I think jeans maybe."

"Can you describe their faces?"

"Not really. I never paid much attention to that, except the big guy had a round face with a thick neck. Nothing stood out about the older guy. Both guys were clean-shaven."

"Notice any tattoos or scars? Anything like that?" Ben asked.

He shook his head. "Can't say."

"Anything else you can tell us?" Morgan asked.

He diverted his eyes toward the front door. "Listen, I got customers coming. You got all I had. Appreciate it if you could leave."

The detectives thanked him for his cooperation, Ben placed the fifty on the table, and they left. It was still raining hard, so they ran the two blocks to their car. They entered it wet as rain splattered against the windshield.

Morgan said, "We definitely have two persons of interest now."

"I agree," Ben answered. "Well worth the money. The barkeep gave us a pretty good description of these guys, and my bet is that these Asian guys were probably Japanese, since Araki was Japanese." He took a cigarette from its box.

"Not in this car, you don't."

"Jesus. You sound like my wife." He reluctantly put the cigarette back in the box.

"You're probably right about being Japanese. Will you get reimbursed for the fifty?"

"Basically, anything under a hundred, if it leads to good info, no problem. But I learned my lesson the hard way."

"How so?"

"It was in my first couple of months as detective, when I believed I would be the next Hercule Poirot. I met with a known informant who, for sixty bucks, gave me some bogus info on a local robbery. I find out he was a junkie who needed his latest fix. I learned to verify the info before handing over any money. I ate the sixty."

Morgan knew she would be learning much from Ben.

He started the car, turned on the windshield wipers, which swatted away the rain, and pulled away from the curb. "If some type of deal, drugs maybe, turned sour, these two could easily be our culprits. Finding them is another story."

They returned to the precinct and asked if anyone remembered arresting or dealing with two men who fit the descriptions given by the bartender. No one did. They would have to wait for something else to turn up.

Ben contacted the police sketch artist, who then met with Ben and Morgan. The bartender's descriptions of the two men gave them a starting point. They were seeking two clean-shaven Asian men—one over six feet tall, weighing maybe three hundred pounds and with a totally bald head, perhaps forty years old. The other man had a regular build and average height, with a full head of gray hair, about sixty years old. They were dressed in everyday clothes, including jeans. Of great importance was that they probably traveled together much of the time, so it was as though they were seeking a Mutt and Jeff pair. When completed, the sketches were then circulated among the entire precinct and shared with surrounding precincts.

Today was the day Mike Kagawa would say goodbye to Amy and Wendy. He had made arrangements for their urns to have their eternal resting place in the Locust Valley Cemetery, only a twenty-minute drive from his home. As was the custom for Japanese, the deceased were cremated, and their urns stayed at the family home for a period of time, awaiting interment. He had chosen the Locust Valley Cemetery because he'd read that it had a beautiful section dedicated to persons of Japanese heritage.

That morning, he would gather the photographs that would be displayed at the funeral. He didn't expect too many attendees since Wendy hardly had time to make many friends in Great Neck. He did expect some family and a few friends, including some from his former school. Some of the staff had asked him if he was considering coming back to teaching. He had told them he needed a little more time to decide his future. They understood.

By that afternoon, the rain had given way to bright sunshine. Mike Kagawa thought it a good sign sent by Amy. She wanted him to be happy, but how could he be without her? He missed watching her comb her hair, how attractive he always thought she looked no matter what she wore, her sense of humor, her smile, her love.

Although Japan had become a more secular society, more than 90 percent of Japanese funerals were conducted as Buddhist ceremonies. He knew that Amy would have wanted it performed as such.

The Japanese section was located on a hill with Yoshino cherry trees and Japanese hollies planted among rhododendrons, native dogwood, and azaleas.

A crowd of about thirty mourners gathered around a makeshift altar, a table laden with fruit, flowers, lighted candles, and photographs of Amy and Wendy.

Two Buddhist priests in long black robes took turns chanting under towering oaks. Kagawa bowed his head as he attempted to hold back sobs, but he could not. His sobbing made the mourners empathize even more with his pain. Tears and controlled crying could be seen and heard among the mourners.

After the burial of the urns, everyone but Kagawa would return to their normal lives, living life as it should be, where children bury parents and not vice versa. Kagawa's life now was anything but normal. He glanced at the empty plot reserved for himself and whispered, *I may be seeing you again very soon, my loves.*

The Chen and Huang families, although Chinese American, would both conduct their funerals over the next seven days, as tradition dictated, with a mourning period lasting for forty-nine days. Chinese could be buried or cremated, and both the Chen and Huang families chose cremation for what was left of their loved ones.

At the service for Patty Chen, twenty-one-year-old Lyle Chen was inconsolable. He had been especially fond of his little sister. He missed teasing her; pulling her pigtails; and how she would playfully smack him on the back of his head and run, daring him to try to catch her. Regardless of the admonition by Detective Kelly, he vowed that if he ever discovered who had defiled and killed Patty, and he had an opportunity to kill them, he would do just that.

After the ceremony, Lyle called an old friend he knew from high school, one he knew had contacts with people of dubious character, and asked about purchasing a handgun.

The next day, the friend said he could get one for $600. Lyle agreed to the price, and later that day, the exchange was made. The heavy, cold weapon felt good in his hand.

CHAPTER 12

THE THREE MEN WHO HAD BEEN SENT BY SATOSHI AKITA TO
find out what they could concerning the encroachment on his territory
by the Triads reported back to him. The Yakuza and the Triads had
been operating in relative peace for several years, but perhaps the Triads
were worried about a strengthening Yakuza.

His men reported that managers of a few of his brothels had been
threatened into working for the Triads. Also, the Triads had intercepted
a package meant for him containing the opioid fentanyl. Somehow,
the Triads must have gotten to a postal worker at the main post office,
informing them of a package from China.

Fentanyl had become far more lucrative than either meth or heroin.
For one thing, heroin had a growing season in the poppy fields. Fentanyl
could be manufactured year-round. Also, one kilogram of fentanyl was
worth fifty kilograms of heroin and thus was easily smuggled into the
States via mail. Both India and China had been prime producers of

fentanyl, but while India had cracked down on its production, China had not.

The Triads, as Chinese, had better connections to Chinese sources. Much of the product was sent through the mail, and much through Mexico via freight. Less than 2 percent of privately owned vehicles and only 16 percent of commercial vehicles were scanned by the Customs and Border Protection Agency.

Then why would the Triads muscle in on the Yakuza? Akita decided it was the age-old lust for power and money. Perhaps the Triads felt threatened by the Yakuza and wanted to put them out of business.

The Triads were similar to both the Japanese Yakuza and the Italian Mafia. Like the Yakuza and Mafia, Triad members were subjected to initiation ceremonies. The typical ceremony took place at an altar where incense was burned, and an animal sacrifice was performed, usually a chicken, pig, or goat. After drinking a mixture of wine and blood of the animal, the member passed beneath an arch of swords while reciting the Triad's thirty-six oaths, which primarily required the member to protect and defend the Triad at all costs. If any of the oaths were not adhered to, the member knew that he would be killed by a myriad of swords or five thunderbolts.

Akita had always known Triad members to be as dedicated as the Yakuza. War always unleashed hell.

Morgan wasn't going to allow Paul to force her to become paranoid, but still, as she stepped into the street, she couldn't be certain he wasn't lurking in some doorway or behind a parked car. Paul owned a minivan that he used for work—that is, when he was sober enough to work—and he probably had followed her taxi the night she met Tyler at the Smith. As a precaution, she decided to walk two blocks north, turn the corner, and hail a taxi there. She felt comforted by the fact that even if he was to follow, in broad daylight she could easily spot his vehicle.

She caught the taxi and followed Tyler's directions. She was certain she hadn't been followed. She stepped inside the ferry building, where she saw Tyler waiting for her. This time, they greeted each other with a brief hug.

Tyler had purchased two round-trip ferry tickets to Governors Island, costing two dollars each. The weather was perfect—clear skies, almost seventy degrees—but it was expected to get cooler by late afternoon. They were dressed accordingly, each wearing long-sleeved shirts and jeans, carrying a light jacket just in case.

They seated themselves on the ferry, and within minutes, it backed out for the ten-minute ride to the island, which was only eight hundred yards from the southernmost point of Manhattan. At the halfway point, Morgan looked back at the skyline of Lower Manhattan. "That's some view," she said. Looming high above the surrounding buildings was the beautiful, angular, silvery Freedom Tower at One World Trade Center, which had replaced the Twin Towers that were destroyed on 9/11.

The cool salt air and the gentle rocking of the boat put Morgan in a relaxed mood. She tilted her head to the side and rested it lightly on Tyler's shoulder. It felt right to her.

They disembarked on the island, where they walked, hand in hand, to the bookstore. Tyler purchased a pamphlet that had a map and a brief history of the island.

Tyler took a moment to scan the pamphlet as they walked the path that would lead them around the island. "Says they constructed three forts here, and during the War of 1812, troops stationed here deterred a British invasion, sparing New York the fiery fate that befell Washington, DC."

"Amazing. So much history in New York that we never hear about."

They passed by one of the forts, and Tyler continued reading. "During the Civil War, the forts were used to house Confederate prisoners of war. The island closed as a fort in 1964 and later became a national landmark, which was opened to the public in 2003."

"I remember learning about Andersonville Prison. Northern captives were kept in ungodly conditions. I hope we treated their troops better." Morgan loved history and was finding it fascinating.

Tyler nodded. "Like they say, war is hell. Do you read much?"

"I like historical novels. A lot of truth in them. How about you?"

"Unfortunately, my reading consists of spreadsheets, tax returns, and the like. But I do enjoy a good movie when I get the chance."

At Blazing Saddles Bicycle Rentals, they rented a two-seater, four-wheeled bicycle with an overhead canopy to block the sun. They sat on side-by-side seats, with one person steering and both of them pedaling. The fun ride took them around the island, where they visited the forts and had spectacular views of New York Harbor and the Statue of Liberty. By the time they returned the bicycle, they were exhausted. They had lunch at the snack bar, eating outside under an umbrella. She had a hamburger and fries; he had two slices of pizza.

After lunch, they strolled around the grassy park area, where Morgan said, "If you don't mind my asking, how old are you?"

He smiled. "How old do I look?" They continued a leisurely walk.

"Hmm. Sixty, sixty-five," she chided.

"Ha. Forty-one. Chivalry prevents us southern folk from asking a lady her age."

"Therefore, the lady will ask. And how old do I look?" She stopped walking, turned toward him, and placed her hands on her hips.

Mimicking her, he said, "Hmm. Sixty-five, seventy. I go for older women."

She laughed. "Then this woman is going to disappoint you. Thirty-seven."

"Good gosh! I'm robbing the cradle." They both laughed.

It felt good to be able to laugh with a man again, and now she felt guilty for having lied to him earlier regarding Paul. She took a deep breath and said, "I'm not officially divorced yet. My annulment will be official in a week or two. I thought it easier to lie when we first met than to say I was still married to Paul."

He smiled kindly. "Understandable."

His one-word response was perfect, she thought.

Hand in hand, they walked to the pier, where they took the ferry back to Manhattan. They decided to grab dinner at a delicatessen on the Lower East Side. After dinner, he asked if she wanted to see where he lived.

Her heart said *yes, go with him*, guaranteed he'd offer a drink and try to get her into bed, but her head said no, since she wasn't quite ready to get into a serious relationship, although she thought if she were ready, it might be with him. Unlike many of her female acquaintances, she'd had few serious relationships, always on her guard against being hurt. She begged off as politely as she could. "I had a great time today. I really did. But I've got to be at work early tomorrow, and I'm dead tired." She saw the disappointment on his face. "But I'll take a raincheck on your offer."

He smiled. "Promise? Cross your heart and hope to die?"

"Promise, without the die part." She gave him something to remember, kissing him on his lips, to which he was a very willing participant. They caught taxis for their own apartments.

After he'd applied the fake beard, baseball cap, and sunglasses, Kagawa had looked at himself in his bathroom mirror. He believed he was staring at one of the most dangerous men on earth, willing to give up his life, but he wasn't expecting to receive seventy-two virgins. Seeing Amy and Wendy again would suffice. He vowed to kill the two men who had defiled and killed Wendy. By killing them, he was probably saving many other girls from lives of suffering and possibly death. Kagawa also felt it highly probable these two men were responsible for the other women whose remains were found along with Wendy's.

Kagawa didn't care if the gun was traceable or not. If it was traced back to Hiro, no harm done. As for fingerprints, he would wipe the gun clean beforehand and wear a surgical glove on his right hand, the one he would shoot with. He was well aware that the actions he was contemplating were the antithesis of societal norms, that people accused of a crime deserved a trial by a jury of their peers. But in taking revenge on Hiro, he knew that he had passed the point of no return where norms were concerned.

Kagawa followed Fujita and Ogura into the room where more than one hundred fifty players were in various stages of preparing for the start of their bridge game. Some were already seated, while others were still signing in or simply milling about, talking with friends.

When he had scouted out the bridge club, he had noticed that several people made their way to their assigned table moments before the game was to begin. Many of them had just come from the bathroom. Therefore, his walking in at that moment and getting behind either Fujita or Ogura would raise no eyebrows.

Kagawa glanced at his watch. Six fifty-nine. The game would start in one minute. He noticed a few players hustling to their seats, and that was his cue. An image of Michael Corleone flashed across his mind. He had wiped the gun clean of fingerprints, and the surgical glove on his right hand would ensure no prints would be left behind. He took a shallow breath as he strode in as though seeking his assigned seat near Fujita and Ogura's table, some forty feet away.

He was only ten feet away from his targets. He reached back under his jacket and stopped directly behind Ogura, hoping to take the larger man out first. In one swift move, he pulled the gun from his back and fired into the back of Ogura's head.

Kagawa didn't wait to see the results of the shot as he saw the look of surprise on Fujita's face. It took only one second between the first and second shots to ring out, with the second shot hitting Fujita squarely in his forehead. Each shot reverberated loudly throughout the cavernous room. Shrieks of terror ricocheted off the walls as the startled people turned and saw blood and skull tissue splattered everywhere. They jumped up and screamed as Kagawa ducked down, dropped the gun, threw his hat behind him, and shouted, "The man with the hat! He has a gun!"

Panicked people were scattering everywhere, knocking over tables and chairs, clawing at one another in an effort to flee the room. Who knew how many more shots could be fired or how many shooters there were? Kagawa was practically carried out of the room with the scores of shouting and running people. Pandemonium was raging. Kagawa threw off his jacket as the manic group rushed into the lobby, with many of them still screaming. Kagawa and many others ran outside into the street, where he heard people shouting such things as "What happened in there? Did you see who did it? Was anyone hurt? How many shooters were there? Is it terrorism?"

Others, who were close to the table, shouted such things as "I heard two shots, and two people were hit. Maybe dead!"

Still wearing the sunglasses, Kagawa calmly but with determination walked toward the corner, where he hailed a taxi a minute before a blue and white turned the corner, its siren blaring and its colorful bright lights flashing. He entered the cab and removed the sunglasses. The taxi drove off just as police cars arrived at the scene.

Morgan and Ben were called to the scene after it was determined that their sketches matched the two dead men. The place was a jumble of overturned chairs and tables, discarded assorted clothing, and cards strewn everywhere. They approached the table where a huge man's head lay. On the floor on the opposite side of the table was another much smaller man. Puddles of blood pooled on the table and the floor. Morgan knew she and Ben would have to interview as many witnesses as possible, perhaps getting the names of witnesses from the bridge club's director.

Morgan studied the huge bald man. She turned to Ben and said, "The officers were right. I think these two were the men that the barkeep said met with Araki. They sure match his description."

Ben answered, "They do. Once we find where these two lived, we might be able to make the connection."

Morgan thought, *If they were involved with the girls' deaths, they deserved to die.*

CSI then took over the collection of evidence.

The bridge club murders had been on the eleven o'clock news the night before, and by the following morning, the deceased had been identified from their IDs as two men of Japanese descent named Hideki Fujita and Tadashi Ogura.

Alice and May Ling saw it on the morning news, as they had just finished showering and preparing themselves for the day's work. They were both stunned and scared.

As they sat on the couch, May Ling asked, "Who pay rent? How get new customer? What happen us?"

Alice tried to gather her wits as best she could. She was as concerned as May Ling and, being only fifteen, didn't know what would happen next. She surmised, "We'll be thrown out into the street, ya know. Maybe not today but soon. We might have to latch onto some pimp, somebody to protect us and supply the drugs."

After a long pause, May Ling said, "This bad. First Hiro, now Fujita and Ogura."

Alice shifted nervously. "Shit. Do you think we might be next?"

May Ling shook her head. "Who kill two whores? We no enemies. We bring money for men. Now bring money for new men."

Alice breathed a sigh of relief. "You're right. Maybe the three of them pissed somebody off. Look at us. Men love us. We make them happy, ya know, and they pay good money for it. Yeah, somebody else will pick us up, and we'll work for them. And you know what? Maybe our new pimps won't hit us as much."

Alice knew to avoid the police since prostitution was illegal, and May Ling could be deported back to China.

"Maybe," Alice offered, "we could run away, ya know? Maybe turn tricks on our own, without some pimp. Keep all the money."

May Ling answered, "We need room and bed. We need shower. We need drugs. We need pimp to give us this."

"Then what do we do?"

"Must find new pimp, or no eat."

A dejected Alice hoped that maybe their luck would change. She sagged heavily into the couch. She expected some regulars to still arrive that day. But she also expected that, once the word got out about Fujita and Ogura, her clientele would dry up. The street would come beckoning. But at least she could keep this day's earnings for herself. She had no idea what the future would hold. She swore to herself that no matter what, she would never go back with her mother. She'd survived this far on her own. She would find a way to go on.

Later that day, after obtaining a search warrant on Fujita and Ogura's apartment, Morgan discovered a wall safe hidden behind a painting. "Look at this." She pointed toward the safe.

Ben saw that it had a combination lock. "We'll have to get a technician to crack this thing open." He immediately called for aid in opening what they hoped might hold invaluable information.

The department's safecracker arrived, and using a drill and a stethoscope, he was able to open the safe in under an hour. Morgan then extracted its contents.

It left no doubt that these two were engaged in illicit undertakings. Over $30,000 in cash was found in the safe, along with two handguns, several ounces of cocaine, and what appeared to be opioid pills. But the most interesting finding was a ledger.

Morgan sat at the kitchen table and viewed the pages. She excitedly turned toward Ben and said, "These pages record the first names of women, the amount of money each brought in, and a letter next to each name. There are over twenty names."

Ben asked, "What do you think these letters mean?"

Morgan perused the ledger. She had some knowledge of codes from her experience in the army, and she believed that, in time, she could decipher the code. "One thing is apparent: not all of them could be housed in one location. I bet there were several locations, and those letters just might indicate which locations these women were or are kept."

"You're probably right."

Morgan then turned to the last page of the ledger. "I got it. On the back page are five street addresses. There are several girls listed with the letter M, which indicates Mott Street. There are four other addresses." She flipped back and forth between the names of the women and the letters next to each one. "They all match one of these addresses. Let's get some squad cars to these locations."

Ben immediately phoned the information to the precinct. Squad cars were quickly dispatched to each of five addresses listed in the ledger. An unexpected bonus was the listing of a girl named only Maria, whose money stopped coming in on September 14. Morgan asked, "Do you remember the exact date Butterfly was found?"

"No. Why?"

"It was around the time that this Maria stopped earning money. If the dates match, I believe that our Butterfly is Maria." She called the precinct and was told that Maria had been found in the dumpster on September 15. She told Ben and said, "Almost definitely, our Butterfly is Maria. If so, maybe we can find a relative."

Ben responded, "But with no last name and no one reporting a girl fitting Butterfly's description, probably not."

Morgan nodded in agreement.

A bonus was that two other girls who had earned good money for these men were listed as Li and Patty. Their address was different from Maria's. It was highly probable that these were the Chen and Huang girls, whose families would have to be informed later that, more than likely, Fujita and Ogura were the responsible parties but were now serving time in the morgue.

Upon further examination of the ledger, Morgan noticed something. She turned to Ben. "There are a number of small payments made to someone named H. I'll bet this refers to our guy, Masahiro. Seems more than coincidental that all three were Japanese, and the bartender had stated that Hiro often met with two men that fit the description of Fujita and Ogura."

Ben nodded. "So, Fujita and Ogura probably paid Masahiro Araki to pimp for them and to find new blood."

"That seems to be the connection. But look at these other payments. They were made on a weekly basis to a person or group listed as Y. Dollars to doughnuts, these were payments made to the Yakuza for the privilege of doing business on their turf. I think a visit with Satoshi Akita might be called for. See what he can tell us."

"Good idea."

Morgan then placed a call to the precinct. She felt energized with the news that squad cars were on their way to five addresses, with prospects of being able to free, and then to help, several girls and young women begin new and hopefully better lives. She was well aware of the changes that had taken place in the government's attitude toward exploited children. The law defined children who were involved in these crimes as victims, not perpetrators. If incarcerated, these youths had no access to services that could address their specific social and emotional needs, and upon release, they would often return to a life on the streets. Morgan vowed to do all she could to help these young victims.

They drove to Satoshi Akita's club, where they flashed their badges to a bartender and said they wanted to see Akita. The man pointed at a table in the rear of the club. Ben glanced at the limber naked young woman performing gyrating moves on a pole on the stage. Morgan playfully poked him in his ribcage.

Ben smiled sheepishly. "Just looking."

As Morgan and Ben approached the table, Morgan said, "That's him. The one in the middle."

Akita sat with Nomura and Harada, all dressed as usual in dark suits and ties. Morgan told herself to remain calm even though she would love to kill the perverted abuser and murderer of girls.

Ben flashed his badge and introduced himself as an NYPD detective. He nodded toward Morgan and said, "You've already met Detective Kelly."

"Pretty miss green eyes seems to like it here." Akita flashed a grin in her direction.

Morgan took a step toward Akita. Ben gripped her arm.

"So, welcome to our humble establishment. How can I be of service? A beer maybe?" He rolled his unlit cigar from one side of his mouth to the other.

Ben said, "We found a ledger that we believe showed payments to the Yakuza from the two men who were assassinated at a bridge club. What can you tell us about this?"

Akita cocked his head to the side. "The payments or the two dead men?"

"Both."

Akita looked at Nomura and Harada and then back at Ben. "Nothing at all, Detective. I run a legal club here. I don't get involved in illegal activities."

"We know you head up a branch of the Yakuza in Chinatown."

"All rumors. I have many persons who simply work for me."

"You never had any contact with Hideki Fujita or Tadashi Ogura?"

"Never heard of them."

Ben nodded slowly. "OK … all right. But if we find that there's a connection between you and them, I guarantee we'll be back."

Akita lit his cigar, took a drag, and exhaled the smoke toward the ceiling.

Ben said, "You do know it's against the law to smoke in bars and restaurants."

"Are you going to arrest me for smoking? Have a drink, on the house, and watch the best part of our organization on that pole."

Ben said, "If you had nothing to do with these murders, who do you think did?"

Akita seemed to be in deep thought before answering. "If I were you, I would look at the Triads. Those Chinese hate that some Japanese are operating in Chinatown." He looked directly at Ben. "Detective Chang. Do you hate us Japanese? Is that why I am being harassed?"

"No, I just hate criminals, especially those who abuse girls and young women."

Akita then eyeballed Morgan, who had chosen to let the more experienced Ben deal with Akita. He said to Morgan, "Quiet one today, aren't you? Are you the *good* cop to his *bad* cop?"

She sternly answered, "I assure you, we can *both* be bad when we want to be."

"Hmm. Nice answer. Can I speak with you for a moment, alone?"

Morgan forcefully replied, "Anything you have to say will be to the two of us."

"OK. I noticed no ring. I happen to love green-eyed women. Here's my card. Call me sometime." He reached into his jacket pocket and held out the card for Morgan.

Morgan felt her adrenaline rising. She snatched the card, ripped it in half, and let the pieces float to the floor.

Akita smugly said, "As I told you before, you're much too pretty to be a cop. If you ever need a job, come see me."

Morgan couldn't hold back her anger. "The next time you see me, it will be to put cuffs on you, you piece of human garbage." She turned to Ben. "Let's get out of this shithole."

Ben said to Akita, "You're messing with the wrong people."

Ben followed a bristling Morgan out of the club, where Morgan said, "That scumbag is responsible for at least the three girls' deaths, even if indirectly, and he uses who knows how many underaged girls. We have to get that creep."

"Him and a lot more like him."

She wouldn't tell Ben, but in spite of herself, getting Akita was becoming personal.

Akita said to Harada, "Throw a scare into the bitch."

Morgan and Ben then paid a visit to Sun Li Fong, leader of the local Triads, and received similar responses. He said he never heard of Fujita and Ogura, and anyway, he would never associate with Japanese men. Ben told Fong that they were being placed on notice. The police would be watching them more closely than ever.

As Alice and May Ling sat topless on the couch, they heard a knock on their door. Alice expected to hear a code word for either one or both girls. She was looking forward to keeping all the money earned, at least until the business dried up. There was no code word spoken. Instead, she heard, "Police. Open the door, please."

The girls glanced wide-eyed at each other, fearful of what might happen to them. Prison? Deportation for May Ling? They ran into the bedroom and quickly threw on some clothes. Alice thought, *Hey, we're just two girls watching television.* She heard the knocks grow louder and a voice yelling, "We know someone is in there. Open up, or we break down the door."

The girls rushed back into the room. May Ling sat on the couch, and Alice answered, "Coming. We were just getting dressed."

She strode to the door and opened it to see two uniformed police officers standing there. A tall African American officer asked in a kindly manner, "May we come in?"

Alice was taken aback, having expected to be roughed up and arrested. She responded meekly, "S … sure."

The officer asked, "Is anyone else here with you?"

Alice replied, "No one."

The officers entered the room. The other officer, a white man with dirty blond hair, searched the bedroom and bathroom and hollered, "Clear." He returned to the two girls. "We know that one of you is Alice, and the other is May Ling."

Alice, surprised that they knew their names, replied, "I'm Alice." She turned and pointed at May Ling. "And that's May Ling."

The black officer said, "Look. We're not here to arrest you. We're here to help you."

Alice cocked her head quizzically. In her world, men lied all the time.

"How old are you?" the white officer asked. "And don't try to lie. We'll find out everything about you, and it will be better for you if you tell the truth."

Alice mulled over his remarks. She looked up at him. "Fifteen."

The officer shook his head. "Jesus." He looked at May Ling. "And you?"

"I seventeen."

The white officer turned to the black officer and said, dismayed, "And she's the *older* one."

The black officer said, "We need you to gather up your things and come with us."

"Where are you taking us?" Alice asked as she bit a fingernail.

"Somewhere safe. We'll explain in our car," the black officer said.

Although not quite certain that the car ride wouldn't lead to something sinister, Alice quickly packed her few things, and she left looking like the frightened girl she truly was.

On the way to the precinct, the officers explained that they would be taken care of and not to worry.

Alice listened but was unsure of her future. At least she wasn't handcuffed, which helped her to believe the officers might be there to help her, not throw her in jail or deport May Ling.

Alice hoped they wouldn't contact her mother. She didn't want her mother to learn that she ended up a prostitute, no better than her mother had been.

The four other sites that were investigated by other police officers netted twelve other girls and young women. They would all receive varying forms of aid and treatment, but only time would tell how many of them would return to a normal life. At least they had a shot at it.

CHAPTER

13

MORGAN AND BEN WERE GRATIFIED THAT FOURTEEN GIRLS and young women had been rescued from the likes of Fujita and Ogura.

Morgan and Ben sat at Ben's desk, reviewing what they knew. Morgan stated, in quiet fury, "One of the girls was just twelve years old, perfect for some perverted scumbag to exploit."

Ben said, "The ledger we found in their apartment made clear the connection between Hiro and the two assassinated men."

"And as the bartender suggested, this Hiro kid worked for them, acting as a pimp in lining up customers and finding new blood to exploit. The question now is, who killed Hiro?"

Ben scratched his head. "Maybe it was Fujita and Ogura who killed him over some dispute. Or maybe it was a competing group who killed the three, worried that Hiro and the two men were horning in on their turf."

Morgan thought for a moment. "Or, since they were making payments to the local Yakuza, and since Hiro had been brought in for questioning, did the Yakuza fear he was spilling his guts about things he might have known? Did the Yakuza execute him after torturing him to see what he had told us? After all, he wasn't shot in the head but was obviously held captive for at least some time, since he was bound with duct tape and suffocated with a plastic bag."

"A great way to send a message to other potential snitches."

Morgan nodded. "That idea makes the most sense, since all three of these enterprising Japanese men are now dead, probably murdered by some group."

She knew they had their hands full in getting to the bottom of these crimes, trying to determine who killed the three men and why.

"Of course," Ben offered, "revenge could have been a motive for relatives of the trafficked females."

"That Lyle Chen made a threat against the killer of his sister, but there was no conceivable way he could know the name of Masahiro Araki since his interviews were never revealed to the public. And no way could he have known about Fujita and Ogura unless he had street contacts who knew something about them. We should talk with him again."

Ben nodded and said, "The Yakuza has eyes everywhere, and they knew Hiro was involved with Fujita and Ogura. My money is still with the Yakuza."

"And on Satoshi Akita," Morgan answered.

They made an appointment to speak with Lyle Chen at the Chen residence. Lyle claimed to have been finishing dinner at home at seven o'clock on the night of the bridge club murders. His parents and siblings attested to that. Could they all be lying? It was possible, but their tone and body language led Morgan to think they were telling the truth.

Morgan asked Lyle, "Do you own a gun?"

Mr. Chen quickly and forcefully answered, "No weapons are allowed in this home."

Morgan saw the two brothers glance at each other. "Lyle. You haven't answered my question."

"No. I don't own a gun. And I didn't kill anyone."

Mr. Chen said, "Enough. We would like you to leave."

They left with the feeling that he might own a gun, but even if he did, their opinion was that Lyle probably didn't kill Fujita and Ogura. But he would still remain on their list of suspects.

Now that the bridge club murders were assumed to be interconnected with Hiro's murder, as well as with the prostitution ring run by the three men in Chinatown, Morgan contacted the two ladies who ran the bridge club, Karen and Jessica. They were asked if they wouldn't mind coming to their precinct in Chinatown. The two ladies agreed and were now sitting next to Morgan's desk.

"Thank you both for coming," Morgan said. "Normally, I would interview witnesses separately, but since you both run the game together, I believe it will help me to understand what happened from both your perspectives."

The two women, still visibly shaken by the previous night's events, merely nodded.

"I know how upset you must be, but I need to ask certain questions, the answers to which might lead to our killer or killers."

A subdued Karen, who appeared to be in her fifties, with reddish hair cut in a shag, answered, "We understand."

"Tell us what you saw and did, beginning prior to the shooting," Morgan said.

"At first, nothing seemed out of place. Nothing unusual. The players come in, sign in at my table, find their assigned tables, and get ready to play. Jessica was handing out the boards—"

"Boards?" Morgan interrupted.

Jessica, who was in her sixties with shoulder-length blond hair, answered, "I give out the boards, which contain four slots, with each slot holding thirteen cards. The boards tell the players which thirteen cards are theirs."

"OK, so what happened next?"

Jessica continued. "I was handing out the boards when I heard the loudest noise I've ever heard."

"In such close quarters," Morgan replied, "a gunshot could be earsplitting."

"Yes, but almost instantaneously, a second shot rang out," Karen said. "I was checking my laptop, that's where the scores are tabulated, when I heard the *bang! Bang!* I looked up as people were jumping out of their seats. All hell had broken loose. People were screaming, running for the exits."

"Did either of you see the shooter or shooters?"

They both answered no.

Morgan asked, "Can you provide us with a list of all the players, with their addresses, who were there that night?"

Jessica answered, "Every player signs in with an ACBL number that matches their name."

"What's that stand for?"

"The American Contract Bridge League. I wouldn't have their addresses, but if you contact the ACBL, they could help you since everyone is on their mailing list."

"How many people signed in?"

Karen thought for a second. "One hundred sixty."

"It'll take some doing, but someone was bound to see something, especially the ones at their table. I'd like to start with them and the tables closest to that one. Can you get me that?"

"No problem," Karen answered.

"Is it possible that some disgruntled player did this?"

Jessica chuckled. "Over a bridge game?"

Morgan offered, "Gamblers have been known to overreact when money is at stake."

"We don't play for money."

"No money? Then what do you play for?" Morgan asked with a quizzical expression.

"We play for points," Karen answered.

"What kind of points?"

"Points that are kept by the ACBL. People use them as bragging rights as to how good a player they think they are."

Morgan scratched her head. "That's it?"

"That's it," Karen answered. "Do you have any clues as to who the shooter or shooters might be?"

"The people who managed to hang around after the shooting, like yourselves, were asked what they had observed. Like most IDs that happen where people are panicked, there were either one or two shooters, who were tall or short, fat or thin, white or Hispanic, and so forth. Not very reliable."

The meeting ended, and the two women left after promising to help with the list of players.

Later, Ben walked over to Morgan. "Forensics is gathering video from the several cameras. Maybe we'll get lucky and get a decent shot of this guy or guys."

Morgan replied, "I hope so. The two women were of no help."

Each of the fourteen trafficking victims was brought to the precinct for questioning and processing. The first order of events was to obtain basic information, including full name, date and place of birth, last known residence prior to being trafficked, parents' names, and any phone numbers that might be of help. The ages of the fourteen ranged from eighteen down to twelve. Their ages would determine what avenues of aid would be available to them.

After the initial interview, the police department would attempt to contact family members or friends who might be able to offer help. Barring this, the next step would be to provide temporary housing through the Social Services Department, where the victims could receive counseling and other services.

Ben and Morgan had agreed to interview several of the girls, including Alice. The girls' stories were, in many aspects, pathetically similar. This was mostly due to their youth and vulnerability. They came from broken homes, had drug addicts for parents, or had been sexually abused. One girl had been abandoned, and even more appalling to Morgan, the twelve-year-old had been sold to traffickers in China when she was only eight years old. Ben had spoken to the girl in Cantonese, and she was pleased to be able to converse in her native language, which set her somewhat at ease with the interview. The things she unabashedly related to Morgan would have horrified even the most hardened of police.

None of the girls had been kidnapped. In one form or another, they all had agreed to go with their trafficker after having been promised a better life. The young and innocent were the traffickers' vulnerable meal tickets.

One of the many pathetic stories was told to Morgan by an eighteen-year-old named Amanda. She had lived in Maryland for the first twelve years of her life. When she was ten, family members abused her. She said that before the abuse, she was a normal little girl who loved to read, collect stamps, and draw. She was also a member of the Barbie fan club. After the abuse, she became a different girl. No one helped her or validated the abuse, so part of her went into hiding, and she became depressed. She didn't want to be around anyone, stopped attending school, and eventually ran away at age twelve, which made her a walking target for predators. It didn't take long for traffickers to find her. Surprisingly, it was a couple, a man and a woman, who found her walking the streets of downtown Baltimore. She was hungry and alone, and they brought her to their home, where they fed her and seemed to care for her—until they initiated her into the world of prostitution. They used her for a few months until she was sold to a man who took her to New York City, where she was sold to Fujita and Ogura. That was six years ago, and in those six years, she had been abused, stabbed, raped, and beaten and had become addicted to drugs, which helped to ease her pain. If the police hadn't found her, she believed she would have been put out onto the street very soon. She had already seen the handwriting on the wall since she had witnessed what had happened to other girls who were approaching the end of their teenage years. As soon as their drug habit became too expensive, they were no longer a valuable commodity and were released to the city to fend for themselves. There were plenty of other young girls to take their places.

Stories such as these made Morgan sick to her stomach.

Morgan heard Alice's story, which was not unique. She said she'd been raped several times over a period of a few months by her mother's boyfriend when she was thirteen, and when she told her mother, her drunken mother threw her out of the house. At a bus terminal, she was approached by Hiro, who promised to take care of her. The next thing she knew, she was working as a prostitute for Fujita and Ogura.

"Ya know," Alice said, "up until I was raped, I was pretty innocent. I never had a real boyfriend. I kind of knew about the birds and the bees, but that was about it. When he raped me that first time, he hurt me, and after it was over, I felt real dirty, ya know? Before that happened, I thought he was an OK guy. He raped me a few more times and did other stuff, and I said I was going to tell my mother. He threatened to tell my mother that it was my fault. I didn't know what to do. I finally told her, and she threw *me* out. That shithead changed my life, ya know? I've had hundreds of men but not one boyfriend." She was bristling.

Morgan empathized with her. "I know where you're coming from."

"How could *you* know?"

Morgan said softly, "Trust me. I know."

Alice stared at her. "Anything like that ever happen to you?"

Morgan had never been asked that question. She didn't want to lie to Alice, but she could never tell her the truth. "Let me just say, I *know* where you are coming from." She nodded her head while staring directly into Alice's eyes.

"Then you know what it feels like."

Morgan could only nod.

Alice said, "I went from being a kid to a grown-up at just thirteen. I have no real friends, no education, and I can't go back to my old school because someone will find out about me. The girls will hate me, and the boys will only want sex from me." Her eyes began to well up.

Morgan reached out and touched Alice on her forearm. "Listen to me. You have a long life ahead of you. Things will get better. You'll see. There are people who are going to help you."

Alice was glad it was a youngish and pretty woman who had interviewed her, especially one who seemed to know how she felt. Alice was still frightened of the future. She often dreamed of going to a movie theater with a handsome boyfriend, where she would munch on popcorn and M&Ms. After, he would take her to a burger and shake restaurant, where she would order the biggest chocolate shake they offered. Maybe she could learn to skateboard. But reality always kicked in. Her next customer would be knocking on the door. Sex was an unwanted burden whose pain was alleviated by drugs. She'd seen so many TV shows with happy families: a husband and wife with two happy kids. She ached for something like that.

Morgan gently asked, "Did you know Patty Chen or Li Huang?"

She shrugged and said, "Should I?"

"These were girls that were being used by Fujita and Ogura but at a different location."

"Never heard of 'em."

"What about Wendy Kagawa?"

Morgan detected a slight flinch.

"Don't know her."

"You're certain? A Japanese fourteen-year-old?"

She answered forcefully, "I told you. I don't know her."

Morgan didn't want to press too hard. Alice had been through so much. "OK. We'll have to get in touch with your mother. Do you remember her phone number?"

Alice was taken aback. "You have to call her?"

"She's your mother. She should know where you are."

Alice shouted, "You can call her, but I won't go back with her! I'll run away."

Morgan sympathetically replied, "I know your story. She won't be able to simply appear and take you back. You'll be under our care for a while. Later, a judge might agree with you, and we'll find a nice home for you to live in."

"You're lying to me, right?"

Morgan replied, "I will *never* lie to you. First, you'll be placed in a detox program to get you off drugs. Get clean, and we'll go from there."

Morgan thought Alice looked like a scared ten-year-old as she softly replied, "OK."

Alice remembered Stephanie Liu's cell number and gave it to Morgan.

At the end of the interview, Morgan wished Alice good luck. She told Alice she had faith in her being able to live a normal and successful life.

At the precinct, Morgan called the mother. "Stephanie Liu?"

"Who wants to know?"

"Detective Kelly. I'm with the Seventh Precinct in Chinatown. We have your daughter, Alice, in our custody."

"No shit. She kill somebody?"

"Nothing like that. We would like you to come to the precinct to speak with us."

"I been real sick. Can't make it over there. Give me your number, and I'll call when I'm better."

After Alice's description of her home life, Morgan wasn't surprised at the conversation. She gave Liu the number to call and wished her a speedy recovery. The call ended.

Morgan thought, *Alice won't have to run away.*

Alice was placed in a detox program in a local hospital. Morgan hoped that, with ongoing treatment, she would kick her habit and thrive. Morgan knew in her heart that there was a good chance that Alice would fail.

CHAPTER

14

THAT EVENING, PAUL WAS ALONE, SITTING ON HIS LIVING room couch and drinking scotch. The job with the construction company had fallen through. He was feeling sorry for himself as he recalled how it all went wrong.

His first wife was a waitress. She was a looker, and he married her after dating for only three months. Their marriage was a disaster from the start. He drank too much, she talked too much, he was out of work too much, and she kept accusing him of seeing other women, all of which was true. They decided to divorce, which led to fighting over who got what.

During that time, he met and fell for Morgan, whom he'd caught on the rebound from a relationship she'd been in. His divorce was dragging, but he knew it was simply a matter of time. He didn't want to lose Morgan, so when the prospect of marriage came up, he threw caution to the wind, and they were married in a private ceremony by a justice of the peace.

Their marriage was good for a while. He managed to hide how much he drank. He turned drinking into a festive act, mixing up fancy martinis, bringing home cheap bubbly, and she bought it, thinking of him as a romantic. He was working construction steadily until his drinking got in the way; too many days of work missed, too many days showing up late.

His fallback position had been Morgan. As a cop, she made a very good salary and had great benefits, including medical. As a detective, her salary was even better. But none of this was any help to him now.

He polished off the last ounce of his bottle of scotch and stared at the gun that lay on the wood coffee table. He thought about whom he might kill first. Would it be Morgan? Or maybe that son of a bitch she was seeing. It sure as hell wouldn't be himself.

That same evening, after checking her refrigerator, Morgan left her apartment and walked toward her car, intending to drive to her favorite grocery store. As she approached her car, she noticed something on her windshield. Taped to it was a one-foot square black piece of paper with a large symbol on it. Morgan tore it off the windshield and stared at it. The symbol appeared to be a Far Eastern letter or word. She was certain it was from Akita, and she believed it had to be some sort of threat.

She scanned the surroundings but saw nothing. She got into her car, but before she turned the key, she wondered, *Will the car blow up?* She'd seen what a car bomb could do to flesh and bone in Iraq. But then she thought, *If there was a bomb, would they make me suspicious by warning me?* She thought not. Besides, if they wanted her dead, one bullet would suffice. She took a deep breath and turned the key. The car started. She exhaled forcefully. She intended to find someone who could interpret the symbol's meaning.

Satoshi Akita was worried not so much for himself but for his organization. He knew that for the past few years, the Triads had been attempting to take over some of his territory. On the plus side, Hideki Fujita and Tadashi Ogura were no longer a problem. More than likely, it was the Triads, since it was obviously a professional hit, although the possibility existed that a rogue Yakuza had a personal vendetta against those two. If so, Akita vowed to mete out the harshest of punishments.

But Akita's main concern was the encroachments by the Triads. Perhaps it was time to demonstrate that the Yakuza wouldn't tolerate any more affronts to their power. Deciding the proper Yakuza response weighed heavily on Akita's shoulders. If there was no response whatsoever, they would appear weak, and that would probably lead to more encroachments on their territory. He ran several legal massage parlors, some posing as spas, which fronted for his brothels. There were over nine thousand illicit massage parlors in the US, with many in Chinatown. About every five years, the NYPD would sweep the massage parlors, resulting in a dozen or so arrests. But charges were often dropped or pleaded down, so new parlors and spas often popped up in the same or new locations.

Akita knew that any response to the Triads would have to be well thought out. It would have to be extremely measured to send the correct message. What would that response be? He would call a meeting with his lieutenants to find a solution to this vexing problem.

The Flying Dragons represented the Triads in New York City. The leader of this group, or Dragon Master, was Sun Li Fong. When he was growing up, Fong's nickname was Baby Buddha due to his being muscular, squat, and with a round face. It was a name that no one dared use anymore. He had been told by one of his followers that three Japanese, who had been operating several brothels, were killed in what appeared to be a mob rubout. He believed that no Triad had anything to do with their deaths, but would the Yakuza accuse them, knowing they were attempting to take over some of their territory? Fong was told by his men of the veiled accusations made toward his organization, but nothing had risen to the level of a threat. Besides, he knew that the Flying Dragons had no reason to kill such an insignificant player as that teenage pimp. But with the death of two far more significant players, he feared that any accusation made now would be taken as a clear threat. Fong knew that some of his men were taking over Yakuza territory, and although there was plenty of money to be made, each group prided itself on showing strength when any of its assets were threatened. Had one of his men independently attempted to take over Fujita and Ogura's territory? He would investigate, and if any of his men had done so, they would regret the day they were born. Also, he would wait to see if any form of retaliation by the Yakuza occurred, and then he would act accordingly.

As a youth, Fong had turned to crime as a means of obtaining the things his parents couldn't afford to give him. With both parents working menial jobs with long hours, the teenaged Fong soon found a surrogate family in a gang of Triads, where he learned to respect his "older brothers." By 1995, Fong had demonstrated leadership qualities, and he became instrumental in bringing in Chinese illegals by plane, truck, and ship, many of whom ended up in New York City. These people paid upward of $15,000 to $35,000 per person to the Triads and syndicates that operated worldwide trafficking in humans, stolen cars, and drugs. Many of these persons became the equivalent of indentured slaves since they needed to pay back the thousands of dollars to their trafficker. In 1995 alone, Fong was part of an enterprise that smuggled more than one hundred thousand Chinese into the US, with most of them ending up in New York City and California, where they provided labor for sweatshops and farms. The major syndicates had ships that carried heroin to Antwerp, Belgium, and whose ships also carried immigrants. The ships then went back to Asia loaded with stolen BMWs, Mercedes, Cadillacs, and Porsches, which were then smuggled into South China and sold to the nouveau riche.

Investigators stated that Chinese gangs had largely replaced the Cosa Nostra in terms of the American heroin trade. In the 1990s, more than 70 percent of the heroin reaching the West Coast of the US was from China. And there was plenty of money to be made selling opioids.

Sun Li Fong was heavily involved in much of these lucrative enterprises, and he vowed to do anything to protect his assets.

At the precinct the following morning, Morgan told Ben, "I found this taped to my windshield last night." She held the paper out for him to see.

Ben examined it. "Looks like some kind of word or letter, but I don't recognize it."

"You wouldn't. I asked around this morning. It's Japanese for death, and you don't have to be a genius to know who it's from."

Ben scratched his head. "It's obviously meant to scare you, but they don't know who they're dealing with. But still, watch yourself. A threat could become some kind of accident."

She slowly shook her head. "I'm gonna get that scumbag first."

Later, Morgan was reexamining the ledger found in the dead men's apartment. One name had been scratched out, almost obliterated, but when she held the page up to the light, she believed it was the name Wendy. She called Ben over and asked what he thought the name was.

Ben held the page up to the light and squinted. "It's hard to tell for certain, but my guess is that it's Wendy." Ben's eyes suddenly brightened as though someone had slapped him on his forehead. "This might be our Wendy Kagawa."

"Exactly what I think."

"Not that common a name, is it?" Ben rhetorically asked.

Morgan continued. "The peculiar thing about this person named Wendy was that her name was the only one that had been entered into the ledger and then scratched out, with no amount of earnings ever credited to her. The date by her name was entered this past September, during the time that Wendy was reported missing."

"Then it was Fujita and Ogura who killed her, aided by Hiro."

"It won't bring her back, but it might give the family closure, knowing what happened to her and that the scumbags that took her were dead."

Ben pushed his chair back from his desk and stood. "Let's get his address from the murder book, and then I think you and I should pay a visit to the family."

Morgan smiled. She was proud of herself. If she could make the pain of the Kagawa family lessen even just a little bit, the trip would be well worth it. She only wished there was some magical pill that could make the pain of her own memories lessen.

"Wait a second," she said. "I interviewed a girl named Alice. She claimed she never heard of Wendy, but the ledger says she worked at the same address and at the same time as Wendy. I'd like to speak to her again."

Morgan contacted the hospital where Alice was undergoing detox. Morgan was told that Alice had had a bad night, and it would be better if Morgan could wait to interview Alice after she was released to a domestic violence shelter, possibly in a few more days. Alice would continue on a drug treatment program there. Morgan understood.

The murder book informed them that Wendy's parents, Amy and Michael Kagawa, lived in Great Neck, Long Island. Morgan dialed Mike Kagawa's telephone number. The phone rang three times and was picked up by a man who answered, "Hello?"

Morgan had thought beforehand how to handle this conversation. "Is this Michael Kagawa?"

"This is Mike. Who's calling?"

"It's Detective Morgan Kelly."

"Detective Kelly. Did you find out something?"

"We have some information regarding your daughter, Wendy."

"What information?"

"Detective Ben Chang and I would rather not discuss it over the phone. We could be there in about forty-five minutes. We have your address. Is that convenient for you?"

"Come by. I'll wait for you."

Morgan and Ben left the precinct and drove to Kagawa's address. Less than an hour later, Morgan rang the doorbell. Kagawa opened the door. "Come in, Detectives." He waved them in. "You'll have to excuse the condition of the house since I'm getting ready to sell it. Moving out as soon as possible."

The two detectives flashed their IDs. Morgan introduced Ben to Mr. Kagawa. Morgan eyeballed the sparsely furnished living room. There were three folding chairs set up in the middle of the room. Kagawa had opened up two more chairs to make it possible for the three of them to chat in relative comfort.

Kagawa pointed at the chairs and pleasantly said, "Please, have a seat. Can I get you something? I have some bottled water if you like."

The two said they were fine as each detective took a seat, and Kagawa sat on the third chair, facing them.

Morgan was the first to notice the large portrait hanging over the mantel. It was an oil painting in which Mike Kagawa was seated in an armchair, dressed in a suit and tie. His wife, an attractive woman, dressed in a flower-patterned dress, was seated on one of the arms. Wendy, who appeared to be twelve or thirteen, dressed in a similar flower-patterned dress, sat on the other arm. They were smiling. "I assume that's your wife and daughter with you?"

Kagawa and Ben turned toward the portrait. Kagawa nodded sadly.

"Beautiful portrait," she continued. "By the way, is your wife home? She should also hear what we have to say."

Morgan noticed him swallow hard.

"My wife committed suicide."

Ben and Morgan responded in unison, "What?"

Kagawa looked down at the floor. "My wife killed herself right after Wendy's remains were found. Killed herself in the garage. Carbon monoxide. Wendy was our only child. A gift from God. Now I feel like there's a cat clawing and scratching at my heart, hurting me persistently and relentlessly. I wake up each morning and pray for deliverance. Perhaps I'll be joining my Wendy and Amy soon in the afterlife."

Morgan clearly saw the pain that was written all over Kagawa's face. Trying her hardest to be as empathetic as possible, Morgan said, "I'm so sorry … for both your losses, but as I mentioned on the phone, perhaps you should seek counseling." Morgan believed she was speaking with one of the loneliest men on earth. She felt deep compassion for him.

Kagawa looked up at them. "What information do you have about my Wendy?"

"Look," Morgan responded in a voice as soft as silk, "I don't know if what we tell you will help you or not, but we believe it will at least bring some closure as to your daughter's fate."

Kagawa paused for a moment, then said, "Go on."

She continued. "From information collected from our investigation into two men's murders, it appears that your daughter was kidnapped by two men named Hideki Fujita and Tadashi Ogura, who wanted"—she didn't want to add insult to injury and chose her words carefully—"to make money by using her. The information we have told us that they didn't make a dime off her. Toxicology reports said she died from an overdose of a combination of drugs." She paused. "We thought you might want to know how she died and by whom and that the bastards who kidnapped your daughter are now burning in hell." As hard as she tried, she couldn't help exhibiting some of her pent-up anger.

Kagawa looked down at his clasped hands. "So, it was two *Japanese* who stole my daughter from me and caused my dear wife to commit suicide. Ironic, isn't it?" His sad eyes looked up at the two detectives.

Ben said, "If it will make you feel any better, the deaths of those two led us to five apartments in Chinatown, where fourteen girls and young women were being used as prostitutes. They lived a life of depravity, in squalor, with drugs, abuse, and so forth. They are now being given government assistance to help them to recover from that life. Perhaps they will be able to start over again. Some of these girls were as young as twelve."

"Thank you for that information. I appreciate it."

Kagawa stood, and, following his lead, so did Ben and Morgan. They shook hands, walked out of the house, and entered their car.

Morgan said, "That poor man is prime for suicide. I hope he seeks counseling. If he believes he'll see his family in heaven, he just might do it."

She recalled Graves's admonition, *Don't take the job home.* She was beginning to think it was impossible.

As was promised, the director of the bridge club, Karen, had sent the full list of players who had signed in that evening. Morgan knew they had their hands full in attempting to find and interview one hundred and sixty witnesses, but the obvious starting point was with the players assigned to east-west at the table where Fujita and Ogura were assigned north-south. Each square bridge table measured only forty inches on a side. The east-west players, a Barbara Davis and a Cynthia Nelson, would have been seated within arm's-length of Fujita and Ogura.

Morgan thought the two women seemed a bit excited to be interviewed. One woman gushed, "This is just like the detective shows on television."

"Sort of," Morgan replied. "Only we don't usually solve our cases in less than one hour."

But other than describing the loud shots, bloody scene, and panicked people, they offered no help in describing the shooter.

The newspapers, television, radio, and social media all ended their reporting of the bridge club murders by asking anyone who witnessed the shooting to please call the police hotline. Over the next few days, they interviewed several more people who might have seen the shooter, but their recollections varied so widely from one another, their descriptions were rendered practically worthless.

Of course, they also received several anonymous phone calls stating they had information on the bridge club murders, all of which turned out to be nothing useful. One of the callers who spoke to Morgan claimed the killing of two Japanese was revenge for Pearl Harbor.

On their agenda was to view the videos collected from the cameras at the bridge club.

Satoshi Akita met with Nomura and Harada at the strip club. As usual, they were nattily dressed in suits and ties. Loud music was playing as an Asian stripper performed on the stage.

Nomura and Harada listened intently as Akita described the situation concerning the Triads. "They have taken over some of our good earners' territory."

"Our rivals have always been the Triads," Harada answered.

Nomura chimed in. "We must do something."

Akita reached inside his suit jacket and extracted a cigar. He bit off the end, spit it onto the floor, and waited as Harada lit a match and touched it to the end of the cigar. Akita blew a smoke ring toward the ceiling and then watched it shimmer and fade away. "I agree." He blew another smoke ring and stated, "But we don't want a war on our hands."

"But if we do nothing, we look weak," Nomura said uneasily.

Akita barked a cough. He placed the cigar on the edge of an ashtray and then clasped his hands together as though praying. Seconds passed. He placed his hands onto the table and declared, "We will send a message, but no one must die. After all, none of the three men were Yakuza. Find one of their men and teach him a lesson, making certain he understands and relays the message we are sending to his superiors. If peace follows, then we all go on as usual. There is enough money to be made for all of us. But if another incident or more encroachments should occur ..." He let that thought hang in the air.

Harada and Nomura stood and bowed. They knew who to call on to deliver the message.

Kagawa stood, head bowed, in reverent silence at his loved ones' graves. He whispered the news that Wendy's death was not in vain. It was she who ultimately was responsible for saving the lives of many other girls and young women. It felt good to be telling her that.

He spotted a nearby bench, sat on it, and began to contemplate these past weeks. The detectives had told him in sketchy detail what had happened to her. And Hiro, who said he wasn't there when she died, only knew that she died from a drug overdose. But there were so many questions unanswered. Where did she die? Exactly when did she die? Did any of the other girls know her? Did she relate anything to them? Did Wendy speak any last words? Did she suffer in death? And as horrible as these thoughts seemed, he believed he needed to know exactly how she died. Was it an accidental overdose, murder, or, God forbid, suicide? If she had committed suicide, it would mean her suffering was unbearable, like Amy's, yet it would make him feel a sense of pride in knowing that Wendy had decided her own fate and, in doing so, denied those animals what they wanted of her.

He looked up at the passing cumulus clouds, wanting to believe her spirit was up there, and he then turned to look at the graves. Then again, did he truly want to know all the horrible details? He pondered his own question for a moment. Yes, he thought, it was better to know than not know. His mind had already been victimized by dozens of terrible and unimaginable visions. Perhaps the truth would be less horrible than the visions occurring in his mind's eye.

But where to find the truth? Of the fourteen people who were freed, it was quite possible that one or more of them had known her and had answers to his questions. He rose from the bench, said his goodbyes, and left knowing his next step. He would contact the two detectives.

Morgan contacted the appropriate people and found that Alice had been moved to a domestic violence shelter on 125th Street. Morgan called the shelter and spoke with the director, Abelina Waters, who confirmed that Alice was indeed there. Morgan asked the director to inform Alice that Detective Kelly, the one who had interviewed her, would be visiting her within the half hour, along with Detective Chang. They immediately drove there.

Upon entering, Morgan was pleased that the shelter appeared clean and well kept. They were met by the director, a tall, thirty-five-year-old African American woman who wore a plaid flannel shirt, blue jeans, and sandals. Her straightened black hair was tied back in a long ponytail. After the introductions, in which she insisted they call her Abby, they were ushered into a small, cluttered office.

"Don't mind the mess," she said. "I've got paperwork up the yin-yang lately. More girls here than we really should be handling."

Morgan smiled as she viewed a framed cartoon depicting a young child holding a roll of toilet paper, with the caption *Nothing is complete until the paperwork is done.*

Abby turned to see what had caught Morgan's attention. She turned back, waved a hand across the desk strewn with papers, and remarked, "Ain't that the truth."

Morgan began, "How did Alice react when you told her we were coming?"

Abby mulled over the question for a moment. "Alice is a tough young lady. Although she's only fifteen, she's seen and been through far more than she should have. When I mentioned you and Detective Chang were coming to see her, her immediate reaction was that she told you all she knew and didn't want to see you. In my experience, when a young person doth protest too much, they are often hiding something. Also, she's not completely recovered from her drug addiction. She's on methadone and is being monitored by our resident doctor. Go easy on her. A show of TLC will go a lot further than badgering will."

The detectives understood completely, having interviewed hundreds of obstinate persons in the line of duty.

Ben asked, "What about her mother? Have you been able to contact her?"

She sighed. "Yeah. Yeah, we did. Alice still remembered her mother's cell number. I informed the mother that Alice was being taken care of in our shelter. The mother is a piece of work. The fact that Alice said she never wanted to see her mother again, *that* I could understand. But to hear her mother state that she never wanted to see her own daughter again, that I *cannot* understand. She sounded either drunk or high on who knows what. So, are you ready?"

The detectives rose as one. "Let's do it," Ben said.

They followed Abby down a corridor until she stopped in front of a closed door and knocked. "Alice, may we come in?"

The door was opened by Alice, who was wearing an oversized blue sweatshirt that read *University of Michigan* and blue jeans. Her feet were bare. They entered the small but fully furnished room.

Morgan immediately said, "Hello, Alice. How are you?" Pointing at Ben, she added, "Oh, and this is Detective Chang."

Alice asked, not in a nice way, "Why is *he* here?"

Morgan answered, "When we're out in the field, we usually travel together."

Ben said, "Hello."

Alice looked at him. "You're Chinese."

Ben smiled kindly. "And so are you, I understand."

"I'm really American, ya know. And I don't speak any Chinese."

Ben laughed heartily. "Me either!" he said, even though he could speak Cantonese.

It seemed to have broken the ice, and Abby said, "I'll be down the hall if you need me." She turned and walked out, purposely leaving the door open.

Alice sat on the corner of her bed. There was only one small chair in the room, but neither detective sat.

Morgan said, "I'm glad you're getting help here. How are you doing?"

She shrugged. "OK."

Morgan studied her. She thought she looked even younger than her fifteen years.

"Alice," Morgan began softly, "I know how difficult it must be for you to have to recall things from your past, but we need information about a girl named Wendy Kagawa, who was only fourteen when she died."

Alice swallowed hard. "I don't know her."

Years of interrogations told both detectives she was lying.

"But you did know her, even if only for a short while, didn't you?" Morgan asked.

Alice bit a fingernail. "Like I said, I don't know anything."

Morgan stared at her. She knew she was lying, but she also knew that the girl had to be treated with kid gloves. Forcing her to remember some horrible event was out of the question. Still, Morgan tried one more time. "You're certain you know nothing about Wendy? Any information would really be helpful to us." Morgan waited for a reply that didn't come and then added, "Oh, and what about Maria?"

Alice blinked. "I don't know anything about her either."

"But she was in that apartment almost the entire time you were there," Ben said in an accusatory tone.

Alice became defensive. "How many times do I have to tell you? I don't know anything."

Morgan asked, "What about Patty Chen and Li Huang?"

"Who?"

"These girls' remains were found at the same location as Wendy. They also worked for Fujita and Ogura but at a different location than yours. You never met them?"

She shook her head.

Morgan knew they weren't going to get any information that day. Morgan handed her a card with her name and phone numbers. "If you think of anything, please call me, OK?"

Alice took the card. "Sure."

The detectives left and returned to the precinct with the knowledge that she knew a lot more than she was willing to say.

CHAPTER

15

YOSHI NOMURA AND TWO OF HIS STRONG-ARM MEN WAITED outside a known hangout for Triads, a small restaurant and bar called Jimmy Woo's on Grand Street. Nomura rested both hands on the wheel of his black Lexus suburban, his breathing relaxed, his heart rate slow. He felt calm before any action, and tonight was no exception. He'd parked almost directly in front of the restaurant, next to a fire hydrant. He knew the faces of many of the Triads and that, sooner or later, one of the Triads would exit the restaurant alone, probably high on alcohol, cocaine, or both. But even if sober, the plan was to allow the man to walk a bit down the street, away from the restaurant, pull the Lexus alongside him, open the rear door, grab the unsuspecting man, throw him into the vehicle, and take off.

The three men were dressed in black, not to appear like ninjas but simply to blend with the night.

They had patiently waited for three hours, watching some patrons enter and exit the restaurant, when the door opened and out walked a man whom one of the strong-arms recognized as being a Triad.

"That's one of them. A guy named Sammy Zhang."

"How much trouble will he be?" Nomura asked.

"Weighs maybe one seventy or so and pretty strong, but this pipe should weaken him a bit." He rapped a metal pipe into the palm of his gloved hand.

Zhang turned and began a wobbly walk toward the street corner. The Lexus slowly pulled away from the curb, drove just ahead of the man, and stopped. The two strong-arms quietly exited the car, watched the man pass by, strode behind him, and then struck Zhang on the back of his head with the metal pipe. As Zhang staggered, he was grabbed by the strong-arms, dragged to the Lexus, and thrown onto the rear seat. The strong-arms got into the rear seat with one man on either side, and they patted down the awakening Triad, extracting a gun that was strapped to his left ankle.

The confused Sammy Zhang looked left and right at the strong-arms, while Nomura drove. He was not confused by the meaning of the two guns that were pointed at him.

He nervously asked, "Who are you? Want do you want?"

From the front seat, Nomura responded, "We want you to give a message to your leaders."

"What leaders?" he scoffed.

Gazing at the man through his rearview mirror, Nomura answered, "You can cut the bullshit. We know you are a Triad."

Zhang asked, "Where are you taking me?"

"Don't worry about it," Nomura answered.

Minutes later, they parked the vehicle and ushered the man down an open metal cellar door, which led them to the basement underneath the strip club. They closed the metal door with a clang and locked it. A strong-arm proceeded to punch Zhang in his face. Zhang immediately went down. While on the ground, the Triad was repeatedly kicked by the two strong-arms until Nomura said, "Enough." The men immediately stopped.

Nomura knelt down next to the moaning man. "Tell your boss that the Yakuza is sending a message. There will be no more taking over of Yakuza territory unless he wants a war. Is that clear?"

Instead of answering, Zhang grasped Nomura's shirt and yanked Nomura toward him as he pulled out a small knife that had been hidden under his belt and began to slash Nomura in the chest. As a bleeding Nomura tried to pull away from the man, the strong-arm with the pipe struck Zhang on his head, once, twice, three times, until his head was cracked open and the knife fell out of his hands.

Nomura ripped open his shirt, revealing several bleeding spots where the small knife had penetrated, and a gash where he had been slashed. "Motherfucker!" he shouted at Zhang, lying motionless on the dirty concrete floor.

One of the strong-arms asked Nomura, "You OK?"

"I'll live."

The other strong-arm checked Zhang's pulse. He looked up. "He's dead."

Nomura's shoulders slumped. He was helped to a standing position. "Akita will not be happy about this."

Nomura ordered the two men to get rid of the body as soon as possible. He said he would go upstairs, wash up, bandage himself as best he could, and seek out Akita.

The following morning found Ben and Morgan having coffee with Mike Kagawa at Ferrara's in Little Italy. Ferrara's, family owned since 1892, was located on Grand Street and was world famous for its cakes, cookies, pastries, and assorted desserts. The word *little* in Little Italy had been taking on more meaning these past few decades as Chinatown continually encroached on it, block by block.

Ben and Morgan agreed to meet with Michael Kagawa at Kagawa's request. He had called the day before. He had a very important favor to ask of them, but he didn't want to meet at the precinct. Morgan suggested Ferrara's. She felt sorry for the man, and she hoped they could be of some help.

The three sat in a booth, with Ben and Morgan on one side and Kagawa on the other side.

Coffee had been served, and Morgan said, "OK, Mr. Kagawa. What can we do for you?"

"Please, call me Mike." Kagawa took a sip of the steaming coffee.

"How can we be of help?" Morgan gently asked.

"There are many questions I would like answered regarding Wendy's death."

Ben responded, "But you already know what happened."

"Yes, the bare details. What I would like to know are things like, when exactly did she die, and where was she killed, how did she die, did she commit suicide, did she have any last words, did she suffer in death? It's possible that one or more girls she was with spoke with her, knew her. They could give me answers to my questions."

"We spoke to one girl who we believe knows something, but she denies it. Maybe one of the other girls might know something. But why put yourself through this?" Morgan asked sympathetically.

Kagawa grimly said, "I have already visited hell. The visions I've had regarding Wendy are worse than you can imagine." His eyes suddenly brightened. "Did I tell you she played the violin? She wanted to play in the Philharmonic orchestra *and* become a doctor! She always had lofty aspirations." He shuddered as he inhaled and exhaled. "If I had asked God before she was born to grant me a daughter, I could never have imagined the joy Wendy would bring me and Amy. I believe finding the truth will help me heal if healing is in my future."

Morgan stared at Kagawa. She could only guess at the pain Kagawa was going through, having lost his only child in horrible fashion, and losing his wife of over twenty years as a direct result of Wendy's death.

"What exactly are you asking of us?" Morgan asked.

"I would like to meet with someone who might have known Wendy. Someone who might have been there when she died." His plea was heartfelt. "Do you know where these girls are now?"

"They've been housed temporarily in domestic violence shelters, where they're getting the help they need to get back on their feet as productive citizens," Morgan answered.

"I would appreciate it if you could find out which, if any, of the girls might be able to give me some answers."

"All right, I think we can do that, but we'll need some time to do the research," Ben said. "Like Detective Kelly just said, we spoke with one of the girls who we thought might know something and got nowhere. But maybe some of the other girls might know something. We can check it out for you."

"I thank you for that." Kagawa threw a ten-dollar bill onto the table, which was picked up and handed back to him by Morgan.

"We got this," she said.

Kagawa nodded and slid out of the booth.

Ben and Morgan watched the forlorn man walk out.

"I hope we can help him," Morgan said.

"So do I," Ben agreed.

Later that day, the detectives received word at the precinct that the cameras in and around the hotel were still being analyzed. But some things were already clear, they were told. One of the cameras had caught the shooter as he entered the room, also as he shot the two men. It appeared from the video that there was only one shooter. Unfortunately, the camera was about fifty feet from the event, and the video was not of the highest quality. But the bloody New York Mets hat and well-worn jacket that was left behind could be seen on the perpetrator, who was also wearing dark-rimmed sunglasses. The one feature that stood out was the man's dark beard. As soon as the shots rang out, the man was seen to be ducking down, the result of which was that, as the frightened players stood and fled, the shooter was hidden by their bodies. It was possible that by the time the hatless shooter reached the exit doors, only the back of his head might have been caught on the video. The video had been shown to the director, Karen, and the assistant director, Jessica, but they could not identify the shooter.

Ben requested a copy of the video, which they promised would arrive the next day.

Morgan sat in a chair next to Ben's desk and said to him, "Let's review what we have. The bridge club murders were probably ordered by Akita because they were in bed with Hiro. Akita believed Hiro was ratting on them because we interrogated him on two occasions."

Ben offered, "So Hiro was tortured, told whatever he could about Fujita and Ogura, and those two get rubbed out, gangland style. Chalk up three more murders by him. Sends a clear message to anyone who thinks of becoming a snitch."

"I'm not going to cry over the deaths of those three. But how can we get to Akita?"

Ben thought for a moment. "I think we should pay another visit to him. Confront him with what we found in the ledger. Maybe we ruffle enough feathers to get him to slip up."

"Let me do the talking. I think I can get under his skin. He likes power over women. I won't give him the satisfaction."

They made an appointment to see Akita at the Happy Hour the following afternoon. Morgan had no illusions as to what to expect this time.

A contrite Yoshi Nomura sat with Ichiro Harada and Satoshi Akita at their usual table in the strip club. A bandaged and sore Nomura had related the events of the night before, and as expected, Akita was extremely displeased. He didn't care that the Triad was killed; only the consequences of the event mattered, consequences he could only guess at, at that time.

The body had been taken and dumped into the Hudson River, with the hope that it would be washed out to sea with his wallet and cell phone. Soon enough, the Triads would realize that he was missing and, more than likely, dead. How they would interpret this was up to them, but it wouldn't take a genius to arrive at the conclusion that the Yakuza were probably behind it. The Triads would have to make the next move.

Right now, he was concerned with one of his massage parlors that had been shut down. Ten Asian women were detained, and the police had attempted to determine which of them were victims and which were perpetrators. Fortunately for Akita, the case fell apart almost immediately because the six workers—all potential witnesses against the organization—were gone. Akita would have to find a new location and six new workers.

Sun Li Fong, the Dragon Master of the Triads, was informed that Sammy Zhang had left Jimmy Woo's around ten the night before but never made it home. Zhang's wife stated that it was unlike him to stay out late and not call or text her. And by that morning, he still hadn't called, and all her calls and texts to him went unanswered. She believed something must have happened to him.

Fong agreed. The forty-two-year-old Zhang was one of his most reliable men. If he was missing this long, something was very wrong. Zhang had the reputation of a man who could take care of himself. There had been no reports of shootings in the area, and no one reported finding Zhang's body. The only conclusion that Fong could arrive at was that Zhang might never be found, and the Yakuza were most likely behind it. There was still the possibility that Zhang could show up. Perhaps he was kidnapped, and the kidnappers would send a message. He intended to wait a day or two. If Zhang didn't reappear, and if no contact was made regarding his disappearance, he would discuss the next steps with his counsel. The loss of Zhang must not go unpunished.

Morgan and Ben arrived at the club and were guided to Akita's table. As usual, Nomura and Harada were by his side. "Welcome once again, Detectives," Akita said, flashing a smile.

Morgan began, "We found a ledger in Fujita and Ogura's apartment."

"Who?"

"Cut the crap. We know you knew them. The ledger showed payments made weekly to the Yakuza. Therefore, the payments were made to you. And you still deny knowing them?"

"Pretty lady—"

"It's Detective Kelly to you." She wanted to wipe that smirk off his face with a shovel.

"Pretty lady, I've already told you, I never heard of those two."

"You knew that we questioned Masahiro Araki on two occasions. You thought he was ratting on you, so you tortured and killed him. Then you killed the two men he worked for. Great way to send a message."

Akita addressed Ben. "I see you're letting the pretty lady call the shots. Is she wearing the balls now?"

Ben kept his cool as he answered, "You're a funny guy. You'll look even funnier when you're wearing an orange jumpsuit."

"You mentioned the Yakuza," Akita said. "You do know of the power they have in Japan. Maybe the two men were sending money back to Japan to help support their families."

Morgan laughed sarcastically. "And your mother wears combat boots."

Akita replied harshly, "You are getting a bit too personal, pretty lady."

Morgan noticed that she was getting under his skin. She liked it. "Wait till you see how personal they get in prison. By the way, you left this on my windshield." She took the crumpled symbol of death from her pocket and threw it at Akita, hitting him on his forehead and rebounding onto the table.

Akita swatted the paper off the table and stood. "This interview is over." He turned, walked into a back room, followed by Nomura and Harada, and closed the door.

Morgan smiled and said to Ben, "Let's go."

Outside, a jaunty Morgan said, "He hates any woman with power."

"Hundred percent."

They returned to the precinct to file a report.

Morgan loved the fact that she could rattle him. But it would take more than that to place a monster behind bars.

In the back room, all three men standing, Akita's dark eyes squinted as he said, "It would be a shame if the bitch had an accident." He then spoke directly to Harada. "Hang out by her precinct. See what she's currently driving and get the license plate. I want to know where she goes and who she sees."

CHAPTER

16

KAGAWA RECEIVED A PHONE CALL FROM MORGAN THE following morning. She informed him that they had contacted the local social service department that was handling the victims' cases. They were then directed to several domestic violence shelters that were often used to provide safe haven for female human trafficking victims. This temporary housing was where the fourteen would receive aid.

After determining which shelters the fourteen girls and young women had been doled out to, Ben and Morgan hit the phones. They contacted the director of each of these shelters and asked only one question. They needed to know if any of these victims had known one of their fellow victims named Wendy Kagawa, of Japanese descent. They gave the director a full description of the Kagawa girl since it was possible her real name wasn't known by the other victims. They asked the directors to call back only if they had something positive. They also called the director, Abby Waters, at Alice's shelter. Perhaps she could try again to get Alice to talk about Wendy and/or Maria.

It didn't take long for Alice's director, Abby, to call back. Abby said that at first, Alice refused to admit that she had known Wendy, but then admitted she kind of knew her. Abby had tried to convince Alice that nothing sinister was going to happen and that cooperating might help other girls. Alice still refused to talk with the detectives again.

But Alice had opened up to Morgan before. Perhaps if she visited Alice without Ben, she suggested to Abby, she might open up again. Abby said it was worth the try.

A short while later, Morgan was seated in Alice's room on one of two folding chairs, facing Alice, who was seated on the other chair.

Alice wore jeans and a T-shirt that read *New York City*.

"How are you?" Morgan asked.

"OK." She bit a fingernail.

"How's the food?"

She removed her hand from her mouth. "It's OK."

Morgan was still learning the tricks of interviewing. Alice's cropped answers did not bode well. She said in a warm voice, "I know I've already asked you about Maria and Wendy, who lived with you on Mott Street. And I know you didn't want to talk about it. But it would help me in my investigation if you could tell me anything about them."

Alice didn't answer. She bit her fingernail again.

Morgan was still sympathetic to Alice's predicament, and she didn't want to press too hard. "Let me ask a big favor. Meet with Wendy's father, Mr. Kagawa. If you don't want to tell him anything, that's OK. But maybe you can find it in your heart to answer the questions he desperately needs to know. Do you think that's possible?"

Alice responded, "Like I said, don't know anything."

"We found a book that said they were both there with you."

Alice's voice was raised as she said, "I don't *know* about them." Her eyes and her body language said differently, but Morgan remembered what it was like to be bullied by adults.

Morgan nodded, said goodbye, and left the room. She explained to Abby that Wendy's father had asked if he might speak with Alice. Perhaps he might be able to get answers that two detectives could not.

Abby said, "It might work. Alice feels threatened by police, but speaking with the father just might work."

Morgan left, called Kagawa, and gave him the news and the name and address of the shelter.

"Appreciate it. I know you told me a little bit, but what exactly happens at these shelters?"

"They provide a temporary safe haven for victims of domestic violence and victims of human trafficking. Depending on the ages of the victims, they try to find permanent housing, help with finding jobs for them, give counseling where needed, and help give them some life skills."

"It sounds like a very good thing for these girls. Maybe give them a start on a new life."

Hesitantly, Morgan said, "Listen. Don't get your hopes up too high on this girl. She said she hardly knew her, and there's still a good chance she might not even allow you to see or talk to her."

"I fully understand, but what do I have to lose?"

Morgan agreed. She was talking to a man who had seemingly lost it all. "OK. Give it a shot. But let me know if you find the answers you're looking for, will you?"

"Absolutely."

The call ended. Morgan hoped this mild-mannered teacher would be able to find some tranquility for his tortured soul.

Kagawa drove into Manhattan, where he parked two blocks from the shelter.

He entered the shelter and was met by the director, who introduced herself as Abby. She sat behind her desk, and he seated himself on a chair in front of the desk. Abby, as gently as she could, informed him that Alice Liu didn't want to see him.

"Please tell her that Wendy was my only child. I only want to ask a few questions, and then I'll be on my way."

"I'll give it a try."

She left Kagawa and went to Alice's room. Alice was sitting on her bed watching a TV show. "Hi, Alice," she said cheerfully.

Alice looked up from the TV. "Hi."

The director seated herself on the one chair in the room and said, "I know you don't want to talk about things that might make you relive some bad memories and are leery of the police. But this man is not part of the police. You won't be in any trouble by speaking with him. His daughter was Wendy, who they say you must have known. Speak with him. See if you can help him. By helping him and talking about the terrible things, not keeping them bottled up inside, I believe you will also be helping yourself."

Alice drew her knees up to her chest and didn't answer.

"I'll tell you what. Just talk with him for a couple of minutes. You don't have to answer any questions if you don't want to. His name is Michael Kagawa. He seems like a very nice person. What do you say?" She reached out and touched Alice on her knee.

Alice pouted. "OK. But if I ask him to leave, he will, right?"

"Right."

"And I don't have to answer questions if I don't want to, right?"

"Absolutely."

The director left and returned with Kagawa. Alice was still sitting on her bed, her back against the headboard, knees still against her chest.

"Alice, this is Mr. Kagawa."

Kagawa smiled pleasantly. "Please, call me Mike." He pointed at the lone chair. "May I sit down?"

Alice glanced at the chair and shrugged.

Abby said, "I'll stay right here," as she stood in the doorway.

Kagawa pulled the chair closer to the bed and sat. Alice reflexively slid farther away from him. He marveled at how much Alice reminded him of his daughter. He leaned in toward Alice. "I know you've been through a lot. And I understand you don't want to relive some of it. But the police told me that you lived in that apartment at the same time as my daughter. Is that true?"

Alice looked away and didn't answer.

Kagawa continued. "Wendy was our only child. She was kidnapped by Fujita and Ogura about a month ago. We searched for her and paid a private detective, but no one found her. My wife quit her job, and I took a leave of absence. We couldn't keep our minds on anything but finding Wendy. We exhausted our savings, and when Wendy's remains were found in a marshland, my wife committed suicide." Kagawa searched Alice's face, but she demonstrated no sign of emotion.

"I have many questions that the police couldn't answer. I believe only you can." He reached into his pants pocket and extracted a necklace. "My daughter would have turned fifteen next month. About the same age as you. She had a necklace that she loved to wear. I would like you to have it." He extended his hand toward Alice and then opened his hand, which held a silver locket and chain.

Alice turned her body so that her legs draped over the side of the bed, close to Kagawa. "You think a bribe with some cheap trinket is going to make me tell you what you want?" she caustically replied. "Men like you spent a lot more money than what that thing is worth, ya know. And they got far more than words. They fucked me. Would you like to fuck me?"

"W … what?"

"Alice!" Abby shouted.

Ignoring Abby's admonishment, Alice continued. "Look how pretty I am," she said seductively and in a manner far more advanced than her years.

Kagawa had no idea how to react. He diverted his eyes, sat back in the chair, and slumped down, defeated. After a silence that seemed an eternity to him, he rose out of the chair and respectfully placed the locket and chain on the bed. "I have no use for this anymore. Wendy would probably want you to have it."

He left the room, slowly shaking his head, followed by Abby.

"Sorry. Maybe she'll come around," Abby said sympathetically.

Kagawa nodded sadly and left the building.

Curiosity got the best of Alice. She picked up the locket and opened it. Inside was a small photograph of Kagawa, his wife, Amy, and Wendy, smiling happily with Mickey Mouse at Disneyworld. She had never been to anything like that. But seeing Wendy as she had never seen her before, smiling at a much happier time, made her regret how she treated Wendy's father. She had admired Wendy's fighting spirit. She never gave in to them no matter what they did. But Alice hated thinking about her because it reminded her of the day Wendy died. Alice had never seen a dead body before Maria's, and she certainly had never seen a person die right in front of her, let alone two within days. Soon after Wendy had received the final shot of heroin, foam began spewing from her nostrils as her skin turned blotchy blue. Her body twitched in spasms until she wheezed and stopped moving. Alice couldn't get those images out of her head. She knew it could be her. She thought about it every time she took the drug. After that, she was more careful.

She got out of the bed, ran into the corridor, and shouted at Abby, "Tell him to stop!"

"You're sure?"

"I think so."

Abby ran outside the building and yelled, "Mr. Kagawa! Come back!"

Kagawa turned and saw Abby. He walked back. "What is it?"

Abby sounded excited as she said, "I believe she'll talk with you."

"Why?"

"I don't know, but come inside."

They entered the building. Alice wasn't in sight. They walked to her room and saw Alice standing there, wearing the locket on her neck. "I never had anything so nice before."

Abby said, "It looks lovely on you."

Kagawa stood still. Alice looked up at him and smiled. "What do you want to know?"

"Whatever you can find in your heart to tell me."

Abby again stood in the doorway.

"May I sit down?" Kagawa asked.

"Sure."

He took his seat, and she sat on the side of the bed.

He began his inquiry. "How long was Wendy with you, and where was this?"

She seemed deep in thought as her nose scrunched up. "I would say no more than a few days before … you know. We lived on Mott Street, above a Chinese takeout."

He sighed heavily. "Did Wendy commit suicide?"

She appeared puzzled. "How would she do that?"

"I … I don't know. Then how did she die?" He swallowed hard.

"Mr. Kagawa. Do you really want to hear all this shit?"

"Please, call me Mike. And yes, as difficult as it will be for me to hear what happened to her, in my mind I have pictured the most terrible things anyway."

She nodded slowly as though she understood. "I'll start from the beginning. Me and this other girl, Maria, were watching TV, ya know, when Ogura and Hiro dragged Wendy into the apartment and pulled her out of a duffel bag. She looked drunk or something, but I'm sure Ogura drugged her. She was kind of awake and didn't know where she was."

Kagawa closed his eyes, and Alice said, "Should I go on?"

He opened his eyes. "Yes."

"She was kind of out of it, but she knew what was going on, ya know? They stripped her naked and threw her onto the bed inside. Big, ugly Ogura went first. He did some bad stuff to her. You know what I mean? This stuff went on for days. Fujita and Hiro had their turns also. They beat her a couple of times because she refused to give them blow jobs. I tried talking to her and told her it was no big deal, that she would get used to it, but she never gave in. It was awesome. I know why. She was different."

He felt both revulsion and pride as he pictured his daughter battling to the very end. Kagawa rubbed his temples with his hands and then asked, "Different? In what way?"

"All the other girls pretty much came voluntarily. We had no place to go. No home, no food, nothing. Wendy had been kidnapped. She had a home, a family ... you."

Tears began to form rivulets down his cheeks.

"Should I stop?"

"Go on," he said as he swatted away the tears.

"They figured that if they doped her up enough, she would eventually start earning money for them, but it never happened. The three of them could rape her, but that didn't get them any money. She was no good to customers if she fought them. They kept increasing the amount of shit they put into her, and she started having a fit, shaking and drooling and stuff, and she just died. Maybe too much shit or just bad shit. Ya know? Happened right in front of me. It was horrible." Alice trembled a bit and looked away. Her arms hugged herself.

Kagawa sat motionless for a minute, full of rage and pity. When she looked back at him, he asked, "Did she have any last words?"

She shook her head. "If she did, I didn't hear them. Besides, by that time, she could hardly speak. She was so weak. Ate practically nothing the whole time. Oh yeah, but she did tell me a couple of times that her father would find her."

Kagawa's head slumped forward. "She thought I failed her." The world had just landed on top of him.

Alice reached out and touched him on his shoulder. He gently placed a hand on top of hers. They remained that way for a few seconds until she gently pulled her hand away.

"Anything else you can remember?" he managed to ask.

She shrugged. "I think that's it."

He remembered something she had said. "You mentioned that you were there with a girl named Maria. What happened to her?"

She took a deep breath before answering. "Maria was with them for years. But her coke and heroin addiction got worse and worse. One day, she OD'd. I really don't feel like telling you what exactly happened."

"I understand. What happened to Maria after she died?"

"They dragged her body out. Put her into a dumpster. Happens to a lot of girls that way. Coulda been me in a couple of years. The guy who killed them did us a favor, ya know?"

He sat in silence for another minute, trying to assemble all he had heard. Were Wendy's last thoughts disappointment in him? Or did she have that much faith in him that she believed he would somehow find her in that godawful place? His mind was made up. He would visit Wendy and beg for her forgiveness.

Kagawa looked at Alice and felt a pang of guilt. He'd been so wrapped up in learning about Wendy he'd almost forgotten what the fifteen-year-old Alice must have gone through. With utmost sincerity, he said, "I'm so, so sorry for what you must have had to bear."

Alice turned and bowed her head, then looked at him through her lashes.

He thought he detected a tear in one of her eyes. He stood, extended his hand, her small hand grasped it, and they shook hands. "I thank you from the bottom of my heart. I know now that Wendy never gave in to them and that those bastards never earned a dime off her. That gives me some comfort."

He turned to leave and then turned back. "Would you mind very much if I visited you again? No questions this time."

"Sure."

He left the room with Abby. When he had the strength, he intended to keep his word and call the detectives to tell them what he had learned.

He would put his suicide on hold.

The requested video of the shooting had arrived at their precinct. Morgan and Ben were seated at Ben's desk in the squad room, staring at a monitor, which they intended to view from the time stamp of 6:45 to approximately 7:10, by which time the room had been emptied out and police units had arrived. By that point, the shooter was certain to have vanished.

Morgan leaned forward in her chair, her eyes riveted on the video.

She saw nothing of note until 6:55. "There they are, Fujita and Ogura walking toward their table."

Ben nodded. "The Davis and Nelson women are already seated."

Morgan saw the boards being handed out to each table. At 6:59, she saw the two women casually looking at the boards. At 7:00, she saw Davis reaching for a slot in the board, as though getting ready to pull her first hand.

"Since the shooting started just before the game started, we should see our shooter any second," she said. She watched as a bearded man wearing a baseball cap and sunglasses walked quickly into the room, striding behind Ogura.

"Bingo!" Ben exclaimed. "There's our shooter."

With no hesitation, the man pulled a pistol from underneath his jacket and, in the same motion, fired point-blank into the back of Ogura's head. Within one second, the second shot was fired from approximately three feet from Fujita's forehead. Fujita had no time to react.

Morgan said, "Jesus. This guy must be a pro. Got them both in about a second. Slow the video down."

Ben slowed the video so that they could concentrate on the shooter.

Ben asked, "How tall would you say the perp is?"

Morgan leaned in closer. "Not tall at all. I would estimate maybe anywhere from five six to five eight. Weighs maybe … one fifty, more or less."

They continued to watch. Within an instant after the second shot was fired, people were jumping out of their seats while the shooter appeared to duck down, blocked from view by the already panicking players.

Ben offered, "Since the gun was found about eight feet from the table, it was probably right there, when he ducked down, that he dropped the gun, took off the hat, threw it into the air, and whipped off the jacket while crouching down and running toward the exit with dozens of screaming and terrified people."

"I wonder if the beard is a disguise."

"Could be."

They continued to watch as the room cleared out. The video ended, but Morgan felt good about being able to narrow down a description of the shooter, even if just a bit. They were now seeking a man, five foot six to five eight, weighing perhaps one hundred fifty pounds, and possibly no beard. Since that description could fit thousands of men, it wasn't much to go on, but it was a start.

Ben said, "I agree that the assassin is probably a professional hitman. Very skilled and efficient."

Morgan nodded. "The Yakuza has no shortage of hitmen. It wouldn't surprise me to find that that scumbag Akita is behind it."

A while later, Morgan received a phone call from Mike Kagawa. As promised, he called to tell them he had gotten information from Alice regarding Wendy's death.

"What changed her mind?" Morgan asked.

"It took some doing, but she opened up after I gave her a locket and chain to keep that was Wendy's. I guess the photo inside might have touched her in some way."

"What did you find out?"

Kagawa related his conversation with Alice.

Then he added, "But my Wendy fought them all the way, right to the very end. They didn't earn a dime off her. I hope the drugs they gave her cost them a fortune."

"I hope so too."

"You said that the death of those two men helped free her and others from those animals."

"Yes, it did. They'll get the help they badly need."

"But what happens to girls like Alice? I understand they can't stay in the shelter forever."

"Social services will try to find a foster home for those underaged kids. If not, perhaps an orphanage. Of course, they will attempt to return these kids to their families, unless they feel that the home life there would be unsuitable."

Kagawa thought for a moment. He'd lost his daughter, who would be almost fifteen now. Her death resulted in the freeing of fourteen victims. Wendy could never be replaced, but would it be at all possible to become the guardian of one of those girls, Alice? Alice had reminded him so much of Wendy. They were both around the same age, and although Alice had endured so much more than Wendy, her jaded manner couldn't hide the vulnerability. She also looked a little like Wendy. He wondered, *Would this make Wendy and Amy happy?* If it would, it might give him a reason to go on living.

"I'm glad," he said. "Oh, about that Maria girl. Alice saw her die in front of her eyes as well. I can see why she wouldn't talk about it, but Alice did say she was addicted to so many drugs that she finally overdosed on her own and was placed in a dumpster."

"Thank you for sharing all this. I really appreciate it." Morgan had already believed that from the butterfly tattoo on Maria. This corroborated it.

"One more thing. I asked Alice if she would mind if I visited her again, only this time with no questions."

"And she said she wouldn't?"

"She did. I think it's good for her to come into contact with an adult who isn't looking to use her. Maybe I could help her in some way."

"I couldn't agree more, Mr. Kagawa."

"Please, not so formal. It's just plain Mike."

"OK, Mike. You take care of yourself. I truly hope you can find some peace in your heart. Life can go on, you know." She was talking from experience. "Maybe you could go back to teaching. We need good men like you in our classrooms."

He pondered her suggestion. "I'll think about it. And you keep up the good work. The city needs good cops like you." The call ended.

Morgan then dialed the shelter and asked to speak with Alice. She thanked Alice again for agreeing to see Mr. Kagawa.

"I don't trust anybody anymore," Alice replied. "But I think I can trust you. You might be getting a call from someone I know."

"Who? And what about?"

"You'll know if she calls. I told her she could trust you."

The call ended with Morgan feeling pleased and intrigued. Who was the mysterious caller?

CHAPTER

17

"DETECTIVE KELLY," MORGAN ANSWERED.

The caller spoke haltingly. "My name … is Brandisha … I live in the shelter with Alice … Alice says I could trust you."

"What is this about?"

"I don't like to talk on the phone. I got information you want. Could you come here, to the shelter? I gotta see who I'm talkin' to."

"Did Alice tell you to call?"

"No. It's my idea."

Morgan didn't want to make the trip for nothing. "Information about what?"

"Some men you should put in jail."

Morgan thought it might be worth the trip. What did she have to lose? "OK, we can be there in less than an hour."

"No. Just you. I'll only talk to you."

She didn't like going without Ben, but it sounded like she had no choice. "All right, just me. See you in about forty-five minutes."

They ended the call, and Morgan spoke with Ben, explaining the situation.

Ben was OK with it only if he accompanied her and remained outside in the car. She agreed as long as he stayed out of sight. She didn't want to lose the girl's trust.

They were about a block away from the shelter when Ben parked the car. Morgan got out and walked the short distance to the shelter. She entered and was once again met by the director, Abby. Abby had been informed by Brandisha to expect the detective. Abby walked up one flight of stairs, followed by Morgan. They arrived at Brandisha's room and knocked on the door. The girl opened it.

Abby spoke first. "Brandisha, this is Detective Kelly."

Morgan smiled. "Hello."

"Hi," answered Brandisha. "Come in."

Morgan walked into the small room, which was a carbon copy of Alice's room.

Abby said, "I'll be at my desk if you need me." She turned and left.

Morgan eyed the young lady. She was a light-skinned African American with a tight Afro that suited her oval face. She was pleasant looking and just a bit overweight. She was wearing a colorful dashiki over ripped jeans, the kind you paid more money to have pretorn at the knees. Morgan could never understand the attraction some people had to those jeans.

Morgan noticed two folding chairs had been set up. "Can we sit down?"

"Oh, sure," she said. "When I told Abby you were coming, she brought in these chairs."

They took their seats.

"Is that a southern accent?" Morgan asked.

"I was born and raised in South Carolina."

Morgan nodded. "Now, what's this all about?"

Morgan noticed Brandisha staring at her. "Do I have something caught in my teeth?" she said jokingly.

"I was just thinkin' how beautiful you are. You're not like the cops I know."

Morgan couldn't help blushing. "You mean because I'm a woman?"

"Yeah, that, and you don't look like the type to rough me up."

"That happen often?"

"Too many times to remember, mostly when I was on the street."

"How old were you then?"

"Thirteen. I looked older. I had this dumb pimp who got tired of me and sold me to some gang."

Morgan leaned in. "You mean Fujita and Ogura?"

"No. Different gang that sold me to Fujita and Ogura."

"What gang is that?"

"Look, I know stuff about these guys. But I don't give anything out for nothin'."

Morgan understood. "What is it you want?"

"I wanna go to someplace nice when I get outta here. And some cash would help."

Morgan mulled over her requests. "If your information leads to the arrest and conviction of some bad guys, I can guarantee some reward money will come your way. And I will do my best, working with Abby, to see that you find a nice place with nice people."

"Abby been good to me." She paused for a few seconds. "OK, deal."

Morgan smiled. "What can you tell me?"

"There's this gang, calls themselves Iron Dragons. They're the ones who bought me from my old pimp and then sold me two years ago to Fujita and Ogura. They said their customers only want white or Chinese chicks. Sold me cheap."

"Did they ever mention the word Yakuza?"

"Heard that name lots of times. These Japs stick together."

"What about a man named Satoshi Akita?"

"I only heard them talk about some Akita guy."

Morgan thought, *This is making my day.* "Where did they house you?"

"A tiny place on Houston. I don't remember the exact address, but it was on the second floor above a bagel store, just off Clinton."

"Do you mind if I ask how you got yourself involved, especially at such a young age?"

She looked down at her clasped hands and said softly, "I trusted somebody."

Morgan instantly knew what Brandisha meant. Trust was very often the first thing a pedophile instilled in a young person. Once trust was established, innocent children became putty in the hands of these men, and sometimes women. "Was it a relative?"

Brandisha's foot was bouncing nervously up and down on the floor, a mile a minute. "It was my family's pastor. I thought he liked me. Asked me to help him out, cleaning the church on weekends, and he would pay me. I was twelve. I don't really want to go into all of it, but let's just say he made me into a woman at twelve. I told my mama ... my pa had run off years ago ... and she told me to hush up. That people would blame me, not him. I ran away. Used my piggy bank money to get on a train that ended up in New York. This young black guy sees me and says all these nice things and that he would take care of me. But then after a few months, he said we needed money, and an easy way to get it was for me to be nice to a bunch of men. I didn't want to, but he was always so nice to me that I felt guilty, his buying dinners an' all, and was scared to be put on the street. So, I did what he wanted."

Brandisha's story was an old one, told time and again. Morgan had known trust in her life too, only to have it shattered. "You can start over, you know. You can take night classes, get your high school diploma, and maybe get into college. Who knows? Maybe become a cop someday and put the bad guys where they belong. Jail."

Brandisha's foot stopped bouncing. She smiled warmly at Morgan. "Wouldn't that be somethin'."

Morgan laughed. "It sure would." Then, with a serious expression, Morgan asked, "Do you remember the apartment number?"

"Sure. Two B."

"How many men ran the place?"

"I saw four different men, all Japanese guys. They would come to collect their money from me and three other girls. If they thought we were hiding some of the money we made, they would beat us.

Sometimes we really did hide some of it and spent it on ourselves. Sometimes for extra drugs that we bought on the street."

"Can you describe these four men?"

"Saw 'em every day for years."

Morgan took a small pad and a pen from her pocket and prepared to write. Brandisha's memory of the four was impeccable, describing hair color, height, weight, facial hair, tattoos, etcetera.

When she was finished writing the descriptions, Morgan asked, "Why didn't you leave?" She thought she knew why but wanted to hear it from Brandisha.

"Where would I go? I was hooked on drugs, I got no education past sixth grade, and until I reached sixteen or seventeen, who would hire me? By that time, it was too late."

"But not too late now," she said reassuringly.

"I hope not. I really do."

Morgan wished her good luck and went down to speak with Abby. She told Abby only some of the conversation, purposely omitting the personal parts and the information regarding her former traffickers. Morgan also made sure to tell her that they had a deal and that Brandisha seemed like she could be saved from the streets.

Since Morgan was at the shelter, she asked Abby if she could stop and say hello to Alice, which she did. She thanked Alice for trusting her enough to convince Brandisha to call with what might be very valuable information.

Morgan then walked back to Ben, got into the car, and drove back to the precinct. If what Brandisha had said was valid, they had some very bad men to catch.

In the car, Morgan told Ben about her conversation with Brandisha. The emphasis was on the possibility of her information leading to some Yakuza and possibly even Akita.

Back at the precinct, Ben sat beside Morgan at her desk. Morgan occasionally glanced at her notes while holding a Styrofoam cup of coffee in her hand.

Ben asked, "Do you think she was telling you the truth? Maybe she's doing this just to make a deal."

Morgan took a sip from her cup. It was burned, as usual. "My impression was that she told what she thought was the truth, but she could be mistaken about some of the details."

"What if she's mistaken about the location? She told you she hadn't been there for about two years. And even if it is the correct location, the traffickers could have moved."

She set her cup on her desk. "She didn't remember the exact address, but she gave a pretty good description of it. And she recalled the exact apartment."

"You know as well as I do the last thing we need is newspapers and TV describing how our investigation screwed up by invading the wrong apartment. I don't want to be on the short end of a wrongful shooting or death."

"What do *you* suggest?" she said sharply, afraid he was taking a jab at her for the shooting of the robber before they became partners.

"Hey," he said. "Nothing personal. We need a stakeout. After all, I'm just a cautious, middle-aged cop."

She smiled. "Sure. You just want to sit in your squad car, smoking and eating doughnuts all day."

He barked a laugh. "I prefer the Portuguese custard tarts from Tai Pan Bakery on Canal. To die for. But seriously, no judge will issue a search warrant based on two-year-old info from a prostitute who wants to make a deal. We'll need to stake out the premises and surveil the comings and goings at that bagel store; see who goes in and out. We especially need to identify one or more of her traffickers. You said she gave you pretty good descriptions of these guys."

"She did." Morgan was excited at the prospect of a stakeout; stakeouts were operated by persons not in uniform or a blue-and-white patrol car.

Ben and Morgan were issued a camera that would be used to photograph the various men. They steeled themselves for a stakeout, which Ben expected to be boring and tedious. Their unmarked vehicle would be parked across the street and would become their crib, where they might spend hours or days. Morgan was eager to have the chance to catch some traffickers.

If they determined they had enough evidence to obtain a warrant, the type of warrant would be discussed with the judge. The usual warrant issued meant that the police, seeking to enter a property, would need to give prior notification to the residents by knocking or ringing a doorbell. In most cases, law enforcement would identify themselves to the residents before they entered the property.

Another type of warrant was the no-knock warrant, which allowed law enforcement officers to forcefully enter the property in an attempt to catch the residents by surprise, hindering the occupants from destroying evidence or taking up arms.

No-knock warrants had to be issued with caution since there had been many incidents in which innocent persons had been killed or injured during the warrant's execution. In Atlanta, Georgia, a ninety-two-year-old woman was fatally shot after she fired a shot toward the ceiling, assuming her home was being invaded. There were many cases such as this where armed homeowners, believing they were being invaded, had shot at officers, resulting in deaths on both sides.

They parked at the corner of Houston and Clinton Streets. They had a clear view of the bagel store Brandisha described. Next to the store was a door that led to three flights above the store.

They settled in with sandwiches and thermoses full of hot coffee. They would take turns for bathroom breaks at a nearby restaurant. Nobody enjoyed stakeouts, but they were part of the job. Ben kept Morgan amused by telling her stories of legendary stakeouts—ones that lasted for weeks and ones the police messed up spectacularly. She wasn't sure she believed them all, but it did make the time pass. They also kept the radio on and argued mildly about what kind of music to listen to.

Morgan said, "I'd love to hear you play your guitar."

"I'm not much of singer, but I can keep tune. Why don't you have dinner at my place some night, and I can serenade you."

"Just let me know when, and I'll be there."

"Sounds like a plan. But no rap crap."

She laughed. "No problem."

They observed the comings and goings, filming every person entering and exiting the doorway. As expected, most of the people entering were men. After sitting and watching for almost six hours, they had identified at least two of the four who fit the descriptions of the traffickers provided by Brandisha.

An hour later, after nightfall, they believed they hit the evidence jackpot. A young woman who, from the makeup she was wearing, could have been anywhere from fifteen to twenty-five years old, wearing a tight halter top and the shortest of miniskirts, exited the building and walked up the block on Houston Street. She stopped at the corner and stood there, apparently trying to make eye contact with every male that walked by. The temperature outside was in the high fifties.

"You'd think she'd be cold, wearing that skimpy outfit," Morgan said.

"She's probably high on something. Doesn't feel it as much."

After twenty minutes, a man of about fifty stopped and spoke with her. The conversation only lasted about a half minute, and then she led the man toward the door, and the two of them entered.

Ben smiled. "That's enough for me. How about you?"

Morgan nodded agreement. "Time to seek a warrant."

Morgan was happy to be able to leave her crib. She would show the photographs to Brandisha to get positive IDs on the traffickers and then contact the gang unit, who would attempt to make the arrests. She might even catch some Yakuza traffickers. She hoped that Brandisha's information would lead to the arrest of Akita. She smiled to herself as she envisioned putting cuffs on that smirking bastard.

CHAPTER

18

KAGAWA COULDN'T GET ALICE OUT OF HIS HEAD. SHE HAD
been a prostitute and a drug addict, but she was only fifteen and had
been used by corrupt individuals for their own illegal gain. Had he
met Alice under other circumstances, he would have thought her to
be like any other fifteen-year-old and, in many ways, like Wendy. But
these weren't other circumstances. Wendy was an intelligent, educated,
talented, innocent girl. Alice was a hardened, street-smart individual
whose resemblance to Wendy ended at age and outward appearance.
Yet he saw something in her. Something that might be redeemable.
She was hard as nails when he first met her, but the gift of the locket
had softened her. He believed that Alice was worth saving. Perhaps he
might be able to help. A voice in his head said he *had* to try. He believed
Wendy was encouraging him.

He had gone to the cemetery and begged for Wendy's forgiveness
for not being able to rescue her from that abyss. He believed with all

his heart that she knew he never stopped trying to find her. He also told her about Alice. Alice had been just one of fourteen saved girls, but he thought he had made a connection with her. She was there when Wendy had passed and had respected Wendy for her will to fight those animals. He needed Wendy's approval in his attempt to help Alice. He had bowed his head in front of her eternal resting place and asked for guidance. He had stood there—head bowed for several minutes, wearily rubbing his hand over his face, seeking some sort of sign—when a monarch butterfly landed on her gravestone. Yes, this was a sign that Wendy approved. He would help Alice as much as she would allow him.

As tears streaked his face, he smiled at the memory of Wendy, at age six, practicing the violin, which made sounds like someone scratching a blackboard with fingernails. But she was a determined little girl, who became so proficient that her playing often made him cry.

Early that morning, Brandisha was shown several photographs of various men who had entered and exited the apartment building. She was able to positively identify three of her traffickers.

Later that day, Morgan and Ben were issued a no-knock search warrant by a judge for the premises that Brandisha had described because it was believed that this might not only be a rescue mission of underaged girls, but there existed a high probability that the perpetrators were armed and dangerous.

The New York City Police Department Emergency Service Unit (ESU) was uniquely trained and equipped to perform tactical and technical rescue duty, otherwise known as Special Weapons and Tactics (SWAT). The Apprehension Tactical Team, or "A-Team," was ESU's full-time tactical element. This unit strictly performed tactical missions, which, on a day-to-day basis, were typically high-risk search warrants.

The SWAT team was to enter the premises at apartment 2B after surveillance determined that at least one or more of the traffickers had entered the building. They hoped not only to rescue the girls and young women but also to capture at least one of the traffickers who, when a deal was cut, might lead them to the others involved.

At 11:15 p.m., Morgan and Ben, watching from their unmarked car parked across the street, spotted two of the men identified by Brandisha enter the building. Ben wirelessly notified the SWAT team leader that in five minutes, it was a go. Morgan could feel goose bumps forming.

At the five-minute mark, the SWAT team's emergency patrol trucks turned the corner, in sight of the vehicle with Morgan and Ben. The team of six men, dressed in black assault uniforms equipped with bulletproof Kevlar vests, silently exited the vehicle, quickly strode to the building, and stealthily made their way to apartment 2B. One of the men carried a heavy battering ram. When the men were positioned in place on both sides of the door, the battering ram was violently smashed against the door lock. The door was kicked open, and the men rushed in amid shouts of "Police! Everyone on the ground! Hands behind your heads!"

Four girls and two men were immediately neutralized by the team, who had caught them all by surprise. The two men were handcuffed, read their rights, and marched downstairs. The frightened girls, who were in varying degrees of undress, were told to put on something warm and accompany the team to the police precinct.

After the raid was successfully accomplished, Ben, Morgan, and the CSI unit examined the apartment for evidence.

Morgan, by this time of night, should have been exhausted, but she was on a natural high, knowing she had accomplished more than catching a couple of traffickers. She had freed four more girls. Morgan was especially gratified since they had two traffickers in custody who might divulge information on other traffickers and, hopefully, on a kingpin or two, perhaps Satoshi Akita himself.

The two men were brought to the precinct, strip-searched, and booked. Being tattooed from shoulder to ankles left no doubt that they were Yakuza. Morgan hoped that the interrogation of these men would lead to the arrest and conviction of the cause of so much pain and suffering—the smirking Akita.

Although it was well past midnight, Morgan was anxious to interrogate each man before they had the good sense to lawyer up, at which time they were certain to be told to say nothing to the police.

Hours of questioning, one man by Morgan and the other by Ben, yielded nothing of value. Each man denied knowing Satoshi Akita. The conclusion was that each man would rather serve time in prison than betray their Yakuza brothers. They were streetwise enough to know that they would serve time. They expected to be rewarded handsomely when they got out—payment for keeping the faith.

Morgan paid a visit to Alice at the shelter the following morning. Alice sat at the edge of her bed as Morgan sat facing her on the folding chair.

Morgan said, "I wanted to thank you in person for convincing Brandisha to call me."

"I knew she wanted to tell somebody, ya know, but didn't know who. I told her about you."

Morgan leaned in closer to Alice. "Because of the two of you, four more girls were freed, and a couple of Brandisha's old traffickers were caught."

"That's great. I hope you can help her."

"I'm working on it with Abby."

"I'm glad."

With utmost sincerity, Morgan said, "I want you to know that you should be proud of yourself. You did a really good thing."

A sad grin crossed her face.

Morgan then noticed a tear forming in Alice's eye.

Alice said, "Could you do me a favor?"

"Sure."

"I … I haven't been really hugged by anyone in a very long time. Could you give me a hug?"

Morgan could feel her heart breaking for Alice. She leaned over, and the two of them tightly hugged each other.

Morgan felt connected to Alice, both being victims of sexual abuse. But Alice wanted to avoid painful memories; Morgan couldn't forget.

Morgan wished she had been lucky enough to have had a cop interested in what happened to her. Maybe it would have helped her heal all those years ago. Morgan left, promising herself that she would help Alice in any way she could.

Later that morning, Mike Kagawa called Abby at the shelter. He knew they couldn't keep Alice there forever and that one of Abby's options was to find a foster home, which wasn't easy when dealing with a fifteen-year-old former prostitute and drug addict. He didn't share his thoughts with Abby, but he believed there was a possibility that he might provide that foster home and possibly become her guardian. Of course, Alice would have to agree. Also, all his plans were predicated on him not committing suicide, which he was now leaning against. Although the pain of living was unbearable at times, maybe he could lessen that pain by helping others.

He asked Abby to tell Alice that he would like to see her that day. He remained on hold until Abby got back to him. She said Alice was reluctant at first but agreed only if it would be a short visit.

Later that day, Kagawa drove to the shelter, and Abby led him to Alice's room. Kagawa knocked on Alice's door. She opened it, and they politely greeted each other. Abby again stood in the doorway. There were two folding chairs now, and Kagawa and Alice took seats facing each other.

"How have you been?" Kagawa asked.

"Good," she replied curtly.

"Are they treating you well here?"

"Yeah, except for the no drugs policy, ya know? Drove me crazy the first few days, but I'm coming around. I'm on medication, which helps." She wore a dubious expression as she asked, "Why are you here? I thought I answered all your questions."

Kagawa shifted uneasily in his chair. "I'm not here for information. I'm here for you."

Her eyes became tight slits. "What the hell does that mean?"

"What I mean is I'd like to get to know you better ... and for you to get to know me better."

She angrily spat, "What the fuck does *that* mean?"

"I mean as just friends," he apprehensively said.

"Older guys like you just want a blow job from me," she scoffed. "Is that what you want?"

"No, Alice. I will never want that from you."

"How can I trust that? How the fuck can we be friends?"

He didn't answer right away. He needed to think. Maybe *friends* wasn't the right word. "OK, not friends, but how about friendly?"

She looked at him skeptically. "What are you getting at?"

He began to stammer. "I … maybe … you know … maybe I could be the one to take care of you." He blurted out that last part.

She stared at him for what seemed to him to be interminable. He dropped his eyes to his hands.

Alice frowned. "Now I get it. You want me to become Wendy, don't you?" She stood and walked toward the door.

He hoped she wasn't about to ask him to leave. He turned toward the door, looked up at her, and solemnly said, "No one could ever replace Wendy. Yes, you do remind me of her. Do you believe in karma?"

"What the hell is that?"

"It's your destiny or fate. Kind of like things from your past deciding your future."

"What's that got to do with me?"

"Things in both our pasts have led us to this point in time. Abby will try to find you a person or persons who might help you. I would like to be that person. If Wendy hadn't died, and if those men hadn't been killed, neither of us would be here right now. I believe it was karma that brought us together." He hoped he had gotten through to her. He held his breath, waiting for her reply.

She walked back to her chair and sat. "Karma shmarma. I hardly know you, ya know. Why would I go with you and not someone else?"

"I realize that you would have to get to know me better before agreeing to anything, and I hope you give me a chance before making a decision."

"How would I get to know you?"

"We could spend a day together. I thought about this. Have you ever been to the Bronx Zoo?"

She answered in a melancholy way, "I've never been any place."

"Think about it. I could set up a day with Abby that's good for you. Any day is good for me." He was optimistic.

She paused for a few seconds. "Let me think about it, OK?"

Her answer was good enough for him. "Absolutely."

He said goodbye and spoke with Abby, who thought taking Alice to the Bronx Zoo was a wonderful idea, provided Alice agreed and they were accompanied by a chaperone. Some men weren't as they seemed.

CHAPTER

19

MORGAN WAS WORKING AT HER DESK IN THE PRECINCT WHEN
a report came in. She walked to Ben, who was sitting at his desk,
drinking coffee.

Ben looked up and asked, "What's up?"

"The Harbor Unit fished a bloated Asian male out of the Hudson.
It's in the ME's office. The body fits the description of a missing person
named Sammy Zhang, a known Triad."

Ben placed the coffee cup on his desk. "Sounds like retaliation."

"If it is, we might have a shitstorm on our hands."

"How was he ID'd?"

She perused the report. "Seems his wife had called the police about
her husband being missing. She ID'd the body at the morgue. The
autopsy report states that there was no water in the deceased's lungs.
Zhang was killed by several blows of blunt-force trauma to the skull."

Ben took a sip of his coffee. "Does the report say how much he weighs?"

She glanced at the report. "One seventy-five."

"Hmm. Sounds like it would take at least two men to carry him and dump him in the river. Probably not random. Sounds like maybe a Yakuza hit job in retaliation for the three dead guys who had ties to the Yakuza."

Morgan nodded. "Let's hope not."

A grief-stricken Mrs. Zhang relayed the information to several of her husband's associates, who then gave the bad news to Sun Li Fong. Since he'd received no ransom note or note of any kind, he had already assumed that Sammy Zhang was dead. The fact that the body was dumped in the Hudson meant that at least two or more persons were most likely involved. Hence, a group that wanted to send a message. And the message Fong received was loud and clear. The Yakuza were playing hardball. He would have no choice now but to retaliate. He would call a meeting of his counsel to decide the proper retribution to mete out.

Satoshi Akita also received the news. He feared that there would be no way to avoid revenge on the part of the Triads. He would call in his lieutenants and tell them to gear up for a war. How long it would take and how many lives might be lost would depend on his men being vigilant in their day-to-day activities. Each man had to watch his brother's back. In the meantime, he would try to set up a meeting with Fong. Perhaps a war could still be avoided. Akita shook his head and thought, *No one will benefit from a war.*

The last war, one that he participated in, occurred some twenty years earlier. It had begun over a high-stakes poker game on Bleecker Street, off Washington Square Park. The game was run by a former bookie who found that taking a percentage of each pot was far more lucrative than trying to go after gamblers who had welched on their bets.

At around two in the morning, one young man, who was attending New York University, was accused of dealing from the bottom of the deck. The young man's father was a Triad and wanted his son to become a lawyer who might one day earn his keep by representing the Triads in business deals.

Stories of what happened next were a mixed bag. There were over a dozen people in the room, with seven of them playing poker. Some of the others were drinking alcohol, smoking weed, and discussing the latest sporting event bets that they either made or planned to make with their bookies. A fight broke out, and the young man was stabbed in the chest. The knife had pierced his aorta. He was dead in minutes.

None of the dozen or so others were ever indicted since no one seemed to have a very good memory of who stabbed the man. The one thing they miraculously recalled was that the person who stabbed him was a member of the Yakuza who fled the scene immediately. The police knew it was probably a fabrication to throw the blame somewhere else, but with more than a dozen witnesses swearing to the same recollection, no one was charged.

But the others knew the reputation of the Triads—someone would have to pay. Thus, they continued to spread the word that it was a Yakuza whose name they didn't know. Not knowing names was not unusual since new players very often wandered in and out of the game. If they had a wad of cash, that was good enough for the house. The larger the pot, the more the take for the house.

Within the week, a member of the Yakuza, and one who was a friend of Satoshi Akita, was found in an alleyway in Chinatown with his throat slit. Akita believed it was his right to avenge the death of his friend, and this was granted to him.

It didn't matter to Akita if he killed the man who had murdered his friend. He knew that that person was doing his job, retaliating for the death of the son of a Triad. In the same vein, he would retaliate for the death of his friend, and it didn't matter which Triad paid for it.

It had taken only two days to find his man. He spotted him coming out of a restaurant at eleven that night with several other Triads. Since the murder of Akita's friend, the Triads were expecting some sort of retaliation and were watching each other's backs when out in the open. Akita, wearing all black, followed along on the other side of the street. One by one, the group dwindled, as some went home, others to a bar, and so on, until the last person was left alone, probably only a short distance from his destination.

Akita silently crossed the street and extracted his knife from its sheath. He held the knife at his side as he closed in on his unsuspecting prey. With catlike motion, he snuck behind the man and, in one swift move, grabbed the man's hair from behind and yanked back his head as the blade slit his throat. Akita could hear gurgling sounds as the man dropped to the floor like a rag doll. Akita heard someone shout, "Hey, what the hell just happened?"

But it was too late. The man was dead, and Akita melted into the night like an apparition.

Revenge was sweet, but Akita knew this was only the beginning. The war finally ended when each side lost five good men. A truce was agreed to by the leaders of both gangs. Each side had shown the other that they would not cower under the other's influence. They had both proven their point. They were men of honor, upholding their oaths to protect their group's reputation at all costs.

Morgan was heading to the briefing room to attend a meeting of the detective squad called by Captain Graves. She expected it to be about the fact that over the past two days, her precinct had responded to calls regarding the deaths of four more Asian men. Several detectives, including herself and Ben, had been assigned to investigate. Two of the victims had their throats slit, one died of blunt-force trauma, and one was shot in the back of the head, probably with a silencer since no one recalled hearing the shot. They had no good leads to the killers.

Morgan walked into the briefing room and took a seat with the rest of the detective squad, who were now seated. Graves stood in front of the blackboard.

He began, "The reason for this meeting is simple. We've now got eight murdered Asian men in the past few days, all of whom appear to be victims of gang warfare. First, it was Masahiro Araki, followed by Hideki Fujita and Tadashi Ogura. All three were of Japanese descent and probably associated, to some degree, with the Yakuza. Next came the floater, Sammy Zhang, known to be a member of the Triads. Now we have four more bodies, two Yakuza members, and two Triads. I don't think it's rocket science to assume we've got the makings of another gang war, which we certainly do not need in our city. We don't know if it's a turf war or what, but we need to end this quickly."

The detectives conveyed their approval by nodding and mumbling, "Sure," and, "Right."

"Unfortunately for us, it's pretty clear that these murders seemed to be mostly random, which means we can probably establish motive, but finding the killer or killers is another story. Hits like these, coming from powerful criminal organizations, seldom get solved without an informant. The perps doing the actual killing are following orders. I hate to sound like Don Vito Corleone, but 'it's a nothing personal, just bus-i-ness.'" It was said with an exaggerated Italian accent and hand gestures, and the group laughed.

Graves continued. "Even if we capture a suspect, they'll never rat out one of their own. They fear their own group more than they fear us."

Morgan asked, "Are you saying to just give up?"

"Not at all. I'm saying we still investigate, but with an eye not so much toward solving these crimes but preventing more of the same."

Morgan continued, "And how do you propose we do that?"

"I'm going to attempt to get the leaders of both the Yakuza and the Triads to meet with me separately. I know how they think. They believe they look weak if they don't retaliate. It's the old eye for an eye, tooth for a tooth syndrome. As vicious as these leaders can be, they're rational individuals. They've both lost men. We've harassed them before over the years, separately bringing in Fong and Akita. But with a war going on, this time is different. If the war continues, innocent people are likely to get hurt or killed. I know it's a long shot, but maybe enough threats by us might cool things down."

Another detective called out, "You got nothing to lose. Go for it."

"If I can get them here … and they also have nothing to lose by showing up … I would like Ben and Morgan to sit in on the meetings since the two of you have been the most involved in these murders."

Ben responded, "Certainly."

Morgan said, "Of course." Morgan wished she could be the one to put them behind bars. She wondered how Graves would treat them—as businessmen or criminals?

The meeting was adjourned. Graves intended to have his street contacts get in touch with the leaders to set up the hoped-for meetings.

CHAPTER

ABBY HAD CONVINCED ALICE THAT IT WOULD BE FUN FOR
her to go with Mike Kagawa to the Bronx Zoo. Despite Alice's distrust
of the male species, she had met Mike Kagawa twice and thought he
might be a harmless, middle-aged man—except she'd dealt with too
many men like that who wanted more than good company. But she had
unexpectedly felt an emotion she hadn't felt for anyone or anything in
a very long time—she felt sorry for him.

Kagawa double-parked his Toyota in front of the shelter, as
instructed by Abby. She, Alice, and a chaperone were waiting inside
the doorway. As the three of them approached the car, Kagawa got out
to meet with them.

Kagawa instantly noticed the chain and locket that hung on Alice's
neck. He felt good about it. She wore a Ralph Lauren navy blue sweater,
blue jeans, and sneakers. "You look nice," Kagawa said with sincerity.

"Abby got me these clothes."

Abby smiled. "She could pass for almost any high school student now, couldn't she?"

"She sure could."

Abby turned toward a heavyset African American woman of about thirty standing next to her. "Mike, this is Sondra. She'll be accompanying you today."

"You think I need a chaperone?"

"It's not about what I think. I'm not letting her spend the day with a man we hardly know."

He nodded and said, "I understand."

"You won't even know I'm there," Sondra replied.

Kagawa assured Abby that they would return before dark. Alice climbed into the front seat of the passenger side as Kagawa got into the driver's side, with Sondra in the rear seat.

After buckling up, he drove off.

Kagawa broke the uncomfortable silence. "You're going to love the zoo."

"You been there a lot?"

"Not a lot. Twice with my wife and daughter."

They both fell silent for the next five minutes until Alice asked, "What was she like?"

The question took him by surprise. "Wendy?"

"Yeah."

He cleared his throat. "She was as good a daughter as anyone could ever hope for. She was a very good student and played the violin. We did everything together, Wendy, my wife, and I."

"You told me your wife committed suicide. How did she do it?"

Again, a question he hadn't anticipated. There was a catch in his throat as he answered, "Ran the car in the closed garage. Carbon monoxide."

"Sorry. I was just curious."

"No problem. Let's talk about something else, OK?"

"Sure."

But other than the circumstances that had brought the two of them together, they shared nothing in common. They rode in silence on the Bronx River Parkway, eventually making their way to Southern Boulevard, across from Fordham University.

The car entered the zoo through the gate, and Kagawa said, "We're here."

He was directed to a parking lot, and they walked to the main entrance, where Kagawa purchased three tickets.

Kagawa asked, "What would you like to see first?"

Alice shrugged. "I don't know. Maybe elephants and giraffes."

"No problem."

Kagawa followed the map to the African Plains area. Alice giggled when a giraffe leaned its long neck over the fence and ate a leaf from her hand. She was amazed at their size and how loving they were to their young. They also saw elephants, zebras, wildebeest, antelope, and other grazing animals.

Alice asked, "Where are the lions and tigers?"

"At another location. These animals are herbivores. It means they eat plant material. Lions and tigers are carnivores. They eat meat, and in the wild, must kill for their food. Here, the zoo feeds them."

They viewed the carnivorous animals that the zoo offered and then had lunch. It all had fascinated Alice, and it seemed to Kagawa that she couldn't get enough of seeing the animals.

Alice never knew who her father was. She had known that her mother was, and still might be, a prostitute herself, and she suspected that she was the daughter of some unnamed john. Her surname of Liu was her mother's maiden name. As a young girl, she saw numerous "uncles" and "good friends" visit her mother at her apartment. Her mother did have occasional true boyfriends, one of whom had taken advantage of the thirteen-year-old Alice on numerous occasions. She wondered if her mother was still seeing that bastard. Knowing her mother, probably not. But the next one wouldn't be any better.

Now, here was this man who said he would like to take care of her. She had spent the day with him, and he seemed to not only enjoy himself but was also very knowledgeable about the animals in the zoo.

Alice's seventh-grade education hadn't served her well. She knew she would eventually be farmed out to foster care, provided they found someone suitable. Otherwise, she could end up in an orphanage and become one of who knew how many other girls. She believed she had gotten to know a little about this Mike Kagawa. He seemed like an OK guy. Maybe she could let him take care of her. But what if she was a disappointment to him? She wasn't as smart or talented as Wendy. And what if he turned out to be a pervert? Did he do something to Wendy? Did she run away? Is that why Hiro found her in Chinatown? But she had no evidence of any of that. Maybe he really was an OK guy. On the plus side, she wouldn't have to work for a living. She could go to the movies, maybe a Broadway show, or Coney Island, where she'd go on the fastest rides. But she also knew she would have to attend school. She feared her lack of education would show, and she might be laughed at. Also, what if someone in school found out that she had been a prostitute? She believed that time would tell, and she was empowered by the fact that the decision was hers alone to make.

Captain Graves surreptitiously spread the word through his street contacts that if the leaders of the Yakuza and Triads did not meet with him, they could expect their legitimate establishments to be raided on trumped-up charges almost daily. Both Akita and Fong were ruthless leaders, but they were also businessmen. Disruption of their businesses would mean loss of revenue. Both men agreed to meet with Graves, separately. First to meet was Akita, at ten that morning. Ben and Morgan were standing and waiting in one of the larger interview rooms where the four of them could sit and talk comfortably.

Morgan sat at the table, her hands clasped in front of her. She glared at Akita as the animal entered the room. The hatred she felt toward him and all others of his ilk was palpable. Recently, she'd jerked awake after dreaming of slitting the man's throat.

Akita made eye contact with Morgan. She stared him straight in the eye until he looked away. She smiled to herself. She'd won the staring contest. The four people sat around a large table: Graves, Morgan, and Ben on one side, Akita on the other.

Graves introduced himself, then said, "And you've already met Detectives Chang and Kelly." Akita stared straight ahead, stone-faced.

Akita then glanced at Morgan and winked at her.

Morgan wanted to slap him silly but controlled herself.

Addressing Akita, Graves began, "I want to thank you for agreeing to this meeting. We believe we might be able to spare some lives, while you may continue to operate any legitimate businesses you might have without undue interference by the authorities."

Akita sat impassively as he listened.

"In the past couple of weeks, there have been eight murders of Asian men, either here in Chinatown or places having connections to it. This stinks of gang warfare, especially since every one of the eight has a connection of some kind to either the Yakuza or Triads. Now, I don't expect you to admit anything here, but what I do expect is that you listen as a rational businessman. As you know, past wars benefitted no one. I realize that there's a macho kind of thing that, in my opinion, has gone far enough. Your organization has lost valuable men, men who might have had families. Men who had children."

With his dark eyes squinting, Akita asked, "And you summoned me here because?"

"Let's assume for the moment that in some fictitious land, the possibility exists that a war has broken out. And let's assume that the leaders have some influence in their organizations, and let's say that each leader might be able to persuade those persons who want to make war that it is in the best interests of their organizations to stop."

Morgan was impressed with Grave's handling of the situation thus far.

Akita offered, "Those are many assumptions."

"Like I said, it might be in their best interests to stop the bloodshed, since both sides of my hypothetical land have lost good men, and both sides stand to lose if they continue their war. Also, in this land are men and women in uniform who are ready to destroy their businesses if the war doesn't immediately end."

Akita put an unlit cigar in his mouth and rolled it from one side to the other. "A wonderful fairy tale."

"I thought you would like it. But hear me out. My threat is a real one. If one more body finds its way to our morgue, all hell will be unleashed upon your businesses. You'll receive violations you never even knew existed." He pounded his knuckles onto the table. "I don't need innocent people caught in a crossfire."

No one spoke for a full minute, one that felt endless to Morgan. She looked at Akita, who displayed no outward sign of any kind.

Finally, Akita spoke. "Will that be all? You have wasted a lot of my time. Perhaps you should write a children's book."

Morgan didn't expect anything else from Akita. He would have to act the macho leader to the bitter end. But she knew he had heard Graves loud and clear. The killings had to end or there would be grave consequences. She hoped that Akita was more concerned with profits than revenge.

Akita turned toward Morgan and smiled. "As I mentioned before, you're much too pretty to be a cop. If you ever think of changing careers, come see me."

Her mind screamed, *Shoot the bastard!* "When I see you, it'll be with a warrant for your arrest. I hope you like men as much as you like women."

Akita stood, ready to leave. He turned to Morgan and asked, "Are you a good driver?"

Morgan stood so abruptly her metal chair fell back onto the floor with a clang. She took three quick strides and got directly in Akita's face. "Are you threatening me?"

He sneered. "I never threaten. I need a good-looking chauffeur."

Morgan shoved Akita with both hands. Akita stumbled back and tripped over the leg of a chair, landing unceremoniously on his rear end.

Graves shouted. "Morgan!"

Morgan stepped toward Akita, stood over him, and shouted, "OK, tough guy. Get up and let's see you take on someone who's not a little girl."

Akita got up, brushed off his pants, and said, "That was very stupid of you."

She glared at him and said, "We'll soon see who the stupid one is."

Akita pointed a finger at her, mimicking a gun. He turned, left the room, and disappeared down the hallway.

Morgan was fuming. "That was *also* a threat, wasn't it?"

Ben said, smiling, "You knocked him on his ass. That was great! But I think he was then trying to get under *your* skin."

Graves added, "I don't think he'd be stupid enough to kill a cop."

"Yeah," Morgan said, "unless I got into a car accident or something."

The three of them let that thought sink in.

Graves changed the subject, saying to Ben and Morgan, "What do you think about the meeting?"

Ben said, "I wonder if it'll have any effect."

A distressed Morgan said, "We're never going to get this guy, are we?"

Graves answered, "As I said before, guys like that insulate themselves."

Morgan shook her head and angrily left the room, knowing that the men who were guilty of the most heinous crimes would probably never see justice. She tried hard not to spiral once again into her mind's darkest recesses. Thoughts of revenge swept over her, thoughts she didn't like in herself. She'd seen many *innocent* people die in Iraq. She knew the world would be a safer place if one *guilty* person were to die after she put a bullet in Akita's head. It was a fantasy she hoped would remain as such.

At his club, Akita said to Harada, "Make plans for an accident."

Later that day, they met with Fong, who was as noncommittal as Akita had been.

CHAPTER

21

IT HAD BEEN A BUSY DAY FOR MORGAN. FIRST IT WAS THE meetings with Akita and Fong. Then it was investigating a possible homicide that was determined to be a suicide and, finally, finishing the paperwork back at the precinct. It was 6:30 p.m., and she was on her way back to her apartment. She was expecting to hear from Tyler. They'd had several phone conversations since their trip to Governors Island, and she found herself looking forward to his calls. He had a sense of humor, and he often made her laugh. More importantly, she now believed that what he had said about himself was the truth—that he was an open and honest person—and she thought his compliments to her were genuine, not a con job. Could this be the start of something more than a friendship? She thought it could, but she still felt she had to go slowly. She had trusted too many men before and had been badly scarred by them.

As she approached the front of her building, she spotted Paul, who was obviously waiting for her. *Oh, shit!* she though, not expecting this to be anything good. She stopped in front of him, placed her hands on her hips, and waited for him to speak.

"Hello, Morgan," he said cheerfully.

"Hi, Paul. What do you want?"

"I just want to talk to you. Is that OK?"

"What about?"

"Us."

"There is no *us* anymore."

"But there could be. I know we're getting divorced, but couples do get back together. Happens all the time."

"What would make me change my mind?"

"Look, for a couple of years, we had a good thing going. Remember?"

"Yeah, until your drinking got you laid off, and you started messing around with other women. And, oh yeah, that little thing you forgot to tell me about, you still being married. Our entire marriage was a sham." She attempted to keep her anger under control but was losing the battle.

His voice was pleading. "I know I fucked up. I'm trying to give up drinking. I might have a few weeks of work coming up, and I'm sorry about the other things."

"Paul, we're no longer a couple. We're not *ever* going to be one again. Get it through that thick skull of yours."

The words came pouring out. "I still love you, always have, probably always will, and I know I can change if you just give me the chance. Please, let me show you I can be a better husband."

She didn't know how to make it any clearer to him that they were through. "I need to go now." She stepped to the side, trying to get by him. He moved to block her path.

"Enough games. Step aside, please."

"Are you seeing your new *honey* tonight?"

"What I do and who I see are none of your business anymore."

"Is it that blond-headed guy?"

She was beyond annoyed. "I know you know because you've followed me. It's time to grow up and get a life for yourself. And you better stop stalking me."

He shouted, "What life? No real job, no more wife who I thought loved me, no nothin'."

"Please step aside—or else."

"Or else what? You gonna pull your gun on me? You're not the only one who owns one. Remember?"

How could she forget? It was she who had gotten him his permit and showed him how to use his pistol. "Are you threatening me?"

"Not at all … *Officer*. Just a reminder, that's all." He stepped aside, she brushed past him, and as she walked toward the apartment building door, she heard him repeat what he'd said before, "It's not over till I say it is."

She stepped into the building, worried that she might be dealing with a powder keg. Another man who wouldn't take no for an answer.

The following day at the precinct, Morgan asked to speak with Ben in private.

"What's up?" Ben asked.

"Paul confronted me last night in front of my apartment building. I think he's becoming irrational where I'm concerned. And he reminded me that he owns a gun."

His eyes flared. "Was it a clear threat?"

"Not really. But he knows about Tyler. I'm not sure what he's capable of."

"You could get a restraining order. Keep him more than five hundred feet from you."

She shook her head. "You know as well as I do that it never works with a crazy person, and I'm afraid that Paul is becoming just that."

"I would watch my back if I were you."

"That's why I'm talking with you. I'm seeing Tyler tonight. I invited him over to my place for a drink, and then we're going for dinner at Lure Fishbar on Mercer Street. I know it's a great imposition to ask of

227

you, but it would set my mind at ease if you could tail us tonight. After the conversation of last night, I believe he'll stalk me tonight, just to see if I'm seeing someone."

He rubbed his chin. "Gee, I'd have to speak with the boss. If she says we have no plans tonight, then I'll be happy to tail you."

"If you do this, I'll owe you one big-time."

"Hey, we're a couple, remember?" He laughed.

She laughed too, recalling her joking with him when they first met.

"I'll call her and maybe let you know right now."

He dialed his wife's cell number, asked if it was OK for him to work that night, and then told Morgan it was a go. She was relieved.

"When should I be there?"

"Tyler is coming at seven. We have a reservation for eight, so we'll leave around seven fifty and walk to the restaurant, which is only five or so minutes from my apartment."

"I'll be there, only you won't know it. And besides, Paul doesn't know me."

"Thanks, Ben. I really appreciate this."

At 6:40, Morgan let the early-arriving Tyler into her apartment. Morgan had shown Ben photos of Tyler that she had taken with her cell phone on Governors Island,. Morgan had also given Ben several photos of Paul, and she hoped Ben was outside, settling in for a boring evening listening to his favorite oldies station on the radio.

At a quarter to eight, after sharing drinks and a few laughs, Morgan and Tyler emerged from the building and turned up the street toward the restaurant, a few blocks away. One minute into the walk, she thought she heard something behind her. She turned quickly but saw nothing.

Tyler asked. "What is it?"

She turned to him and smiled. "Nothing." She grasped his hand and continued to walk. She recalled Ben saying that he would be there, but that she wouldn't know it. She hoped he was. She had meant to call Ben to make certain, but Tyler's early arrival precluded that. What if something came up and he couldn't make it? But, she thought, so far so good.

Morgan and Tyler entered the Lure Fishbar Restaurant, which had a maritime décor, with a luxury yacht-like interior, including wood-planked floor, yacht-style windows, and curved ceiling. Morgan and Tyler were seated side by side in a padded booth. They each ordered a glass of wine from an overly polite, uniformed, middle-aged waiter.

The waiter returned with their wine and asked if they were ready to order.

Tyler said, "We're going to share the kale Caesar salad."

He bowed slightly and said, "Certainly. And what will the lady be having for her main course?"

It had been a long time since she'd dined in a fancy restaurant. Never with Paul. Something struck her funny bone. Maybe it was the waiter's phony demeanor, the wine, or both. She smiled broadly as she replied, "The *lady* will be having the miso-glazed salmon with sugar snap peas and mushrooms."

He nodded. "Excellent choice."

Morgan believed that, had she ordered a rat burger, he would've said, "Excellent choice."

The waiter looked at Tyler. "And for the gentleman?"

Tyler glanced at Morgan, who was suppressing a laugh. He turned to the waiter and said, "The *gentleman* will have the steamed red snapper with bok choy and jasmine rice."

"Very nice." The waiter took their menus and left.

Morgan and Tyler looked at each other and laughed.

Almost two hours passed with Morgan enjoying the time with the two of them acting like lovebirds. Tyler paid the check, and the couple walked hand in hand toward the exit. The Soho streets had become more crowded with diners, drinkers, and residents out for a postprandial stroll, and Morgan reassured herself that everything will be fine.

As soon as they left the restaurant, Morgan was startled by the looming figure of Paul standing in their way, appearing fidgety. She could smell the alcohol on his breath.

"Jesus Christ, Paul!" she shouted, her face turning red. "Get out of our way!"

He didn't move, staring at them with bloodshot eyes.

Where's Ben? Morgan thought. *He should be here.* What if something had happened to him?

Tyler stepped in front of Morgan and said, "The lady just asked you to move aside."

Paul wore a crazed and drunken expression as he addressed Tyler. "Go fuck yourself, asshole." He stepped toward him.

Tyler shoved Paul backward.

Paul stumbled, then half turned, and Morgan hoped he was leaving, but he was only grabbing a gun from his pocket. He pointed it waveringly at Tyler. "You wanna get tough? That's my woman you're fucking."

Morgan yelled, "Paul, put the gun away. We're just friends. Put the gun away!"

Morgan then saw Ben rushing forward from across the street with his weapon drawn. He shouted while pointing his weapon at Paul, "Police! Drop your weapon, now!"

Paul turned to see Ben running toward him, and he immediately fired a round that hit Ben in his torso. Ben fired back, hitting Paul in his shoulder. Morgan yelled and grabbed Paul's gun as he staggered backward. Morgan then tackled Paul, who attempted to wrestle with her, but with only one good arm and intoxicated, he was no match. Morgan held a screaming and cursing Paul down on the sidewalk as many curious people began streaming out of the restaurant. She shouted to Tyler, "Hold him! I have to check on Ben!" Tyler, still flustered from the attack, bent down and took over, allowing Morgan to run over to Ben, who was lying in the street on his back. She shouted, "Call nine-one-one. Tell them police officer down. Send an ambulance. Call nine-one-one!" Several people began dialing the number.

She knelt at Ben's side. "Ben!" she cried. "Are you OK?"

Ben opened his eyes. "Got me good, didn't he?"

"You hang in there, partner. Help is on its way."

She could see Ben's breathing become labored. Fear and remorse gripped her. She promised herself that if he died, she would resign from the force.

Paul was screaming expletives, still struggling to extricate himself from Tyler's grasp. Tyler shouted for the crowd to help him control the man who had just shot the police officer, and one young, muscled gym rat with a shaved head and gold earrings knelt and grabbed Paul's good arm. In his condition, Paul was no match for the two men.

Within minutes, several police cars and an ambulance, with their sirens blaring and top lights flashing, pulled up to the scene. Morgan immediately identified herself as a detective with the Seventh Precinct and told them to arrest Paul. He had shot Detective Ben Chang.

Ben was placed on a gurney and deposited into an ambulance that sped away, its sirens screaming.

Another ambulance pulled up, and a handcuffed Paul was placed in it, with two police officers accompanying him. Morgan and Tyler watched as it left for the hospital, sirens blaring.

Tyler put his arm around a visibly shaken Morgan. "Are you OK?"

"I will be if Ben is." Tears were streaming down her face. She looked at a sweaty Tyler. "Are you OK?"

Tyler was still breathing hard. "A bit unnerved by all this, but yeah, I'm good." As the crowd was dispersing, he asked, "What happened here? Who is Ben, and what was he doing here?"

She explained, her story clear but her voice showing her distress. She hadn't expected Paul to pull a gun and shoot someone, especially not Ben. She had obviously underestimated just how distraught he was, and she'd thought he had more sense of self-preservation. She asked Tyler to accompany her to the hospital. She didn't want to face Ben's wife alone, and he agreed, telling her he would drive her there.

"You own a car?"

"I'll explain on the way. It's parked in a garage, two blocks away."

He told her he'd bought a used Nissan Altima in 2005 in North Carolina that he moved to New York in. He kept it parked on the street and used it very infrequently, usually only if he left the city. Tonight, he thought she might not mind going for a drive after dinner, so he had parked the car in a nearby garage. They retrieved the car and drove toward the hospital.

On the way, she had time to reflect on her life. Was she cursed? If Ben died, he would be her third partner, including her partner in Iraq, to be killed in the line of duty. She didn't know how she would cope.

As he drove, Tyler asked, "How are you doing?"

She audibly exhaled. "A bit numb and really scared."

He looked at her and tenderly said, "You're safe now."

She shook her head. "Scared that if Ben dies, I don't think I could handle it."

He reassuringly said, "Ben will live. I feel it."

She choked back a sob as the car pulled up to the New York Presbyterian Hospital. She flashed her badge at the emergency entrance, and Tyler was able to park in a no-parking spot. They hustled inside, asked at the desk where Ben was, and rushed to the waiting room.

Ben's wife, Doreen, was already in the waiting room when Morgan and Tyler entered.

Morgan introduced herself while Tyler stood back, then nervously asked, "How is he?"

Doreen wiped her eyes with a tissue. "He's in the OR. The doctor said he's in critical condition. I only know that he was shot in his chest or stomach. He was supposed to be working tonight with you." She glanced at Morgan's outfit. "But you're dressed up. What happened out there?"

Morgan took a deep breath before answering. "Ben knew I was being stalked by my future ex-husband, Paul, who made some veiled threats toward me. I asked Ben to tail me and my friend here"—she pointed at Tyler—"just in case he tried something stupid. I never expected him to pull a gun on us. Ben shouted for him to drop his weapon. Paul turned and fired. So did Ben. Ben got the worst of it. Paul will live. If Ben dies, I will never forgive myself." At this point, the entire night had taken its toll. Morgan began to sob in a manner that she hadn't done since she was thirteen, when her mother moved the family away from her nightmare. Tyler put his arm around her.

Doreen reached out and gently touched Morgan's damp cheek. "My husband is a big, strong man. I know he's going to make it." She pulled her hand away.

Morgan looked at her as she began to control her sobs. "I pray … he's OK."

"All we can do is just that, pray and wait for the doctors to come out and give us some good news." Tears welled up in Doreen's eyes.

Morgan attempted a smile, but her quivering lips didn't allow it.

They settled in for the wait. Several members of the police force began to file into the waiting area with Doreen, Morgan, and Tyler.

As uncomfortable as it was for her, Morgan had to explain what had happened several times over. The officers seemed to understand, but Morgan believed that they felt it should never have happened. Guilt was not something she had learned to live with.

The wait seemed like an eternity for Morgan. She sat with Tyler, mostly in silence, since there wasn't anything anyone could say to her that would change things. After four hours, a doctor appeared, dressed in greens, with a mask pulled down under his chin.

He looked around the room and said, "Mrs. Chang?"

Doreen was helped to a standing position by one of the officers. "Yes."

The doctor called her over to a corner of the room and spoke with her, while everyone in the room stood up and held their breath. They could see her nod to the doctor several times. The doctor turned back toward the double doors.

Morgan felt her heart pounding in her chest as Doreen approached the group. "The doctor said he lost a lot of blood, but he's going to live!"

A cheer went up from the crowd as Morgan slumped into Tyler's arms. He gently sat her down onto a chair as she said, "Thank you, God. Thank you."

Doreen said she would stay the night but that the rest of the crowd should go home. Morgan wanted to stay, but Tyler convinced her that she should go home and try to get some rest. She agreed, knowing she would need her strength when it came time to file all the reports she would be required to fill out.

They left in Tyler's car.

While Tyler drove, Morgan sullenly said, "I almost lost another partner."

He waited for more, but it wasn't forthcoming, so he asked, "What do you mean?"

She sighed, inhaled deeply, and explained, "About four months ago, a different partner and I responded to a robbery. He was killed. I believe some of the department blames me in some way, even though I was cleared of any wrongdoing."

"Then that's their problem."

"I think they think that if I were a man, this wouldn't have happened."

He turned toward her and said, "Again, that's *their* problem."

"Maybe so, but it's in my head, so it's also *my* problem."

Tyler drove her home. They got out of the car, and he kissed her cheek. As he turned to leave, she grabbed his arm and said, "Thank you."

He forced a smile. "Nothin' more than any southern gentleman would do for his lady."

She watched him as he drove down the street and out of sight. She hoped the shooting and her being on the police force wouldn't make him skittish about seeing her again. She wouldn't blame him after what he'd witnessed that night.

If he would let her, she vowed to try to make it up to him.

She was dead tired but still had trouble falling asleep. Images of that evening were haunting her; she visualized the event over and over. She should have anticipated the possibility of a gun and didn't because the murders she was investigating made Paul seem like small potatoes. Could she have done something differently? Should she not have asked Ben to follow her? Could she have grabbed Paul's gun before he turned and shot Ben? Would everyone think she placed Ben in danger unnecessarily?

Her last thought before sleep mercifully arrived was that maybe she should resign from the force. But before doing so, she would find a way to kill Akita. After all, she was an expert with a rifle.

Tyler called Morgan on her cell the next morning, trying as best he could to make her feel better. He invited her to have dinner at his apartment that evening, to which she readily agreed. She looked forward to not having to spend the night alone with her painful thoughts. The rest of her morning was spent filing incident reports and filling out forms. She was thankful that Ben was going to be OK, but she still felt extremely guilty at having been the one who had placed him in jeopardy.

Doreen had given Morgan her cell number. Morgan called and asked how Ben was. She was told that he was still asleep, under a lot of medication, but should be awake by tomorrow. The good news was that he should have a complete recovery.

Morgan asked, "Is it OK if I come by tomorrow?" She felt as though she were pleading, but she didn't care.

"OK? I'm certain he would love to see you." The call ended.

Morgan was introduced to her new temporary partner, Chris Grabowski, a veteran detective with more than twenty years on the force, who had recently been transferred from another precinct.

Morgan brought him up to date on the cases she had been working on with Ben, and he did likewise regarding the cases he had been working on with his former partner, who had recently retired.

The one case that could never be hers was the one involving Paul. She was told he was recovering nicely in the same hospital as Ben and would be arraigned as soon as possible. Shooting a cop would get him many years in an upstate prison.

In spite of herself, she felt sorry for Paul. They had shared some good times together in the beginning, but he had brought it all down upon himself. At least he was out of her life now, hopefully for good.

The remainder of her day was spent finishing her paperwork. She hadn't gotten much sleep the night before, and she was exhausted, both physically and emotionally, but she was glad to be able to see Tyler later.

That evening, Morgan drove her Ford to Tyler's address and parked. On the way there, she had the distinct feeling that the vehicle behind her was following her, mimicking every turn she made. Before exiting her car, she observed the vehicle passing her and caught a glimpse of the man behind the wheel. The vehicle made a turn at the next light and disappeared. She thought, *Was that Harada?* Or maybe she was being a bit paranoid.

Tyler opened the door, and Morgan entered the one-bedroom condominium that he had purchased years prior.

She glanced around the apartment. "This must have cost a small fortune."

"Got it at a great price, after the housing market collapsed."

She was impressed with the decorating and asked, "How did you manage to do such a great job?" She swept an arm across the room.

He smiled appreciatively. "It was easy. Hired an interior decorator."

She could see from the fine furnishings that he was probably doing well at his job as an accountant.

To her surprise, he hadn't ordered food from a takeout but had cooked the meal himself. He explained that he'd had some practice in southern-style cooking while growing up in North Carolina. He served homestyle chicken gumbo soup, southern-fried chicken, which he personally breaded and fried, with mashed sweet potatoes and marshmallows. And for dessert, homemade key lime pie.

They each had several glasses of wine, and by ten that evening, Morgan was feeling more relaxed than she had been in a very long time. She had expected that sometime that evening, Tyler would make his move on her. In fact, she had hoped he would, since she was finally truly falling for him, and she believed he felt the same way about her. She would take a risk with this man, with the hope he wouldn't be the disappointment so many men before him had been.

He made love to her that night in a manner she wasn't used to. Tyler was very gentle and eager to accommodate all her sexual needs. Paul had always been concerned with himself. He'd always been aggressive and rough, very often climaxing in minutes and falling asleep, leaving her to finish the job on her own. Tyler ... Tyler kept meeting her eyes during sex. Paul had certainly never done *that*.

After their lovemaking, Tyler said, "Stay the night."

She thought about it. "I really can't. I have work tomorrow, and I need to be home to get ready. And I promised to visit Ben at the hospital before going to work."

He understood. "Rain check?"

She smiled. "Absolutely."

He kissed her tenderly on her lips, and she left.

In her Ford, she felt like she was floating on a cloud. She intended to see more of Tyler. A lot more.

As she pulled away from the curb, she noticed through her rearview mirror that another vehicle pulled away from the curb, a few parked cars behind hers. Was this more paranoia? Or was she actually being tailed? She couldn't make the type of vehicle or see the driver due to the vehicle's headlights. She made several turns, followed by the vehicle. At the next red light, she decided she'd had enough. She unclipped her piece, stepped out of her car, and approached the vehicle. The vehicle suddenly backed down the street and turned onto a different street.

Morgan was bristling as she entered her car. She managed to catch a glimpse of the Asian man, the same man she thought might have been following her earlier. Now she was almost certain it was Harada. Exactly why he would follow her was unclear. But she knew it couldn't be for anything good. Placing a bullet between Akita's eyes seemed more and more like something she might do.

Graves called a meeting the following morning. He was happy to announce that for the past few days, no more bodies of Asian men, killed indiscriminately, had been found. He believed that the war was over. One sour note was that, in all likelihood, no one would ever pay for murdering any of the eight dead men. On the positive side, there were eight fewer criminals to worry about.

Morgan knew that unless some new evidence was presented, the bridge club murders and the murder of Masahiro Araki would also go unsolved and be relegated to the cold case files, although she was certain that Satoshi Akita was ultimately responsible, even if indirectly, for these deaths and the deaths of so many girls and young women, including the

Kagawa, Chen, and Huang girls. Taking down that smug Akita was still a major priority.

After the meeting, Morgan approached Graves and said, "I think we need to get on TV again to ask the public for help with the bridge club murders. With so many potential witnesses, or perhaps some snitch, if we offer a reward of some kind, maybe we can catch a break."

Graves pondered her suggestion. "Not easy to do, but I'll pass it by the powers that be."

"Thanks."

Tyler called her and asked if he could take her to dinner that evening. She told him it was fine as long as they finished early enough for her to visit Ben. Dinner and an early evening were OK with him. She was liking him more and more.

Tyler took a taxi and met her at her apartment. They caught a quick dinner at Five Napkin, primarily a burger place that was within walking distance of her building.

While waiting for the check, Morgan said, "I wasn't certain you'd want to see me again."

"Why is that?" he answered with a curious expression.

"Me being a cop, the shooting and all that, would scare off a lot of people."

"I have to admit, it wasn't quite how I thought the evening would go, but how would it look if I bailed out the first time someone I like very much got into trouble? Not my style. Besides, growing up, my dad used to take me hunting in the Smoky Mountains. Guns don't scare me, so long as they're not pointed at me. And besides, the way you wrestled Paul? I'm impressed. I'm sure you can take care of me." He smiled warmly, and she laughed.

"Serve and protect," she said.

He asked if she wanted him to accompany her to the hospital, but she thought it best she go alone. He understood. "You guys are close. You need to see him, and I'm sure he needs to see you."

She was definitely falling for this southern gentleman.

They left the restaurant. Tyler caught a cab home while Morgan went for her car.

Morgan arrived at the hospital at eight. Ben was still in the ICU but was awake. It was expected that he would be in a hospital room in the next day or two, depending upon his recovery status.

Morgan walked in, greeted by Doreen—her kids had left for the evening—and saw Ben smile at her. She walked over to him and kissed him on his forehead. "How are you?"

He smiled. "Doing as good as anyone who's been hit by a Mack truck."

She chuckled. He hadn't lost his sense of humor, and that was good. She inhaled deeply. "I'm so sorry for what happened."

"What's there to be sorry about? I was doing my job."

"No, you were doing me a favor. I should never have asked."

"And if I hadn't been there, maybe he would have shot you or your friend or both. And how would that have made me feel if I thought you didn't think enough of me to ask me to protect you?"

Tears were flowing down her cheeks. He was consoling her! God, how she admired Doreen to have married such a magnificent man. "Listen, you just rest and get better. They stuck me with some guy named Chris Grabowski. He seems OK, but I need you there with me. And besides, you promised to play the guitar for me."

He smiled. "I'll be back soon enough to serenade you. Don't you worry. How big could a bullet be? Not easy to get through this big body."

Doreen and Morgan both laughed. Morgan said her goodbyes and left for home.

She hoped Tyler would be the one to fill the void she felt in her heart. She believed there were still some good men out there, and she thought Tyler might be one of them. But she was focused on one *bad* man as an intense desire to get that destroyer of young lives, Akita, still held her in its grasp.

That evening, she drove to the shooting range. She continually looked to see if she was being followed. She believed she was, but the vehicle in the distance wasn't the same as she had observed outside Tyler's building.

As soon as her Ford entered through the gate to the shooting range, she saw the vehicle turning around and driving off.

Later, after visualizing Akita as her target, Morgan finished target practice and left for home. She was certain she wasn't being followed this time since she made several evasive moves. She intended to confront Akita.

CHAPTER 22

MARYANN SILVERSTEIN HAD BEEN MARRIED TO HER HUSBAND, Jerry, for almost thirty years, and she believed she knew all his moods. These past few nights, he'd been tossing and turning in bed, and she knew something was bothering him, but he had said it was nothing. She could tell he was lying, and now it was time for her to press him on it. Was he involved with another woman and feeling guilty? She didn't think he would do such a thing, but then again, he was a man, and their sex life wasn't what it used to be. She had stared at herself in the mirror. She had gained about twenty pounds since their marriage but still believed herself to be attractive.

Jerry was sitting at the kitchen table, finishing his coffee and reading the morning newspaper when Maryann sat at the table and demanded, "I want to know what's been bothering you these past few days. Is it another woman?"

Jerry looked up from his newspaper with an astonished expression. "What? Where did you get that idea?"

She rapped her hand on the table. "If it's not another woman, then I want to know what's wrong with you."

He pushed the paper and coffee mug to the side, sighed heavily, and said, "About a week or so ago, Mike Kagawa called me."

"Mike? How is he doing?" She had met Mike and his family and had empathized with Mike, thinking about her own family.

"He said he was trying to survive. A tragedy like that …" Jerry shook his head slowly.

"Is that what's been bothering you? Thinking about poor Mike?"

"No. It's something he asked me to do."

She leaned in closer with a concerned expression. "What could he possibly ask of you that would upset you?"

"He asked questions about bridge."

She shrugged her shoulders. "At a time of grief, he wants to learn bridge?"

"Let me clarify. He asked if I could find out where two men that he had met played bridge. I asked if they played duplicate, and of course Mike had no idea what that was, so I explained a bit, but it was way over his head. He said he had lost their phone numbers, but he knew they played at a bridge club in the city, and if he knew where they played, he could meet with them again."

Maryann shook her head, confused. "Where in the world are you going with this?"

"I told him that if they played duplicate, they were probably ACBL members, and I could look on the internet, and if they played recently, I would be able to tell him at which bridge clubs they played."

She placed her hand under her chin. "OK."

"I got back to him and told him they played at a club in Chinatown."

"OK." She removed her hand from her chin, waiting for some sort of punchline.

"The men he was asking about were named Hideki Fujita and Tadashi Ogura."

The names rang no bells for her. "OK."

"These were the two men who were killed at that bridge club."

Her eyes flew open wide. "The same men he asked about?"

"Exactly. I called Mike and mentioned the unbelievable coincidence. He sounded as surprised as I was."

She reached out and touched his arm. "I still don't understand what's bothering you."

"I read in the paper that these two men were the ones who killed Wendy."

Maryann sat in silence, trying to digest what she'd just heard. Finally, she leaned back in her chair and exclaimed, "Holy fucking shit!" She felt as though vertigo held her in its grasp. "Are you telling me that Mike Kagawa, the guy who taught across the hall from you all these years, might be the man who shot those two in the head, like some mafia hitman?"

"Now you know what's been bothering me. I haven't told anyone and have been struggling with calling the police. But maybe it is just coincidence. The newspapers and TV believe it's gang warfare. Makes more sense, but ..."

She nodded in an understanding way. "What are you going to do?"

"On the one hand, how could I accuse an old friend, especially after what he's been through? On the other hand, I'm now guilty of ... I don't know what. Possibly harboring a murderer? Withholding evidence, or who knows what?"

"But he might be a murderer, Jerry. Can you live with that knowledge?"

"He might spend the rest of his life behind bars, but I've thought of another scenario."

"What?"

"If he killed the men who murdered his daughter and, indirectly, made Amy commit suicide, it might be too much for anyone to handle rationally. Maybe he gets off for temporary insanity. It has happened before."

"You know that his life would still be ruined. He could never get his teaching job back."

He waved his hand dismissively. "I know, I know."

"And he would never forgive you."

"I thought about that. I could call anonymously from a phone booth."

She pondered his suggestion. It would relieve him of some of his worry and guilt about withholding evidence. "I think that's what you should do."

He nodded. "Let me think about it."

Jerry felt better having gotten some of the burden off his chest by sharing it with his wife. But he was still in a quandary as to what to do. Perhaps he should let the police handle it, clear him if he was innocent. Jerry Silverstein had known Mike Kagawa ever since they were both probationary teachers twenty-five years earlier, each teaching science in the same high school. He knew Mike to be a compassionate, caring, highly competent educator who had a passion for science and who loved teaching it. Of course, there were days when every teacher had problems with students, but Mike never lost sight of the fact that these were kids, all of whom deserved a chance to learn and make something better of themselves.

Mike would often remain after school, offering extra help to his students. He also ran the chess club every Wednesday, teaching students the game he learned as a kid and loved to play. Some of his students became so good at it that they often beat Mike, which to Mike was the greatest compliment a teacher could receive—having the student become more proficient than the teacher.

There were even times when Mike felt the need to pay a visit to a student's home, which often gave him insight as to why that student was doing poorly. Too many students had a home life that was anything but conducive to an atmosphere of learning. Mike would often state that the most frustrating thing about teaching was the inability to have much of an effect on too many of the lives that needed it most.

Like Mike Kagawa, Jerry was well into middle age. He didn't feel much different than he did some twenty years ago, but when he stared into the mirror, he realized he wasn't thirty anymore. His brown hair had receded and was turning silver, he had gained about twenty pounds, and his face had added some wrinkles where there used to be none.

And like Mike Kagawa, he was a family man. He had two teenaged daughters whom he would do anything for, and he knew Mike to be the same way. He had met Amy and Wendy on a couple of occasions, and he saw the love that Mike had for them. Jerry thought, *What would I do if my wife and kids were murdered?* This thought made his dilemma that much more vexing. How would he react if he knew who had murdered his entire family? Hadn't he read the novel *A Time to Kill*, in which a distraught man shoots and kills one of the men who tortured and violated his young daughter? Didn't the jury find him not guilty? Of course, that was fiction, but temporary insanity might be a way out for Mike, although his life as a teacher would probably be over.

Later that night, Jerry saw a public service announcement on TV asking for the public's help in solving the bridge club murders. It made Jerry's struggle with his perplexing problem even worse. Should he call the police and tell them what he knew, which might lead to years of imprisonment for Mike? Or keep silent and risk the possibility that he might be prosecuted for withholding evidence that could have led to the capture of the killer of two men?

It was a dilemma that would keep him tossing and turning that night.

The TV public service announcement regarding the bridge club murders was yielding few results. Since it was Morgan's idea, she was nominated to field the calls, of which most were the usual crank callers. Morgan answered her phone, "Detective Kelly."

From a pay phone in Queens, Jerry Silverstein said, "I have information regarding the two murdered men at a bridge club."

She stifled a yawn. "OK, and what is your name?"

"No names. But I might know who killed those two."

Morgan had already received many calls like this. Another disgruntled person with a chip on his shoulder, or some crank caller who had nothing better to do with his day, was making the call simply to please his sick self. She expected to take with a grain of salt whatever this anonymous person was about to tell her. "OK, Mr. Anonymous. Let's have it."

"The man you might be looking for is Michael Kagawa, Wendy Kagawa's father."

She almost dropped the phone. "Who is this? And how do you know this?"

The line went dead.

A myriad of thoughts raced through her. Michael Kagawa? Impossible. The caller would have seen the names of both Wendy Kagawa and Michael Kagawa in the news. Sick people very often picked out a name at random and called to say they knew something. No, it couldn't be Mike Kagawa. It was just another crank caller who saw the TV announcement.

But the more she thought about it, the more suspicious she became. Those two men had murdered his daughter. Motive to kill was certainly there. But a mild-mannered high school science teacher committing double murder gangland style? It just didn't fit the pattern. But then again, he had lost everything—his whole family, his savings, his house—great reasons to want to take revenge. But how could he have done it? He couldn't have known that Fujita and Ogura were Wendy's kidnappers or that they played bridge at that club.

Since it was an anonymous caller, with no details whatsoever, she intended to keep the call to herself, at least for the time being. Besides, she didn't believe it, and she didn't want to add fuel to the fire that Mike Kagawa was trying desperately to extinguish by helping Alice— unless, of course, there was some hard evidence that pointed to him as the killer. But for now, her suspicions still lay with the Yakuza and that piece of shit Akita.

CHAPTER 23

ALICE WAS NOW OFF DRUGS, AND SHE WOULD HAVE TO BE placed in a foster home. Kagawa had discussed the possibility of becoming Alice's guardian with both Alice and Abby. Even though Abby thought it a long shot, she had agreed to set up a hearing in family court.

The biggest stumbling block was that Alice had a mother, whom the court would usually side with if the mother objected to the guardianship. Morgan had been asked by Alice if she would attend the hearing in family court. Morgan agreed, primarily because the phone call accusing Kagawa compelled her to observe the proceedings. She hoped the judge wouldn't grant Kagawa's guardianship of Alice. The consequences for Alice could be devastating if it was later found that Kagawa was indeed guilty of two murders. If it appeared as though the guardianship would be granted, Morgan felt that she might have to testify. She couldn't accuse him of murder, but she could testify to the fact that Kagawa's losses made him potentially unstable to the point of his talking of suicide. She expected Alice and Kagawa to be furious with her. She hoped her testimony wouldn't be needed.

Abby accompanied Kagawa and Alice to the courthouse, where they sat in pews, waiting for their case to be heard by the judge.

Morgan entered the courtroom and sat in the last pew.

A few minutes later, Alice's mother, Stephanie Liu, stepped into the courtroom wearing a man-tailored shirt and blue jeans, torn at the knees.

Alice exclaimed, "That's her! Damn it!" She turned away.

Kagawa and Abby turned to look.

Stephanie Liu saw Alice, walked over to her pew, and while standing in the aisle said, "Alice, where have you been? I've been searching everywhere for you. Thank God, I found you. Come on, honey. Let's go home." She put her hand out for Alice to grab hold of.

Morgan thought, *Yeah, right. Another adult who could boldface lie to a child.* Father Timothy had promised her a place in heaven next to God. She hoped he was burning in hell.

Alice turned the other way and said nothing.

Abby addressed her. "Ms. Liu. We have a hearing to discuss where Alice will live."

Liu was indignant and said way too loudly, "Who the fuck're you?"

The judge, in his sixties with silver hair, dressed in a black robe and wearing a pair of glasses that rode the end of his nose, looked up from the current case he was hearing and admonished the gallery. "There will be order in this court, or some of you will be asked to leave. The lady standing, please take a seat and be quiet."

Liu snarled at Abby and took a seat in a pew on the other side of the aisle.

A while later, Alice Liu's case was called. All parties involved were asked to come forward.

The judge, sitting behind his raised desk, looked down at them and said, "I see a Michael Kagawa is petitioning for guardianship."

Kagawa answered, "That's me, Your Honor."

Morgan stared at Kagawa, a man who wanted to take care of a person in need. *Could this man be the cold-blooded killer of two men?*

"And that a fifteen-year-old, Alice Liu, filed the petition. Is that correct?"

Alice answered in a barely audible voice, "That's me."

"And I understand that the mother of Alice Liu is also here."

"Me, Your Honor, and these people are trying to steal my loving child from me!"

The judge glanced at his papers. "Let me understand this situation. We have a mother who is contesting this petition and a daughter who has filed it. The two are apparently at odds with each other. I'll hear from the petitioner first. Young lady, why are you seeking the guardianship of Michael Kagawa?"

She had been biting a fingernail. She removed her hand from her mouth and cleared her throat. "He's a nice man. He wants to take care of me."

The judge gently said, "But you have a mother who also wants to take care of you. The law is clear on this. I can appoint a legal guardian only if a living parent is unable to take care of her child. Thus far, I have a parent standing before me who appears fit and willing. Do you have any reason to believe that your mother cannot care for you?"

"She threw me out of the house over two years ago," she firmly said.

"That's a lie, Your Honor!" Liu loudly interrupted. "She ran away, and now I found her again."

"Ms. Liu. You'll have plenty of time to testify," he said in a commanding voice. "Right now, I want only to hear from Alice."

She threw her hands up and said unapologetically, "Sure."

Abby interrupted. "May I say something, Your Honor?"

"And you are?"

"Abelina Waters, Your Honor. I'm the director at the shelter on 125th Street that's been taking temporary care and custody of Alice. I spoke with Ms. Liu several days ago and informed her that we had her daughter safely in our shelter. She told me she never wanted to see her again."

A fuming Liu shouted, "I was still angry at Alice for running away. That's why I said what I did. I love my daughter and need her with me. When she called a second time and told me someone wanted to take my daughter from me, I realized how much I loved and missed her."

The judge asked, "Did you visit with Alice since that first call?"

"I … I was intending to but wasn't feeling well."

"Do you have a job?"

"I get a government check every month."

"And why is that?"

"I got a bad back. I'm on disability."

The judge jotted down a few notes.

The judge then continued his query. "Alice, did you run away, or did she throw you out?"

"She threw me out."

"And why would she do that?"

Alice turned toward the gallery and then back at the judge. "You really want me to tell you everything?"

"If you think it will help your case, yes. By the way, I have the right to exclude the public from this courtroom, depending upon the privacy interests of the two parties. Shall I clear the courtroom?"

Morgan leaned forward and thought, *Go ahead, girl. Tell your story like I never did.* Morgan had always believed she couldn't have been the only girl to be molested by Father Timothy. Perhaps if she had reported him to the authorities, he might have been stopped.

Alice shrugged. "I don't care."

Ms. Liu said, "I have nothin' to hide."

"All right, then," the judge concluded. "We'll proceed. Alice, you may continue."

"OK. My mother was a prostitute and a druggie my whole life."

"Liar!" Liu shouted.

The judge firmly said, "Ms. Liu. I told you, you'll get your chance." She said nothing this time. She turned toward Alice with a sneer.

"Alice, please continue."

"We had men she called 'uncles' and 'friends,' ya know, go into her bedroom all the time. She also had boyfriends sometimes. One piece-of-shit boyfriend ..."

The gallery laughed, and the judge said, "Try to control the language, Alice."

"Oh, sorry. One day, this bastard boyfriend of hers ... can I say bastard?"

Again, some giggling could be heard.

The judge glanced sternly at the audience and then back at Alice. "Sure. Continue."

"He asked if he could come into my bedroom to show me something. I said OK. I was thirteen, ya know? The next thing I know, he was showing me his dick. He threw me on my bed, held his hand over my mouth, and ripped off my clothes. I tried to scream, but even if I could, my mother was so drugged out she wouldn't hear me anyway. I was raped and smacked around, and he threatened me that if I told anyone, he would kill me. But about a week later, it happened again. Only this time, he made me do other things, ya know? Do I have to say what?"

"I get the picture. Go on."

"Finally, after being raped and other stuff for a couple of months, I was angry enough to tell my mother, ya know. She said her boyfriend would never do those things, and I must be lying. We fought. She told me to leave and never come back. I went to this building with a lot of travelers and was picked up by someone who promised to take care of me. I was turned into a prostitute until the police rescued me and put me in a shelter with Abby here." She shrugged. "That's it."

Alice's testimony conjured visions of the past for Morgan; Father Timothy using her for his pleasure; the soldier at Ft. Hood who attempted to rape her. After being deployed to Iraq, she was assigned as a driver. One day, her truck came to a fork in the road. Her partner, a fellow soldier sitting next to her, thought the left fork was safer. She said she thought she heard that the left fork was potentially IED territory. She made the decision to take the right fork. A few minutes later, a sniper's bullet passed through the passenger side window, striking her partner, killing him instantly, and scattering blood and brain tissue all over her. He died in her arms. She came out unscathed physically but not emotionally. She felt guilty. Perhaps, had they taken the left fork, he would still be alive.

Now it was the judge's turn to clear his throat. "Ms. Liu. You may now speak."

"All lies, Your Honor. Everything." She pointed a menacing finger at Alice.

"Your daughter claims you threw her out."

"She ran away. I tried everything to find her." She took a tissue from her pocket and dabbed her eyes.

"And you, of course, filed a police report?"

"A what?" She stopped dabbing her eyes.

"A missing person's report. Your daughter had been missing over two years. It's normal for a parent whose child has run away and not returned after a day or two to get help from the authorities in finding that child. If you filed a report, I would like to see it."

She looked bewildered. "I don't remember." This brought some snickering from the audience.

"You don't remember if you ever spoke to the police in the two years that your daughter was missing? It would have behooved you to follow up on their progress on a daily basis."

She stood silently.

"Would you mind stepping forward?"

She did so.

"Would you mind rolling up your sleeves, please?"

She stammered, "W ... why?"

"No particular reason. The sleeves, please."

She hesitated and then proceeded to roll up her sleeves, exposing her arms. The judge leaned forward and nodded. "You can roll down your sleeves. Thank you."

She rolled them down and stood back.

"Alice, who is Mr. Kagawa to you?"

"He's a friend. A nice man who wants to take care of me."

"If I were to approve this guardianship, I must be convinced that you understand what happens when a legal guardian is appointed. What have you been told?"

"I was told that Mike, Mr. Kagawa, would act sort of like a parent. He would tell me the right things to do and take good care of me until I'm eighteen, ya know. Then I could stay till twenty-one if I want to."

"Mr. Kagawa. Why do you wish to become Alice's guardian?"

Kagawa cleared his throat again. "I met Alice under the most terrible of circumstances. My daughter was kidnapped and killed by the men who were using Alice and many other girls. She was kind enough to talk to me about my daughter's last days, and we have formed a bond. I had taken a leave of absence from my teaching position here in the city, searching in vain for my daughter. I intend to return to teaching as soon as possible. I will be more than able to care for Alice, Your Honor."

"Is there a Mrs. Kagawa?"

In a barely audible voice, he answered, "My wife committed suicide after our only child was found murdered."

The judge jotted down some notes and said to Kagawa, "The court generally assigns minors to families where both husband and wife are present. You've suffered a double tragedy, and I would be remiss if I were to grant guardianship to someone who might need counseling himself."

Ms. Liu called out, "Right on!"

Kagawa pleaded, "But I'm a teacher and can help give Alice the education she lacks."

The judge looked at Abby. "Ms. Waters. What is your opinion?"

"Alice will have to leave the shelter very soon. I believe the two of them have formed a relationship that will benefit Alice greatly."

"Be that as it may, I must be cautious where minors are concerned." The judge sat in silence for a minute. After deliberating, he looked up and stated, "I cannot in good conscience grant guardianship to Mr. Kagawa."

Ms. Liu raised her fist in triumph and shouted, "You go gi ... Your Honor."

Alice glanced at her mother and said, "Oh, shit!"

Kagawa stared at the floor.

Morgan breathed a sigh of relief. She wouldn't have to intervene.

The judge continued, "But the evidence is overwhelming that Alice's version of what happened between her and her mother is the truth. I therefore cannot render Alice to the custody of her mother."

Ms. Liu shouted, "What the fuck! She's my daughter. You can't fucking do this!"

"Officer, please escort Ms. Liu out of the courtroom." A court officer then ushered Liu out amid several curses.

Alice smiled broadly.

The judge said, "Ms. Waters. Is it possible for Alice to remain in your shelter until we can find a suitable situation for her?"

Abby answered, "Certainly, Your Honor."

"We'll look into a state-appointed temporary guardian and then look for a suitable licensed foster family." The judge saw how unhappy Kagawa and Alice looked. "I know my decision is not what you wanted to hear, but it's in Alice's best interest. Mr. Kagawa, this does not preclude you from having contact with Alice. Perhaps once she gets settled, you can tutor her."

Kagawa looked up at the judge. "That would be nice, Your Honor."

The judge said, "Next case."

Alice and Kagawa hugged. Then Abby joined in on the hugging.

Morgan believed the judge made the right decision. Was Kagawa a killer? After watching Alice and Kagawa hug, she certainly hoped he wasn't, knowing how horrible that would be for Alice.

By the end of that day, two Triads and another Yakuza had been found murdered. Threats by police were having less of an effect than the ageless and sometimes all-consuming motivation of revenge. Morgan wondered how much longer the two groups would continue to cannibalize each other. That remained to be seen. But these were mostly lower-echelon players. How to get to Akita was still a major concern.

That evening, she rushed into the Happy Hour, stopped in front of Akita's table where he sat with Nomura and Harada, and pointed a finger at Harada. With raised voice, she said, "That man's been following me. If I see him following me again, I'll assume my life is in danger and I might have to discharge my piece in self-defense. Is that clear?"

She stormed out of the club.

Akita said to Harada, "You have to get rid of her—and soon."

At ten the next morning, after seeing Ben at the hospital, where he seemed to be recovering nicely, she was at the precinct reviewing the video that she and Ben had already seen of the bridge club murders. The video had shown a man in a baseball cap, wearing a jacket and sunglasses, and with a dark beard. All they had determined from the video was that it appeared to be a short man, about a hundred fifty pounds. But that description would fit thousands of men in Chinatown alone, providing he was wearing a fake wig and beard. Even if the beard was real, the killer could easily have shaved it off.

She put the video on slow motion, hoping to see something that would provide further evidence that it indeed was Kagawa, or perhaps something that might eliminate him from suspicion. She intently watched the screen as she played the video several times over, but she saw nothing that would sway her either way. She still had her doubts that it was Kagawa, believing instead that it was as they had suspected, a gang war hit. But the anonymous accusation still nagged at her. The caller would have had to have known that Wendy had been killed by Fujita and Ogura and that Michael Kagawa was Wendy's father. Would a crank caller take the time to connect the dots? Should she call Kagawa in and confront him? She hated to accuse him of something so dastardly at a time when his life was so fragile. Perhaps if she mentioned it to him almost in passing, as though she didn't believe it and assumed it was some crank caller. *Can you believe it? Ha, ha.* Yes, that might work, and she would be able to assess his reaction.

She decided to meet with him, but not at the precinct since she wanted this conversation to be as casual as possible. She picked up the phone, called Kagawa, and asked if he could meet with her. He asked if this was about Alice, and she replied that it was something she needed to clear up. He agreed, but he asked if it could possibly be at his home since he was expecting his real estate agent to come by with a potential buyer sometime later that morning. She said she would be there in about forty-five minutes or so. She left the precinct for her car.

Within the hour, she parked her car in front of Kagawa's house and rang the bell. Kagawa opened the door and immediately asked, "How is Detective Chang doing?"

She stepped into his living room. "I saw him this morning, and he's progressing nicely. Might even be out of the hospital in a few days."

"That's wonderful news. Come, sit down."

They sat on two folding chairs, facing each other.

"So, Detective. What is this about?"

"First, let me say how happy I am for both you and Alice. I think it's a wonderful thing you're doing for her."

He nodded. "I expect it to be mutually beneficial, you know. At this point in my life, I need her as much as she needs me."

"I can see that." She shifted uneasily in her seat.

"You've traveled a distance to come here ... for?"

She forced a smile. "You are not going to believe it, but I received an anonymous phone call saying that you were the man who shot the two men at the bridge club." She watched for his reaction.

Kagawa cocked his head to the side. "I bet you get a lot of calls like that."

"We do. And as absurd as the accusation is, it's my duty to follow up, even on calls that are probably crank calls."

"Well, here you are. Do you think I could do something like that? It's not in my nature."

"That's exactly my thought, but I had to ask. You understand, don't you?"

"Of course. Someone makes an accusation, and you follow up on it. It's your job."

As much as she tried, she detected nothing in Kagawa's words or body language that would lead her to the conclusion that he was the killer.

"Well, thank you for your time. I wish you all the luck in the world. And I have high hopes that Alice will flourish with you as her tutor."

"I appreciate that."

They said their goodbyes, and Morgan left for the precinct.

Kagawa thought, *The walls are closing in*. He Googled where to purchase poison and found a site that advertised suicide pills that he could receive by mail. He intended to use one if he was ever arrested. Death in minutes.

Back at the precinct, Morgan was still bothered by the anonymous caller. She asked herself, *How would it be possible for Kagawa to know about Fujita and Ogura?* She took a pad and wrote what was now known, that Alice had more than confirmed their suspicions that Hiro had kidnapped Wendy with the help of his so-called father, Ogura. Next, she thought about the photo of Hiro taken by Wendy. It was how she and Ben were able to initially confront him. Could Kagawa also have found Hiro through the photo? Hiro had promised to stay away from that school, but maybe he went back anyway. Could Mike Kagawa have somehow kidnapped Hiro and tortured him into divulging the names of Fujita and Ogura? It seemed unlikely. And as horrible as Wendy's death was, Kagawa still had a wife to share his grief. But perhaps with the wife's suicide, he was pushed over the edge into the abyss of vengeance. He had stated he had nothing to live for. Perhaps it was thoughts of vengeance that kept him alive. Hiro had been found in his trunk with no weapon. If he had a weapon, whoever killed Hiro probably would have taken that weapon. Was it Hiro's weapon—found at the murder scene—that was used to murder the men at the bridge club? No way of knowing since it was unregistered. Did Kagawa own a handgun? If he did, he had probably purchased it legally and therefore would have registered it. She immediately went to her computer and pulled up the names of people who had licenses to carry a concealed weapon. She searched for Michael Kagawa's name, but as expected, there was no match.

But the wheels kept turning. Suppose it was Kagawa who had killed Masahiro Araki and taken his gun. He might need bullets for that piece. And not owning one, perhaps he would need to practice using the gun. The gun that was used was a Glock, which required 9mm bullets. Gun shops were forbidden to sell bullets to anyone who was not licensed to carry a concealed weapon. Would he purchase bullets online? Would he have them sent to his home in Great Neck? The likelihood was slim but still a possibility.

She Googled online sellers of 9mm bullets. Unfortunately, there were numerous purveyors of those bullets, such as Walmart, Amazon, Lucky Gunner, Ammograb.com, and dozens of others. It might take some doing, but she was determined to send a fax on official department letterhead to every one of the dozens, with a warrant demanding whether any bullets were sent to either a Michael Kagawa or to an address in Great Neck, New York. It was a long shot, and it would take time for them to get back to her, but it would set her mind at ease in knowing that Kagawa had not purchased the 9mm bullets.

CHAPTER 24

MORGAN RECEIVED THE NEWS SHE HAD BEEN DREADING THE
following day. An online seller of 9mm bullets, American Eagle, had
overnighted a box of fifty 9mm bullets to an M. Kagawa at Kagawa's
Great Neck address, and it had been delivered two days after the death
of Masahiro Araki.

She sat at her desk at the precinct and buried her head in her hands,
feeling the wind being sucked out of her. It was undeniable now. Mike
Kagawa was possibly the bridge club murderer, and if so, was more
than likely the killer of Masahiro Araki. Motive; anonymous accuser;
fits the general description of the murderer; and purchaser of 9mm
bullets two days after Araki was murdered. With the evidence she had,
she was certain that if Kagawa was indeed the killer, she could get a
full confession from the unfortunate man. He probably would never
have hurt a fly if his life hadn't been so incredibly shattered. But, she
further thought, did he merely intend to carry out the murders? Did

someone else, like Lyle Chen, or some group like the Yakuza actually commit the crime?

She was too upset to see anyone at that moment, and she told her new partner, Chris Grabowski, that she was going downstairs to get some fresh air. She left and walked to a nearby park, where she sat on a bench under a maple tree whose leaves had turned to orange. She viewed young mothers pushing toddlers in strollers, young kids playing games, and a few older men playing chess. She thought, *Life can seem so simple when viewed from a distance, but is anyone's life truly simple?* No, simple wasn't possible. Every life had its bumpy roads to travel, with some unfortunate souls traveling a great deal farther down those roads. She'd had her own tribulations and had not come out unscathed. What would she have done if her entire family had been killed and she had the chance to avenge that loss? She felt she really couldn't answer the question. But could she have killed many years ago, when her nightmares began? She believed she might have been able to do it if she'd had the opportunity. Some killings were categorized as justifiable homicide. If Kagawa did the deed, would his murders qualify? She thought not. Could it be considered temporary insanity? The murders were separated by days and so calculating that, once again, she thought not. No, if Michael Kagawa was guilty of the murder of three men, although each of the murdered men might have deserved to die, America's system of justice allowed for a trial by jury for even the most heinous of crimes committed by the most despicable people. The murderer had afforded them none of their rights, and it would be that person who would have to face a jury of his peers.

She thought about sharing her evidence with Grabowski, but she knew that Ben was being released from the hospital later that day. She felt she owed it to Ben to share the news with him first.

Morgan was back at her desk at the precinct when Alice called. Alice excitedly said, "Detective Kelly, I just want to thank you."

"For what?"

"For making me meet Mike, Mr. Kagawa. He wants me to call him Mike. If it wasn't for you, I wouldn't have such a nice man tutor me, ya know? He's going to give me remedial something that would help me catch up. And, ya know, Mike is a teacher. He thinks I'm really smart, and maybe one day I'll go to college. Wouldn't that be great?"

"Alice, it sure would, and I'm certain you'll do well."

"I gotta go now. But ..."

"But what, Alice?"

"But ... if I could choose a mother, it would be you!" She immediately hung up.

Morgan was still holding the phone in her hand, stunned by Alice's remark. *Wow* was all she could think. *Wow*. Alice's remark came totally out of the blue. Morgan was aware that Alice trusted her, but to say what she just said? *Hell of a compliment*, Morgan thought.

Morgan was certain she would someday make a good mom. Maybe it would be with Tyler, but she knew she was jumping the gun, even though she was falling in love with him. Did he feel the same? She hoped he did.

But now she was bothered by Alice's call. Alice was certainly on a natural high and looking forward to a better life. And Kagawa was putting the pieces of his life back together. If Kagawa was the murderer, the evidence she had would probably be enough to put Kagawa behind bars for years. Knowing how Kagawa felt about the afterlife, she believed he would never make it to prison; he would commit suicide and join Amy and Wendy. And Alice would lose a friend and tutor. How would Alice react if she learned that the man she came to like and trust, and one who would help her achieve success, was a cold-blooded murderer? It might lead to a promising life wasted.

Morgan felt as though she were getting a headache. Her mind vacillated between doing her duty as an officer of the law, which would more than likely destroy two lives, and ... and what? Not reporting her suspicions of the bridge club murders? Either way, she believed she would be the loser. But she had always done her duty, whether it was in Iraq or on the streets of Chinatown. She had sworn to uphold the law. She could never look at herself in the mirror in the same way if she didn't do exactly that.

She hoped he only thought about becoming a vigilante and that it was the Yakuza or someone else who did the deed. But until she obtained some form of corroboration, she would treat Kagawa as a person of interest.

Morgan visited with Ben at his apartment later that afternoon. She was gratified that he was home and well on his way to a full recovery. The apartment was filled with his family, friends, relatives, and other detectives and police officers. Morgan stared at the beaming Ben, who was thrilled to be home and happy to be among so many well-wishers.

Morgan left the apartment without saying anything to Ben about Kagawa. She didn't want to ruin his homecoming with shop talk. At this point, she couldn't wait much longer to confront Kagawa as a person of interest.

She went back to the precinct, where she called Kagawa's cell. "Hello, Mike. It's Detective Kelly."

"Detective Kelly. I was just thinking about you."

"What about?"

"I'm leaving for the cemetery in about fifteen minutes, where I'll tell Amy and Wendy all the great news about me and Alice and how much you helped us."

"I was simply doing my job, that's all." The last thing she needed now was a compliment from him.

"No, you went above and beyond to help Alice. I will never forget you for it. And the reason for this call?"

Morgan took a deep breath. Proper procedure dictated that she not tip off the accused that he was about to be arrested, but she was there to probe, not to arrest. She knew he would arrive at the cemetery in about half an hour. She planned to speak with Kagawa, and if it was at the cemetery, so be it. If he was arrested and was innocent, the system would clear him.

"I wanted to ask if you'd be home for me to speak with you in person, but is it okay if I meet you at the cemetery?"

"That would be wonderful. You could pay your respects to Amy and Wendy."

The call ended.

She left the precinct with a heavy heart. She could have asked Grabowski to accompany her, but she wanted to do this interview alone.

Kagawa sat deep in thought. Why would she have to meet in person? The cemetery was at least an hour away, and that was with no traffic. Kagawa thought his heart had stopped beating. She knew. She knew it was him. He mentally prepared himself for the worst, but he took solace in the fact that he would never see the inside of a prison. He walked into a bathroom, opened the medicine cabinet, extracted a suicide capsule from its vial, placed it in his pocket, and left for the cemetery where, as soon as he'd see Morgan approaching, he intended to place the capsule between his cheek and gum. If she was there to arrest him, all he needed was to place the capsule between his teeth and bite down. He wouldn't commit suicide in front of Amy and Wendy—that would be disrespectful. He would wait until he got close to the detective's car, close his eyes, and envision joining his beloved wife and dear sweet Wendy in just minutes.

A while later, Morgan arrived at the cemetery and asked the director where Amy and Wendy Kagawa were interred. She followed the directions, walking a winding path through dogwood trees, cherry trees, and rhododendrons. She spotted Kagawa in the distance waving at her while sitting on a bench, which was situated under a canopy of towering oak trees whose leaves had turned to red. The beautiful setting felt incongruous to the uncomfortable conversation she was dreading.

She approached Kagawa, who immediately stood up. "Detective. Amy and Wendy will be so happy to know that you are paying your respects. I've already informed them of your wonderful deeds." He pointed at the bench. "Please, sit down."

She fingered her handcuffs and sat down. He sat next to her.

He faced her. "I'm so happy to see you."

She smiled grimly. "I'm here to ask you some uncomfortable questions."

Kagawa ignored her statement and continued. "You know, I really believe that Alice will turn out OK, even though she's been through a personal hell. I don't think you or I can ever truly understand what she has been through. Being raped repeatedly as a child. It's beyond my comprehension how she survived all that."

But not beyond mine, Morgan thought. A sadness that she hadn't felt in a very long time suddenly permeated every cell in her body.

She gazed into the distance with what the military referred to as the thousand-yard stare. Morgan knew the pain he had gone through, and she believed his was even greater than what she had known.

Kagawa looked down at the ground. "I hope I can be the one to help Alice find peace and a positive direction in life." He looked up at Morgan.

Morgan touched the handcuffs that hung at her side. "Let me tell you a story."

Morgan shifted on the bench so that she could look directly at Kagawa's face. After making eye contact with him, she spoke slowly and deliberately. It was time to confront him with her suspicions. "There was this girl named Wendy, who was kidnapped and killed by her traffickers. Her father was so distraught that he decided to murder them. This was accomplished with a gun that he took from a young man whom he had also killed by placing a plastic bag over his head."

He glanced at the graves, sighed heavily, and said, "I told Amy and Wendy that I might soon be joining them."

Morgan knew what he meant. She made eye contact again with Kagawa and said, "My story doesn't end here. I saw a movie a couple of years ago called *Spotlight*. Maybe you saw it."

Kagawa merely blinked.

She continued. "It's about the scandal in the Catholic Church involving hundreds of priests who molested both boys and girls. All the church did was move them to another parish. After seeing that movie that was based on true events, I learned that there were hundreds, maybe thousands of kids who were molested over the past several decades. And what happened to all those priests? Practically nothing. Most of them got away clean or with a slap on the wrist. You see, the guilty parties got away."

The two of them sat quietly. A strained silence filled the crisp autumn air.

Morgan's mind was clogged with conflicting images. Reflecting on her past, she saw the face of Father Timothy. She asked herself, *Did he pay for his sins?* Did the person who attempted to rape her ever see justice? Did the person who killed her comrade in Iraq pay a price for killing him? And how many innocent victims never find justice, such as the children killed by soldiers in war due to collateral damage? And did men like Satoshi Akita and Sun Li Fong ever face justice? So many young lives wasted by men like them. It didn't seem right that someone like Kagawa might go to prison for killing men who deserved it, while someone like Akita, who caused so much mayhem and death, should go free. She had been trained to kill in the army and in the Police Academy. So much of her life had been steeped in thoughts of revenge, but she had never acted upon those thoughts. And she hoped she never would. Perhaps the arrest and conviction of men like Satoshi Akita would provide a modicum of justice for all those ruined lives. Would her thoughts of vigilantism end, or would she become what she was trained not to be—judge, jury, and executioner? She prayed those thoughts would stop here and now.

She had sworn to uphold the law. If she suspected Kagawa and didn't arrest him, she would be guilty of a crime. And if she arrested him, and he committed suicide, which also might do irreparable harm to Alice, would she feel guilty? The answer was yes, and either way, she would have to live with guilt.

The only question she needed to answer was, which guilt was she more likely able to live with? Then, in a confession she needed to make, to the only person she believed she could, she added, "One more thing. I learned that the main perpetrators of the trafficking would never pay a price for the suffering and killing of so many girls and young women." She paused, took a deep breath, and continued. "So, one day, I planned to make use of my marksmanship skills by shooting and killing a leader of this trafficking group, Satoshi Akita, who, indirectly, was responsible for Wendy's death." She paused, deep in thought. "Fortunately, my better angels took hold, and I could never carry out the deed."

Silence reigned for thirty seconds until Kagawa said, "I truly believe that it was karma that led us both to this place and time. Yes, sometimes the guilty get away, and sometimes they get caught. My father taught me that to exact revenge is not only a right; it is an absolute duty." He drew a deep breath. "I did my duty." He smiled sadly and nodded at her.

She gazed at him with an understanding expression, but now she was absolutely certain he was guilty of three murders.

A stiff breeze began to blow from out of the north, pelting them with falling leaves. Morgan stood, turned toward Kagawa, who was still seated on the bench, and ordered, "Mike, stand up and place your hands behind your back."

Kagawa solemnly said, "Disgrace and prison is nothing I will ever endure." He stood and placed his hands behind his back. Morgan cuffed him and read him his rights, to which he responded that he understood and said, "It had been a good and satisfying life until tragedy struck. I was a dedicated teacher and loving husband and father. Every life ends."

Morgan led him away from the graves and began a slow walk toward her car. Her mind was a blur of conflicting thoughts. She knew he would find a way to kill himself and be reunited with his loved ones. And Alice might eventually end up on the streets. He had killed the men who caused him so much pain, men who deserved to die. She had learned at an early age that life wasn't fair. She thought back to the quote she had mentioned to Ben, *It is forbidden to kill, therefore, all murderers are punished unless they kill in large numbers and to the sound of trumpets.* She had helped fellow American soldiers kill in large numbers and to the sound of trumpets. Unfortunately, too often it was innocent civilians who were killed. Collateral damage—too flippant a phrase, she thought, to describe such horrible carnage.

As they approached her vehicle, Kagawa unexpectedly stopped walking and closed his eyes.

Morgan stopped her slow walk, turned to Kagawa, and saw tears streaming down his contorted face. She said with utmost sincerity, "Mike, sometimes the guilty *do* get away."

He opened his eyes. His face suddenly bore a curious expression.

She turned him around, uncuffed him, and said, "Try to enjoy your life. It can still be worth living. I'll follow up on Alice's progress from time to time, if you don't mind."

Kagawa coughed with his left hand covering his mouth. He turned to face Morgan and extended his right hand for her to shake, which she did. "Thank you, Detective Morgan Kelly. Thank you from the bottom of my heart. I might have to postpone joining Amy and Wendy in the afterlife. I believe they will understand."

She nodded, turned away, and finished the slow walk to her car.

She had lived with her own secret stories for so long, and she intended to keep another story to herself, forever.

With conflicted thoughts, Kagawa walked back to the graves and sat on the bench. He looked at the capsule in his left hand, dropped it on the ground, and stepped on it. He had gotten away with the murder of three men. Could he have gone another way? Could he have helped the police to put the three men in jail? Would that have assuaged his urge for revenge? What if Alice knew he'd murdered three men? Would she think of him as a monster? Would his acts encourage her to take revenge on people who had abused her?

Detective Kelly had given him a free pass that he now promised to repay in some fashion. He would help not only Alice but possibly other troubled girls as well. He didn't know how, but he was certain there were many ways he could help, and he vowed in front of Amy and Wendy that he would accomplish it in their name. He also felt regretful in being a part of Detective Kelly's remarkable and difficult decision to give him his freedom. Was his relationship with Alice the deciding factor in letting him go? He tried to put himself in Detective Kelly's shoes, but he knew he never fully could. He believed his release had to weigh heavily on her. He would be forever grateful to her.

Morgan also had conflicted thoughts. She had let a man get away with murder. She felt she had good reasons, but those reasons wouldn't make it right in the eyes of the law. What if it became known that she could have arrested a murderer but didn't? She understood the chance she was taking but felt there was no other way for her to go. If arrested, Kagawa, an otherwise good and decent man, would probably soon be dead, and Alice would be devastated to know that the one man she was beginning to trust was a triple murderer. Morgan knew, as difficult as it was, that she had to try to let go of the past. She would concentrate on men who truly deserved to be behind bars, men like Satoshi Akita.

CHAPTER 25

THE FISH WEREN'T BITING THAT DAY. ALEX KAZAN, HIS WIFE, and five-year-old daughter had taken their twenty-seven-foot Doral past the Statue of Liberty with hopes of catching something. Although they had been shut out, it was still a fun day.

The power boat's engine was off, and the boat was drifting with the tide—while the family was finishing sandwiches and drinks—when Alex noticed something floating in the water. He stood up to get a better look as the boat slowly drifted toward it. A moment later, he sternly told his wife, "Take Julie into the cabin, now."

"What?" she answered.

While Julie was concentrating on her sandwich, Alex pointed at the floating thing.

His wife gasped and understood. "Julie, honey, it's getting chilly. Let's go downstairs." She made sure to stand between her daughter and the thing as the two of them stepped into the small cabin.

Alex immediately dialed 911 and told them his location and the color and make of his boat. He said he would wait for someone to arrive.

Minutes later, a Harbor Unit speedboat pulled up alongside Alex's boat. He quickly pointed at the object in the water. The police recorded his personal information and said they would handle the situation. Alex was more than happy to get his family out of there.

The grossly bloated body that had been weighted down with not enough rocks was taken to the morgue, where it was determined to be a young Asian woman who was about five months pregnant. She had been strangled with some type of wire. The killer obviously believed the rocks would hide her body forever, but they weren't heavy enough to counter the gases that had built up in the decaying body. She had several tattoos that the police hoped would make her identification easier.

Morgan had received a missing person's report filed by a Katy Wu, who stated that her pregnant friend was missing. The description she gave matched the age, appearance, and tattoos of the deceased. She had left her name and cell number. Morgan called and asked if she could meet at the morgue for a positive identification. She reluctantly agreed.

After positively identifying the deceased at the morgue as Chunhua Zhao, Morgan interviewed the young Asian woman.

"How did you know her?"

The nice-looking Katy, with a dancer's body, was clearly disturbed by the events, but she was able to hold it together. "Me and Chunhua worked together. She was my best friend."

"What about her relatives?"

"No one. She was sold in China and wound up here."

"Where did you work?"

"At a strip club."

"Which one?"

"Happy Hour."

Morgan's eyes opened wide. She then asked, "How old are you?"

She put her hand up. "Don't worry. I'm legal. Twenty."

She nodded. "How old was Chunhua?"

"Nineteen." Rivulets of tears began to flow down Katy's cheeks. "Did you know she was pregnant?"

She handed her a tissue, which she wiped across her eyes. "Yes, and that leads to my next question. Do you know who the father is?"

She hesitated. "I could be in big trouble for telling you. Soon as I heard she was missing, I quit working for him. Moved out of my apartment and found a different one."

"You're not a witness to the crime. Anything you say will be held in complete confidentiality. It would certainly help if we knew a name."

She inhaled a shuddering breath. "Satoshi Akita."

Morgan couldn't hide her surprise. "Are you certain?" She understood why Katy quit and moved.

A wry smile crossed her face. "I wasn't exactly there when she got pregnant, but it's what she told me. Why would she lie?"

"OK. Any ideas who might have killed her?"

"You're the cop. You figure it out. But whoever did this, I hope you kill the fucker."

"If I were you, I wouldn't tell anyone you came to the police."

"I'm not crazy."

Morgan thought to keep the identification of the deceased under wraps for the time being, since they didn't want Akita privy to their information. She met with Graves in his office and gave him the news.

Morgan said, "That cocksucker, excuse my language, knocked up one of his strippers and probably killed her."

Graves thought for a moment. "It's my first reaction too, but even if he was the father, it doesn't mean he killed her, or even had her killed."

"What's your gut telling you?"

"Same as you. He did it. But proving he was involved is another story. And we can't be certain he's even the father. She could have lied to her friend to cover for someone, or maybe she just *thought* it was Akita's. Maybe she had sex with multiple men and didn't know who the father was."

"OK, all possible. But first we need to get a DNA sample from him and match it to the fetus."

"You know as well as I do that unless we arrest him or are about to arrest him for some criminal offense for which he might do jail time, we can't force him to do the test. We could try for a court order, but that would take time, and Akita has enough resources to fight this for years. And even if he is the father, we need to find proof that he was involved in her death."

Morgan thought, *One step at a time.* She just might be the one able to get Akita's DNA.

After her shift was over, Morgan placed a call to the Happy Hour strip club. She asked the woman who answered whether Satoshi Akita was there.

"Who's calling?"

"Simone. I was told he was looking for a new stripper and to call this number, that he might interview me today."

"If you want to see him today, you have to hurry. On Mondays, he leaves at six sharp. Otherwise, call back tomorrow."

"Thanks. I'll call back tomorrow."

Morgan hung up and glanced at her watch. It was five thirty. She had called from a pay phone in a Chinese takeout from across the street. She waited in her unmarked Ford for twenty-five minutes and then entered Akita's club at 5:55. She flashed her badge at the door and proceeded to Akita's table, where he sat with Nomura and Harada.

Akita was ready to light up a Cuban when he looked up, surprised to see Morgan approaching. He looked behind her and said, "Pretty lady. No partner today?" He placed the unlit cigar on the ashtray.

"I'm off duty. I was hoping to speak with you in private."

He studied her and then devilishly asked, "Are you thinking about taking me up on my job offer, or is it just my good looks you are interested in?"

She felt her muscles tightening. "Like I said, in private."

Akita stared at her. "OK, follow me to my back room."

Morgan laughed abrasively. "You think I'd go back there with you? It needs to be out here, in the open."

Akita glanced at his watch. He turned to Nomura and Harada and said, "Wait in the front. I'll be along in a minute."

The men obeyed.

Akita addressed Morgan. "OK, green eyes. What can I do for you?"

She sat on one of the chairs, near Akita. Leaning in close, she said, "I'm appealing to your better angels. I know even *you* had a mother, maybe some sisters or daughters. I'm asking you to stop using underaged girls for any and all of your operations."

Akita smiled crookedly. "And here I was, hoping you needed a job. Are you wearing a wire, Detective? Are you that naïve to think I would tell you I would stop doing something I don't ever do? Check out my girls here. You'll see they are all of age." He checked his watch again. "If that is all, I need to be going."

"I'm not wearing a wire. I just thought I might be able to appeal to your better angels."

He snorted and stood. "Go have a drink, pretty green eyes. And my job offer still stands."

He shot her that smug look of his and exited the club with Nomura and Harada.

Morgan almost felt like taking him up on his offer of a drink in order to celebrate. On the table was an ashtray full of Akita's spent cigars. She discreetly bagged them and left the club.

In her car, she immediately tagged and sealed the evidence bag and then drove back to the precinct, where she called Graves on his cell and said, "I have a present for you."

While waiting for Nomura to retrieve the SUV, Akita tapped his breast pocket and said to Harada, "My cigar. Be right back." He went back inside and picked up his cigar. His eyes opened wide as he viewed the ashtray. He shouted, "Did anyone clean my ashtray?" The responses were negative. He mumbled, "Fucking bitch," and then rushed outside, where Nomura was waiting in the SUV.

Harada opened the rear door, and he and Akita got in.

Akita said, "That sneaky cunt took my cigar butts."

Nomura looked through the rearview mirror and said, "Butts? What for?"

"My spit. She wants my DNA."

"Why?"

"I don't know, but I guarantee it isn't for anything good." He turned to Harada. "Get it done by tomorrow night."

The following morning, the chewed ends of the cigars were given to the lab for a possible DNA match with the fetus. Morgan was told it would take one to two days for the results, but by the following afternoon, they had their results. Satoshi Akita was the father of Chunhua's fetus.

Morgan was ecstatic at the news. She spoke with Graves again. "At least we now have a possible motive. Maybe she refused to have an abortion. After all, she was five months pregnant. Most of these young women would have had an abortion in the first trimester."

Graves scratched his head. "He's a married man. Having her baby might have threatened his marriage."

"What do you think? Enough to arrest him?"

"Let me run it by the DA's office, but don't get your hopes up. We have a *possible* motive and not much else. The DA doesn't bring murder charges easily. And we can't use DNA as evidence that we obtained without his consent."

"Run it by them. He's the father. She's dead. Motive and opportunity. Maybe they'll see it our way."

The next day, after speaking with the DA, Graves spoke with Morgan. "No dice. They need something more substantial. He was the father, so what. Anyone could have killed her, even an old jealous boyfriend."

"You and I both know he did it."

"In our gut, yeah. But a jury won't find him guilty based on a feeling."

Morgan nodded. She knew he was correct. Unless they found more evidence, Akita would be free to run his organization, using and abusing girls and young women.

The desire to kill that animal washed over her once again. Shooting him would be too easy for him—too swift, not enough pain. Maybe she could make his eyes pop out as she strangled him with a garrote, just like he'd done to Chunhua. Or maybe she would have dozens of his underage girls use razor blades to render death by a thousand cuts.

She hoped one of her fantasies would come to fruition.

Later that day, she called Tyler and asked if he had time to see her that night. He said he was free and asked her what she wanted to do.

Morgan replied, "Have you ever been to a shooting range?"

"I've done some shooting, mostly with a rifle, but never at a range. Old beer cans were my targets."

"I'm doing some target practice. Want to come along?"

He quickly answered, "Love to."

"Great. I'll pick you up at eight."

Later, Morgan picked up Tyler, and they arrived at the range.

Wearing eye and ear protection, Morgan watched admiringly as Tyler handled his pistol with confidence. He fired off several shots, most of which hit the target.

Tyler grinned as he turned to Morgan. "That was great. I haven't shot a weapon in maybe … twenty years."

"My turn." Morgan stepped up to the fire line. She aimed and peeled off eight shots in eight seconds, all hitting the bull's-eye.

Tyler was duly impressed. "Man, that was great shooting."

Morgan reloaded and peeled off another eight shots, with the same good result, visualizing the image of Satoshi Akita as she fired. It felt good to relieve some aggression. "Learned that in the military."

"You've never spoken much about your time there."

She turned to face him. She placed her hand on his cheek and said, "One day. One day, I will."

It was almost 11:00 p.m. when they finished at the range.

As soon as they entered the Ford, Tyler said, "I made a reservation for Friday at eight at the Smith, to celebrate our one-month anniversary. I hope that's OK."

She was pleased. "Wow, a month already?" She smiled and said, "Friday is good, except I might have to work late. I'll pick you up at your building at about seven forty-five."

She drove past the gate and toward the Pelham Bridge. The Ford was in the right-hand lane when she turned to Tyler and sweetly said, "Want to cash in on that rain check I owe you?"

He smiled, but before he could answer, a black Cadillac Escalade with its lights off, riding in the left lane, shot from behind her Ford and suddenly swerved violently into the left front of her cruiser. There was a terrific jolt, and the Ford careened over the short, two-foot barrier and plummeted fifteen feet into the Hutchinson River. Morgan screamed.

The vehicle landed with a huge splash. Before she had her wits about her, it was sinking rapidly, water seeping through cracks in the windows. Morgan and Tyler were strapped into their seats. It took a moment, but then the hard focus of battle returned, and Morgan was able to get her bearings, note the speed of the car's descent and the water's ingress, and unbuckle her seat belt. She shouted at Tyler, but he didn't move or respond, apparently unconscious. Time was short. She leaned over and frantically worked to unbuckle Tyler. The water was cold and, combined with the unfamiliar angle, made her hands fumble. She shouted, "Tyler, wake up!" The water had risen to the level of their chests.

The vehicle sank farther into the shallow river. There was still an air pocket above their necks, but it was shrinking fast. Her shaking hands managed to free Tyler. She reached over him and yanked the door handle. She struggled with opening his door against the rush of river water. *At least*, she thought mordantly, *nobody is shooting at us.*

Unable to open it, she draped her legs across Tyler's lap and pushed as hard as she could. Screaming, "Goddamn it!" she was able to shove the door open. She pushed the limp Tyler through the door and followed him out into the dark, cold water. The river was only two feet above the vehicle's roof. She wrapped her arm around Tyler's neck and started to swim to the nearest shore, about fifty feet away, dragging Tyler along behind her.

She had to save Tyler, although she knew it might be too late. She silently prayed he was alive as she swam toward the shore, which was now only twenty feet away. Her arms were lead weights as she struggled to continue swimming. *I used to be tougher.* Her strength was ready to give out when she realized that she could stand up, about ten feet from shore. She dragged Tyler onto a grassy area where, out of breath, she laid him on his back and frantically began performing CPR.

Several breaths into his gaping mouth had passed, and still no visible sign of life from Tyler. She muttered, "Dear God, don't let him die," and continued CPR.

Seconds later, Tyler choked and spit up some water. She screamed, "Tyler! Can you hear me?" He was alive! Her shoulders sagged with relief.

Tyler coughed and sputtered. His eyes were open as he softly said, "Wha … what happened?" The initial impact had whipsawed his head against the passenger door window, rendering him unconscious.

She placed her hand behind his head, hugged him tightly, and then gently laid his head down. "We went into the river. But don't worry about that now. We need to get help. Can you sit up?"

"I think so." He put his hand to his aching head.

She helped him into a sitting position. "Think you can stand up?"

He sat for a few seconds before trying. Morgan placed her arms under his shoulders and helped him to stand. "How are you feeling? Do you think you can walk? Otherwise, I can leave you here, get help, and come back for you."

Tyler took a few unsteady steps and stopped. He took few more steps and said, "OK, but you better hold on to me."

Dripping wet, they made their way up the embankment to the road. After a few minutes, Morgan was able to flag down a car. She identified herself as an NYPD detective, and she and Tyler were driven to the nearest hospital, where Morgan contacted her precinct.

While sitting in the emergency room, waiting for Tyler to be called, Morgan explained what had happened. She was exhausted and wrung out but still revved from the adrenaline of successfully saving him and herself. She kept talking, jittery and angry. She was certain this was Akita's doing. She wanted revenge. Finally, she noticed he had something to say. "I'm sorry. I'm rambling. How do you feel?"

Tyler's voice was hoarse and drained as he said, "In the past few days, I've been threatened with a loaded gun, I saw two people get shot, and I was almost murdered by drowning." He turned to face her and solemnly said, "I've fallen in love with you … but I'm not sure I can do this anymore." He looked down at his feet.

She was shocked. She had just saved him … *Okay.* She understood. Kind of. Not really. They had made it out of the river. The moment when her mother told her that her father had left the family came rushing back—one afternoon after school—that same weightlessness and scorching feeling of inadequacy. Her whole body vibrated with the knowledge of not being enough. The first man she had ever loved had abandoned her—never again to see her or ask about her until she confronted him in Florida. She would never be the same person after his unexpected departure from her life.

She wasn't expecting this from Tyler, but she instantly thought she should have, given what he'd gone through. A civilian. An accountant. Pleading as though she was a little girl again, she said, "But I owe you a rain check."

Sadly, he said, "Will we be alive to cash it in?"

She desperately needed him to not give up on her. "Paul's no longer a threat, and I guarantee Akita won't try anything again." She knew she couldn't guarantee anything.

He thought for a moment. "Give me a night or two to get my head on straight."

She nodded and tightly grasped his hand. She was so glad he was alive. She would have felt that about anyone, but she knew now how deeply she felt about this man. Maybe it wouldn't work out—lots of things didn't work out—but for now, her hopes were pinned on this relationship.

Tyler was diagnosed with a concussion and was admitted overnight for observation. She kissed him goodbye. "I'll be back first thing tomorrow." A police car was waiting outside for her.

She knew Akita wouldn't have personally driven the vehicle. It was part of his system of insulation. She envisioned putting two bullets in that smirking face—one for her and one for almost killing Tyler.

The following morning, she was told the Escalade that had hit them had been found but was stolen the day before. She filled out her report and picked up Tyler in a new Ford Taurus. He had been released from the hospital with instructions to rest. She drove him home, mostly in silence. Before he got out, she said, "The doctor said you'll be as good as new with another day of rest."

He smiled and said, "I never thanked you for saving my life."

Mimicking him with an exaggerated southern accent, she replied, "Nothin' more than any *northern* lady would do for her gentleman."

He laughed, kissed her on her cheek, and left.

She wouldn't blame him if he never wanted to see her again. As she pulled away from the curb, she felt as though couldn't suck enough air no matter how deeply she inhaled. She drove back to the precinct.

At the precinct, Morgan called Ben and informed him of the events of the previous evening. Ben was stunned. "Damn, partner, I thought I had it rough. You are something else." Ben reflected on his doubts about her not being as effective as a two-hundred-pound male, doubts that were now erased. "I agree it was Akita. But proving it is another story. How's Tyler handling all of this?"

She smiled sadly and said, "I hope I haven't become a pariah to him. Accounting is far less dangerous." She needed to change the subject. "And how are *you* doing?"

"In a few more weeks, I'll be as good as new, maybe better because they started me on a rehab regimen that's killing me but is supposed to get me into better shape than ever. And you'll be happy to learn I'm quitting smoking. Doctor's orders."

"That's great to hear. When you get back, we've got a lot more to catch up on."

"I'm already hearing stuff through the grapevine. And only good things about you. I better get back soon before you take all the glory for yourself."

She laughed. "Yeah, some glory. All the major bad guys are still at it. I don't know if we'll ever get them."

"Good things happen to those who wait. Maybe they'll cannibalize each other."

"Don't count on it. Maybe some of us have to take drastic measures."

He paused. "Morgan, what the hell does that mean?"

His question startled her. "Nothing. Just venting." *Waterboarding*, she thought. She would love to introduce Akita to that reviled practice.

"Don't go do anything dangerous or stupid. Wait for me to get back and be stupid."

She smiled. "Don't worry, you big lug. Can't do anything stupid without you. Just take care, and I'll see you soon."

The call ended. Images of girls being abused were haunting her. Two skinny eleven-year-olds in particular flashed through her mind—the frightened Ashleigh and herself.

CHAPTER

AKITA, NOMURA, AND HARADA, SITTING IN AKITA'S CLUB, had expected to learn of the deaths of Detective Morgan Kelly and the man she was seeing. Nothing was reported on TV or in the newspapers. It was assumed they had survived.

Akita turned to Harada. "You definitely saw it sink?"

"Absolutely. But a car was approaching, so I had to get out of there. They must have gotten out and swam to shore." Harada was sweating.

Akita waved his hand. "It's OK. I taught her not to mess with me. And we destroyed her vehicle. Some chauffeur, huh?" The three men laughed and left the club.

Akita's normal routine differed on these recent nights. He had finished dinner with his wife in his posh, three-bedroom condominium. His two boys were grown, and he was proud that he had sent them both to fine universities, after which they had both begun their own careers. Akita's life was his own, borne out of hardship, whose rewards had been huge but not without great risk to himself, a risk he never wanted his sons to face.

Yoshi Nomura and two other bodyguards waited outside his building. Normally, only Nomura would be picking him up, but these past days had been anything but normal. Akita was well aware of the unwritten rule that the leaders were off limits. But now, as a precaution, as the doorman opened the door, each bodyguard immediately positioned himself on either side of Akita, with Nomura in front of Akita, shielding him to the waiting SUV. They all drove to the strip club, where Akita would meet with his lieutenants to discuss business. Of course, drinking and smoking his favorite cigars, and the occasional escapade in a back room with one of the strippers, was part of the attraction for him.

The main topic for this night was the possible truce with the Triads. Would it hold? No one was certain, but the consensus was that it probably would.

It was after midnight and time to go home. Nomura retrieved the SUV from the parking lot and pulled the vehicle up to the club, ten feet from the club's entrance. He got out and opened the passenger-side door as Akita, with the two bodyguards by his side, stepped out.

Akita took two steps toward the vehicle when he suddenly clutched his chest and fell backward onto the sidewalk.

Nomura shouted, "Satoshi!" As he knelt down by Akita's side, his immediate concern was heart attack, but within seconds, that thought was erased by the sight of blood oozing from Akita's chest. The two bodyguards instantly drew their guns and quickly scanned the surroundings, while Nomura frantically shouted, "Satoshi! Can you hear me?" Akita's eyes were wide open. Nomura quickly dialed 911 for an ambulance.

At the hospital, Akita was pronounced dead on arrival. Two gunshots to the chest had killed him instantly. The police had been notified.

Nomura wasn't concerned about the police. With Akita assassinated, certainly at the hands of the Triads, the war wouldn't be over and would potentially reach new heights. And of great concern was that the loss of their leader would weaken their presence in Chinatown, at least for the time being.

The next morning, Morgan and Grabowski were notified by Graves of the incident.

Grabowski's eyes opened wide. "I thought the leaders were off limits."

Morgan, appearing surprised, sarcastically said, "Couldn't have happened to a nicer guy."

Graves noticed Morgan's grim expression. "Something wrong?"

She inhaled deeply and said, "I wanted to be the one to bring him to justice."

"I know how you feel, but now we've got a potential shit storm brewing. More than likely, it's another Triad assassination, except this time, their revenge was taken on a leader. Two shots through the heart by a skilled marksman from a rooftop."

Appearing puzzled, Morgan asked, "How do you know from a rooftop?"

"CSI used a trajectory kit very early this morning."

"Remind me, how exactly does that work?" Morgan asked.

"Through the use of tubes and lasers, from the angle that the bullets entered his chest and exited his back, forensics was quick to determine that the shooter probably fired from the roof of the four-story building across the street, and apparently with a silencer since no shots were heard."

Morgan asked, "Wasn't one of the murdered Yakuza killed with a silencer? Maybe ballistics could determine if it was the same gun used to kill Akita."

"Already in the works," Graves answered. "They'll get us the results ASAP. In the meantime, I've sent a car to pick up Fong. We can't let this escalate."

Morgan smiled to herself, knowing that vengeance had played its part in Akita's demise.

An hour later, Morgan was surprised to see Graves approaching her desk with a grinning Ben at his side. She immediately stood, smiled broadly, and ran over to Ben. She gave him a hug, pulled back, and said, "Shouldn't you be home, resting?"

"The doctor said walking is good for me."

Graves said, "I'll leave you two lovebirds to reminisce. I have a ton of paperwork on my desk." He strode away.

Ben sat in a chair next to Morgan's desk, while Morgan sat behind it. Morgan asked, "How are you feeling?"

"Better every day."

"And how's your family?"

"All doing well, thanks. How's it going with Tyler?"

"Still going." At least she hoped so.

Ben moved his chair closer to the desk and said, almost in a whisper, "I need to hear something from you."

He seemed to be fumbling for something to say. Morgan asked, "What is it?"

He sighed before replying, "I'm not sure how to say it."

She cocked her head to the side.

"I feel horrible asking you this. Did you have anything to do with Akita's death?"

She leaned way back in her chair. "Why would you ask something like that?"

With a pained expression, he answered, "Because I know how badly you wanted to get him and what you said to me the day of his killing. I just need to hear from you that you had nothing to do with it."

She paused for several seconds before answering. "I swore an oath to follow the law, and that's what I've done." She said it even though she knew she hadn't followed the letter of the law with Mike Kagawa.

Ben studied her for a few seconds. "Then that's good enough for me. I just had to hear it from you. I hope you understand."

"Fully. If I had heard you make veiled threats, I might have asked you the same question."

He breathed a sigh of relief. "Then we're all good?"

"Of course. Just get better, and we'll work on getting Fong and all the other dirtbags."

Graves had sent a car to locate Fong with the hope of averting an escalation of the war, but Fong was nowhere to be found, and none of his cohorts seemed to know—or were unwilling to divulge—where Fong could be found. It was assumed by Morgan and the other detectives that upon Fong's hearing of Akita's murder, or perhaps after ordering his assassination, Fong took off for safe haven. But no matter where he was, Morgan knew he was still calling the shots.

With Akita gone, Morgan began to concentrate on getting Fong. But something inside her was changing. For the past eleven years, she had worked in a world where too often she saw the darker side of humanity. Now, with the elimination of a kingpin, she felt a liberation that allowed her to focus on the better angels of humanity. There were certainly plenty of good people out there—like Graves, Ben, and Abby. And she believed Tyler was also one of them. She vowed to do her best to focus on the good that people did. Revenge would be for others to take.

Several known leaders of the Triads were swiftly brought in for questioning. Each man disavowed any knowledge of Akita's murder, which Morgan and the other detectives expected. But it was made clear to these men that a police task force was being assembled to monitor the movements of every known Triad, and that their places of business would be swarmed by Department of Health officials, making good on Graves's promise to Akita and Fong that, if the war didn't end, their legitimate businesses would be targeted.

Several lieutenants of the Yakuza were similarly rounded up and brought in for questioning, but since they were the perceived victims of Akita's murder, they were told that their legitimate businesses would be spared the Triad's fate of interference by the Health Department, provided that the war ended now.

There was no way for Morgan to know if any of the department's efforts would prevent further bloodshed.

As Morgan sat at her desk, an idea crossed her mind. She brought the files up on her computer of the recently murdered Yakuza and Triads. Would the spouse of a murdered man reveal more than the men they had interviewed? She examined the profiles of each murder victim. Hiro, Fujita, and Ogura had no spouse listed. Of the other men—mostly in their twenties and early thirties—only one was listed as having a spouse, and that was Sammy Zhang. Olivia Zhang was the one who had reported the forty-two-year-old as missing and who had identified the body at the morgue that had been fished out of the bay. In her statement to the police, she claimed her husband was an important man who might have been killed by the Yakuza. Of course, she had no evidence of it, but her gut told her that. This had been surmised by Morgan since his death occurred soon after the deaths of Hiro, Fujita, and Ogura. The tattoos on the body led her to believe he was a Triad, although the wife denied any knowledge of it.

Morgan found Olivia Zhang's phone number and address, and she called and asked if she could come to her apartment and speak with her. Mrs. Zhang was reluctant at first, but Morgan assured her it would be brief and that she needed answers that might help shed light on her husband's killers. She left the precinct for her car and arrived at the Zhang residence.

Mrs. Zhang led Morgan into the living room of the well-furnished apartment. They sat on couches facing each other.

Morgan said, "Thank you for seeing me."

Olivia Zhang was a diminutive Asian woman with streaks of dyed blond in her jet-black hair. "What do you know of my husband's death?"

"We believe it was revenge for the murders of persons related to the Yakuza."

In a droll way, she responded, "Tell me something I don't already know."

Morgan's brow creased. "How do you know this?"

"Who else would it be?"

Morgan nodded. "We also believe he was killed because he was a member of the Triads."

She shook her head. "I know nothing about my husband's business."

Morgan stared at her. She had expected the Zhang woman to plead ignorance of her husband's association with the Triads, but still it was time to pop the question. "Do you know Sun Li Fong?"

"He's my brother-in-law."

Morgan hid her surprise as best she could. "How is he related?"

"Don't you know?"

"I just want it confirmed by you."

"My husband was Sun Li's wife's only brother."

Morgan's mind raced as she tried to quickly digest the revelation. She asked, "Do you know where Fong is?"

She sadly stated, "No one tells me anything anymore."

"Did you know that the leader of the local Yakuza, Satoshi Akita, was shot and killed yesterday?"

She forcibly said, "He deserved it. I'm sure he ordered my husband killed."

"Do you know of any place that Fong might hide out?"

"No, and if I did, would I tell you?"

After pressing Mrs. Zhang with a few more questions concerning Fong's whereabouts, Morgan left—still with no knowledge of Fong's location. Suddenly, a serendipitous feeling washed over her. She couldn't wait to get back to the precinct.

Sun Li Fong had rented a farmhouse situated on thirty acres in Upstate New York. He had surrounded himself with several bodyguards, and he intended to monitor events from there. He would wait until things calmed down before returning to Chinatown, where he would be on close guard, hoping to avoid the circle of death. He knew it would take much planning and far more protection.

Fong was well aware of the age-old tradition that leaders were off limits. After all, it provided him with a fair degree of protection, but his wife had come to him, reminding him that blood was thicker than water. Sammy Zhang was his brother-in-law, his wife's only brother, and it was she who had shamed him into assassinating Akita. He knew the risk he was taking, but on the plus side, he would now face a weakened Yakuza—at least in the short run.

More importantly, he and his wife had taken their revenge.

While driving back to the precinct, Morgan's thoughts again turned to the topic of revenge. She now believed Graves was correct. Revenge did not have to be taken upon the actual perpetrator to satisfy the powerful urge for retribution. Stopping perpetrators of crimes against girls and young women, similar to the crimes she had suffered, seemed to assuage her quest for revenge. Her life's work, drawing her in like a siren's song, would now include focusing on freeing these victims from their bondage.

As soon as Morgan returned to the precinct, she immediately sat at her desk and began to outline the events of the past weeks. It was as if the pen had a mind of its own as she feverishly drew arrows from one name to another of all the major players. After observing what she had outlined, a look of great satisfaction crossed her face. All the pieces were now coming together. It was a chain of events—started by her—that had led to Akita's assassination.

Her investigation into Wendy's kidnapping and murder inadvertently helped lead Mike Kagawa to Hiro, which then led Kagawa to Fujita and Ogura. Their deaths helped to spark a gang war that led to the murder of Sammy Zhang, which then led to the assassination of Satoshi Akita.

She smiled contentedly to herself because she'd gotten that bastard after all—but getting Fong and other sex traffickers would remain her primary mission.

Her work had kept her mind off Tyler. She remembered that he'd made a date for the two of them for that evening. Was it still on? Would he ever want to see her again? She tried calling him, but his phone immediately went to voice mail. For the next hour, she tried several more times, with the same result. Did he turn his phone off so he wouldn't be confronted by her? It didn't seem like Tyler. *But then*, she thought, *is he just another man who isn't what he seemed?*

As she aimlessly drove her car, she recalled how good he made her feel. How they often laughed together, so different than with Paul. How she'd thought of the possibility of having children with him, especially when she watched Mike Kagawa with Alice. A man who'd lost so much but was still willing to try. Tyler would be a great father. Wouldn't that be something to see?

It was 7:30. A thought suddenly occurred to her. They both had gone into the river. Her cell phone was waterproof. What if Tyler's wasn't? With a heavy heart and a glimmer of hope, she drove toward Tyler's address. She turned the corner onto his street. It was almost 7:45. Up ahead was his building. She apprehensively approached the front of his building ...

And Tyler was waiting for her.

Printed in the United States
by Baker & Taylor Publisher Services